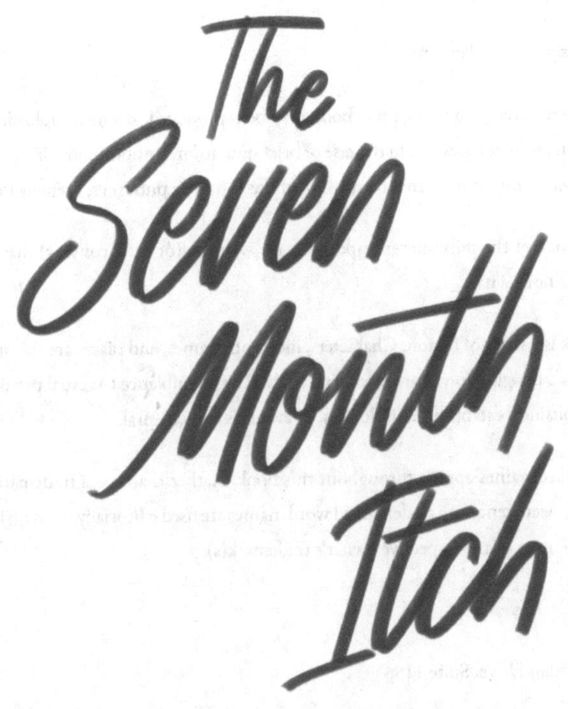

The Seven Month Itch

TANVIER PEART

frenchy
PRESS

The Frenchy Press

5325 Sheridan Drive, Suite 1196

Buffalo, New York 14221-9998

thefrenchypress.com

ISBNs: 979-8-9875061-0-3 (trade pbk.), 979-8-9875061-1-0 (ebook)

Library of Congress Control Number: 2023912999

First Edition: January 2024

Printed in the United States of America

1st Printing

Also by Tanvier Peart

Chance at Love Series

The Seven Month Itch (available as an audiobook)
Miles Apart
Tender Offer

Standalone

Ella Gets the D
Untitled Mafia Rom-Com (coming 2026)

Buffalo Steel Rugby Series

One Knight's Stand
Buffalo Rugby Romance Book 2 (coming 2026)

AUTHOR NOTE

The Seven Month Itch is a romance novel about love and second chances. While full of quirky moments and steamy scenes, this story mentions early pregnancy loss (off-page) and forcible touching (over the clothes and not between the couple) during a '90s party. Take care of yourself.

You'll never be too much for the one who can't get enough.

THE PLAYLIST—PART I

#1 – "Somebody Already Broke My Heart"—Sade

#2 – "Focus"—H.E.R.

#3 – "Forever Don't Last"—Jazmine Sullivan

#4 – "Freak Like Me"—Adina Howard

#5 – "Confidently Lost"—Sabrina Claudio

#6 – "All I Have"—Amerie

#7 – "Whenever You're Around"—Jill Scott

#8 – "Come Close"—Common

THE PLAYLIST—PART II

#9 – "No Ordinary Love"—Sade

#10 – "La Vida Es Un Carnaval"—Celia Cruz

#11 – "Let's Stay Together"—Al Green

#12 – "I Want You Around"—Snoh Aalegra

#13 – "Get You"—Daniel Caesar (feat. Kali Uchis)

#14 – "Oceane"—RINI (feat. Olivia Escuyo)

#15 – "All I Want for Christmas Is You"—Mariah Carey

#16 – "Nice & Slow"—Usher

#17 – "This Is"—Ella Mai

Chapter 1

Justice

The *thwap* my head makes startles me awake. I wince at the sting and peel myself off the cold, hard glass that offers zero protection from a throbbing jaw or the stream of light aimed at my eyes, ready to burn my retinas. So this is the life of a crash test dummy on the verge of blindness.

Christmas on a cracker, that *hurt*. At least there's no drool.

Snow-covered pines race past the shuttle in a blur. My breath paints a fog across the window when I lean in for a closer look. I'd smile if it didn't hurt.

On any other day, a winter wonderland would excite me. I'm a sucker for Hallmark, and this view has all the ingredients for a movie set in a scenic small town with nosy townspeople and a feel-good ending.

But today is a nightmare. I'm not in a holiday movie, escaping the big city to save my family's tree farm—nor in my childhood home, in front of the fireplace with a book, hot cocoa, and a frosty view of our yard, which is covered in a fresh blanket of snow. Heck, I'm not in the comfortable bed I left in Texas this morning.

I'm...where are we?

Emma, my captor, shakes me like an exorcist from my attempt to go back to sleep. This is the bowels of Hell. Everything hurts. My face. My eyes. The shoulder her manicured talons grip to keep me in place.

She's one glossy fingernail away from getting tossed out of this fancy Sprinter to become one with nature. Unless she has a hot shower and a warm bed in that bottomless designer bag she calls a purse, we have nothing to discuss. I've never been to Kansas, but the urge to click my heels together three times to wake up from this bad dream masked as a getaway wrapped in "good intentions" is tempting.

Very tempting.

Regret isn't a third wheel on our annual girls' trip, but after our plane touched down in Denver three hours ago, she is present and accounted for today. And do you know what she thinks? This singles' retreat is a big mistake. The kind that requires holy water and a tetanus shot.

A *singles' retreat.*

My enthusiasm is right up there with a rectal exam. What does one do at a singles' retreat anyway, besides act single and retreat when necessary?

How Emma convinced me to come remains an unsolved mystery. Oh, that's right—I had no choice.

The artist formerly known as my best friend forced me to step away from work and go on vacation. Not by gunpoint, thank God, but to reclaim my time from the mess that's become my life.

Sounds good, right? It was, until I read the fine print that included random men with unlimited access to this awkward Black girl in the middle of the woods for a week. Em thinks we'll have an unforgettable time. I think black-and-white photos of our younger selves will pan across a screen as a narrator describes the events that led to our deaths.

Two best friends dared to have the adventure of a lifetime. But little did they know their snow-filled escapade would end in a bloodbath and their heads mounted on snowmen.

Can't wait!

My chest tightens at the driver's alert. We're ten minutes away from our destination, which might as well be a murder cabin with no cell reception. I stare out the window and scowl at the grin in the reflection. Spoiler: it's not me.

Heifer.

It's all fun and games until we find ourselves in some sex dungeon with leather head harnesses, greasy granddaddies, and a steel door to mask our screams. A singles' retreat is *not* what I had in mind when I told Em I would *think* about life as a single woman.

A blind date? Doable, if there's a swipe left function that teleports me back home and drops me in a pair of sweats.

One of those Christian dating apps so I can try out the username @PsalmLikeItHot? Sure, why not?

What happened to meeting someone in the grocery store bread aisle or at the post office? We share a "hello" and a laugh over jams and stamps. That's more my speed. Baby steps that lead to coffee weeks later, *not* a singles' retreat. But, you give an inch, and your overbearing friend signs you up to run a marathon in heels that rub your baby toes raw.

Emma threatened to stage an intervention if I didn't get on the plane. I questioned her sanity and asked if an air marshal was on board. This was *after* she posted an ad online for a Good Samaritan to escort me to the airport. An ad. As if human trafficking and serial killers aren't a real thing. Thank Baby Jesus someone—me—had the sense to remove "Operation Save Her Coochie" before I landed in the back of an unmarked van, or she ended up in a federal prison.

But did that stop her? Not a chance.

She booked flights to our snowy retreat behind my back and flew to Austin from Malibu to make sure my butt was on the plane. She even worked with my assistant to guarantee I had this week off so I could make the trip. In the forest, in the middle of winter, God knows where.

Was there no place available on the beach? Bikinis and mai tais got Stella her groove back. Why not me?

I pull myself up from the cocoon of my reclined leather seat. These windows do nothing to block out the sun. "You should be thankful this little stunt didn't pan out like a *Law & Order: SVU* episode, Madam Kidnapper."

Her chin dips to lower the designer shades now on the bridge of her nose. Moss green eyes dare me to look away. "Let Detective Stabler try," she says with a smirk.

Emma Douglass is as unapologetic as the day I met her two decades ago. We enjoyed detention on our first day of high school after our homeroom teacher overheard Em say he looked like a predator on *America's Most Wanted* who kept young girls chained up in the closet. In her defense, Mr. Shaw did give off magic potion vibes. His wild beard and unkempt gray hair favored Dr. Vink—with a va-va-va—from *Are You Afraid of the Dark?* But mad scientist living in his mother's basement was more his speed, not kidnapping. At least, I hope not.

She told me we'd be friends that day, the same way she told me to get on the plane with no sudden moves today. Em gets under my skin, and she'd have zero issue committing a felony offense, but I can't live without her.

Emma grew up the daughter of a US senator and a mom who gives the Beverly Hills Housewives and their Botox dealers a run for their money. Her parents are Blair Underwood and Milla Jovovich look-alikes—the ultimate DC power couple, fit for a Shonda Rhimes drama.

With her mom and dad lusting after private jets and crustless sandwiches, our bond strengthened over the years. She spent many nights at my house, which translated to home-cooked meals my mom would whip up on days her middle school class didn't suck her soul. My dad, God bless him, has a brilliant mind as an engineer, but he couldn't boil water in Hell. He did his best to step in and make dinner for "his girls," but we kept the fire department and local pizza shop on standby.

Our home was humble compared to Emma's, but it was comfortable, full of laughter, and the occasional burnt meal. It was a far cry from the fancy political galas she endured, but a place she called home. Em will lose a limb before she parts from her designer labels, but with us, she felt seen. Not like some heirloom her parents showed off for the cameras and later ignored.

We took the same classes in high school and attended Bodie University together, much to her father's disappointment. Senator Douglass wanted Emma to go to his alma mater back in DC, but he lost that debate to his iron-willed daughter. She stayed in California after we graduated, left the San Diego area for Malibu, and never looked back. I packed up what little I owned and headed to Texas as a newlywed.

Our annual girls' trips became a tradition during spring break. We plan them together, so it should've been a red flag when she asked for my credit card but never revealed the itinerary. February is the month of our trip—or so I thought. My soul almost fell out of my butthole this morning after her attempt to break down my door with stilettos like we needed to leave for witness protection.

Emma was wise to wait until we were midair and I was two drinks in to tell me we were off to a singles' retreat. First, who has a weeklong singles' retreat? Second, what inspired her to spend our girls' trip looking for love? I'm fresh from the Land of the Broken Heart, and she...well, she hates romance but seems determined to get me back on the dating scene. No matter how many times I tell her I'm okay.

That's because she knows you're not.

Whatever.

It's not that I *haven't* thought about it. I've been...busy.

Is a swan dive into work after your marriage hits a brick wall an unhealthy coping mechanism? Sure, I'll admit it. But at least I scored a promotion and a fancy new title. That has to count for something, right?

Seven months of grief and resentment passed in a suffocating haze that never relaxed its grip. The wounds are still fresh, and I'm not ready to face the music. Divorce is a foreign tune I don't want to learn, at least not yet.

The urge to hit the reset button after a relationship that started when I was a freshman in college isn't there. Who in their right mind gets their heart stomped into the ground and jumps at the first chance to give it to someone else—at a retreat, of all places? Not me.

My pulse trumpets as we turn down a private entrance. Gravel and ice crunch in a symphony under the weight of the tires. I grip my armrest and steady my breaths. Everything clenches, including my vagina for good measure.

"Stop preparing for a crash landing and open your eyes," Emma says next to me.

Post lights and white fencing lead to a hotel the size of the place in *The Shining*. I don't need to look at a map to know I'll freeze to death in the hedge maze if there is one. With my luck, terror twins with pigtails in matching outfits will follow me around the halls. Perverts might be more survivable.

My eyes lift to a view that takes my breath away.

The resort sits at the bottom of a valley. It's a mountain scene straight out of a Christmas movie—the kind where you kiss in slow motion as snow floats from the sky. Maybe if I rent a car and drive it into a ditch, I'll meet some hot local who's good with his hands and builds rocking chairs for elders in his spare time. I'll bake cookies for the rest of my life if it erases all reminders of my failed marriage.

Okay, this place is gorgeous. I bet Mariah Carey has a chalet off the property and yodels her Christmas songs to wake up the town during winter. It's that over the top.

Maybe I *will* recharge and clear my head here. Christmas was painful back home with my parents, who flooded me with questions about my ex, if I'm okay, and my daily fiber intake. They meant well, but they treated me like a wounded animal in one of those commercials with the Sarah McLachlan song, the kind you can save with the change in your purse. It was my first Christmas as a woman on the road to divorce, and I didn't have a chance to sulk with a bottle of wine and watch *The Holiday* like I wanted.

A change in scenery in a place that doesn't remind me of my ex will do me good. If that means I entertain the company of strangers like a twisted *Bachelorette* episode with true crime potential, so be it.

The shuttle door swings open, pulling the heat and the last of my patience with it. A man in a gold-and-black uniform with a fancy row of buttons dips his head inside. He's missing the white gloves and tiny hat, but the pompous look is present in his glare.

"Welcome to The Ravine. Please watch your step on your way out. We hope you enjoy your stay," he says to me. Or the sky. It's hard to tell who he's talking to with his nose in the air. What a charmer this one is.

"She"—I nod back at Emma—"took me against my will. But I promise not to press charges if you turn the heat on outside." I take his hand to get out and smile. His scowl etches deeper into his features, and I shrug.

Guess sarcasm isn't a language they speak in these parts.

Em and I join the small group that files out the Sprinter and trudges over a path of snow toward the entrance.

Ropes of garland curl up the entrance's four columns like holiday ribbon. The first-floor windows still have wreaths in the center that I know cost more than a month's salary. It's not hard to picture this resort in its full glory during Christmastime.

How Emma found a seven-day retreat in the middle of nowhere still baffles me. Come to think of it, maybe this trip has nothing to do with me. She watches videos of men chopping thick slabs of wood in suspenders and pants that squeeze their cheeks. She would die a happy woman if she found herself a mountain man who's the perfect blend between the Brawny paper towel guy and Chris Evans.

She'd *still* haunt me in the afterlife for not getting under a new man fast enough, but there'd be a postcoital smirk. "Tie yourself up in pleasure, not a relationship" is her mantra. She enjoys all flavors of men the world offers without the need to settle on one.

A gust of wind scrapes up my spine. Our friendship can freeze outside by itself. Where are those *Shining* twins to take their first sacrifice?

"Did you have to pick a place below freezing for us to visit? The feeling in my toes is still back in Austin." I pull my jacket against my chest for warmth, but it's pointless. There's no escape. Mr. Uptight walks along the plowed path with a gold-plated luggage cart and gestures for us to follow.

"Enough with the complaints, Jay. Is it too hard for you to say thank you?" Em breezes into the foyer on the stilts she calls heels and checks her Cartier watch like she has somewhere to be. "By the way." She turns to me. "You only have thongs to wear while you're here. Thank me later."

I'm sorry, *what?* A tundra *and* booty floss. The thing will grow icicles by the time I peel it from my crack. "Emma!" I say in a stage whisper.

Her leather heels screech to a halt on the wide plank floor. She raises a hand and levels me a stare. *Here it comes.* "Save it, your majesty. You had months to move on. You don't want your man back—or so you say—fine. Jay, you're cranky. You need dick—*good dick*—to knock those cobwebs off that coochie before it closes up for good."

Good dick reverberates through the immaculate lobby. Heads turn to stare at the woman who hasn't had sex in months.

Me.

Pay no attention to the lady in Prada with the mouth of a trucker, folks. What you see is what you get. My face is numb, but my cheeks aren't red from the cold.

Kill me now.

So it's been a minute since I had sex. Seven months, one week, and four days to be exact, but who's counting? Do I miss it? Of course. Is it necessary for everyone to know my neglected vagina is about to go on life support? Nope, it's not.

Seven months isn't *that* long. Is it?

She cuts me off again. "I make no apologies for who I am. Now pick your jaw up from the floor so we can check in." It's pointless to argue. I grab her arm in a rush and follow the bellperson with a knotted stomach in tow.

I stumble when we turn a corner and enter the great room. *Holy shiplap!* I died and went to HGTV heaven. This resort is all about luxury and doesn't pull any punches.

Windows stretch to the angled ceiling, which has too many exposed beams to count. There are three stone fireplaces with mantels draped in garland. Clusters of tufted sectionals and oversize chairs in a palette of creams and taupes invite guests to the warming stations. I don't know whether to grab a novel from one of the bookcases or prep for high tea.

"Give it to me." The corners of Emma's mouth curl in triumph.

I roll my eyes and bite back a smile. "You were right. Thank you."

Check-in is a breeze, with no signs of hedonism, and I thank God for small favors. A nap, a good meal, and a thick pair of wool socks are at the top of my scavenger hunt list.

The front desk attendant hands us our key cards. "You're in one of our grand suites on the seventh floor, which should accommodate your every need."

"Does that include a mountain man with a giant—"

"Tool belt!" I cover Emma's mouth and flash a smile. "She has a love for flannel and appreciates skilled tradespeople." Wrong answer.

She rips my hand from her face. "Yes, this one needs someone to snake her drain. *Deep.* Send him up with the thickest *tool belt.*"

God, it's me again. Where is my friend's off switch?

We stumble to the elevators next to the desk, out of view of the attendant, who has turned an impressive shade of white. "Can we *please* put the peen talk on hold until we get upstairs?" I push the button in a huff.

Emma meets my eyes and sighs. "Okay. No more dick talk for today." She motions to me. "Just do me a favor and do *something* with that hair and that outfit when we get upstairs."

I frown and look down. Black jeans, a khaki-colored knit sweater, and black motorcycle boots. Did she expect New York Fashion Week after she gave me two minutes to change out of my PJs? If she wanted a "moment," as she calls it, she should've picked out my clothes while she packed my suitcase.

She ignores my glare. "There's a kickoff mixer tonight. I need more from you than that 'don't touch me, I'm on my period' outfit. It's fine for riding a plane—but not a man."

I don't pretend to take offense. Emma is the senior creative director of a luxury lingerie company. They sell crotchless panties that cost more than the GDP of a small country. The Kardashians look like nuns compared to the people she's around on an average day. My friend stands tall in six-inch stilettos, ready for the runway and not the snow. Her crimson blouse plunges to her cleavage, which gold chains hover over in a sultry trail to black leather pants that grip her hips.

"You never know who you'll meet here." Her voice trails off to a place far away, one I'd like to be instead of at this singles' retreat. Back home, in my queen-size bed, safe from stranger danger and mounds of ice.

A side glance at Emma's hand to her throat draws my brows together. Does she need the Heimlich? I follow her line of sight and freeze.

Terrence, my soon-to-be-ex-husband, is here.

Chapter 2

Terrence

The elevator's whine ruptures my daze. Every thought scrambles to make sense of the woman in front of me, whose stare is a stab in the gut. The woman who left and never looked back. My heart punches into my chest. The will to take the first step doesn't register until the elevator screams.

Silence thickens the air. Guests move around the hall, oblivious to the showdown about to happen. I can't take my eyes off her, so what do I do? Gawk like it's the first time we met fifteen years ago.

Justice's voice wrapped around my neck when she'd said her name in our History 100 class. It had such force it was impossible not to turn in her direction. She tucked one of her black curls behind her ear, a nervous habit, and looked down at her desk to organize her textbook and papers. She was too innocent, with too many colored pens and note cards, not to be a freshman.

Our eyes met when she glanced at me under those thick lashes after I said my name. Stares came with the territory as a starter on the Golden Eagles football team, but the way her curious brown eyes held mine did something to my heart. I'd never reacted to a woman like that. *Ever*. So what did I do? Followed her out of class like a lovestruck puppy in need of a belly rub.

She's always the most beautiful woman in the room, the person who sees me for *me*.

Emma's gaze bounces between us. "Oh, this trip just got better," she says with a smirk.

Justice's glare will burn my skin if I stare any longer. Heavy breaths rise and fall from her chest. Her chin lifts, and behind those chocolate eyes is a volatile mix of hurt and fury she tries to mask.

Even in a fit of rage, she's gorgeous.

One of us needs to speak, so I break the ice with the first thing that comes to mind. "Since when do you wear motorcycle boots?"

Smooth. Real smooth.

Her lips twist, but her scowl stays in place. I should say more—I want to—but the words taste like wet sand caught in my throat. This is the first time I've seen her up close since our split. Minus her clenched jaw and her fists balled at her side, Justice looks good. *Really* good. Her chestnut skin still has its glow, and she hasn't parted with that messy updo she does when she's fed up with her natural hair.

I break eye contact to take a trip down the memory lane that is her body. That sweater does nothing to show off the curves I know hide underneath, though her jeans fit like a glove around the hips and ass I love to grab. *Loved*. Heat rushes her cheeks when my eyes drag up her form. The swipe of her tongue over her plump lips gives them extra color. Everything around us becomes a blur.

All I see is *her*.

Why hasn't she said anything yet? We haven't seen each other for seven months, and *this* is what I get? Silence? Let's try again.

"Why the hell are you here?" Stern, but it works.

If looks could kill, I'd be a dead man in this life and the next. "I'm here for the singles' retreat with Emma," she volleys back.

Well, that stung. My dick jerks in recognition of her voice but doesn't register the intended blow to my ego. Justice is soft-spoken at times, but she likes to get a rise out of me. She did, just not where she thought.

Focus, T.

I brush past her and shake my head. "Best of luck with your next husband. Might want to get a divorce first."

"You son of a—"

Got her.

It amazes me how real that transference of energy shit is. Because now, the woman who ignored *me* for almost a year is on my tail.

Let's see how you like it.

Justice takes rushed steps to match my casual pace. She's adorable when flustered, but I keep quiet to dodge a knee to the balls.

"You've got some nerve." It's meant to be a whisper but isn't. "Aren't you here for the retreat? I didn't realize what this was until Emma told me on the flight. What's your excuse?"

Huh.

For someone hell-bent on divorce, she seems...rattled. The pain buried in her words is a direct hit to my heart. Part of me wants to wrap her in my arms. The other part—the one still pissed she left—won't let me do it.

I shrug. "Don't need an excuse, princess. I'm here for the festivities, same as you. Now, if you'll excuse me, I have someone at the bar."

There go those white-knuckled fists again. This whole "I don't care" act is bullshit.

Justice has no right to question me after she ended our marriage the way she did. She wanted us to separate. I gave her space. She refused to respond whenever I reached out. I stopped reaching out. I can't win for trying, and I'm sick of it.

It wasn't a lie when I said I have someone waiting. Who cares if I embellished a bit?

— ❧ —

"There he is!"

A long whistle becomes my soundtrack for the walk to the bar, now twice the length, thanks to every head swiveled in my direction. *Dick.* Miles, a man I've known since we were in diapers, when my abuela watched us, wears a grin as broad as his chest. There's only a handful of people here to witness his antics, and they should count their blessings. This bastard will make my life hell this week.

I need a drink. Or four.

"Think you can bring it down a notch?" I nod at the ice queen in the booth across the bar with wrinkled brows raised to her scalp and smile. She has on one of those Stepford wife blazers and is two seconds from calling security or sending us to the Sunken Place with her teacup.

Miles turns and winks at Cruella, whose focus drops to the menu in front of her. Pink sweeps across her cheeks. When she glances back at Miles, there's a twinkle in her eye.

Jesus. Don't kill the woman.

He cocks his head and shifts his eyes to me. "Get your period, sunshine?" The stool grumbles under his weight. The flimsy thing probably costs thousands of dollars. "Thought you stood me up." He fakes a shudder.

"You don't look hard up for company."

His smile deepens. He lifts a shoulder, like flirting with someone's grandmother is typical Sunday behavior. Maybe it is.

Miles could pass for the guy in *Moonlight* and that *Predator* movie that's a ticket into the hearts and panties of women. There isn't a fitted shirt he won't wear to show off the biceps he swears are panty-droppers. We've aged a bit since our football days at Bodie, when he was an inside linebacker and I was an outside linebacker. But he keeps himself together, as do I.

"What the hell took you so long to get down here? Wait. Hold that thought." He snaps his fingers at the bartender on the other end of the long granite countertop. "Garçon! Another Blue on the rocks, and one for this guy"—he thumbs in my direction—"who looks like he's seen that little white girl come out the TV."

I give the bartender a look to say, *It's not his mother's fault he came out like this* and drop a large bill on the counter. Even with a good tip, no amount of money will apologize for the words out this man's mouth. I'm bad, but not *that* bad.

"So, what supernatural entity caught you by the balls?"

I let out a breath and sip the scotch. "Ran into Justice."

He chokes on his. "No shit? She's in this hotel?" His eyes scan the room like she'll appear if we chant her name in front of a mirror.

"No, she's in the *other* hotel down the road. Yes, man, she's here!" And it's throwing me for a loop.

After Jay and I split, Miles did everything but hire someone to crawl into my bed to get me out of my "funk." He didn't hate my wife. They had a complicated relationship in a sibling-I-never-asked-for-but-here-we-are kind of way. Miles didn't want the downfall of my marriage to consume me. How could it not? Justice and I were together for fifteen years, married for eleven. That woman was a thorn in my ass, but she took a piece of my heart the day she moved out.

"You good?" He studies me with a raised brow, ready to call bullshit if I lie.

Smoky flavors from the Johnnie Walker coat my lips on a gulp. This is damn good, but not enough to wash down the lump in my throat. "Why focus on the past when you can't change it?"

If only it were that easy.

My drink spills over the rim at his slap to my back. "That's right, bro. Drink up." Miles eyes me again. "No better way to get over your ex than with another woman's legs over your shoulders, right?"

What's with that look?

He locks eyes with something across the bar before I get the chance to ask. I follow his gaze to see a brunette and sigh. He's the closest thing I've got to a brother, but we don't call each other for a shoulder to cry on. Not that I need one.

I swallow the rest of my drink to head back to my room. This week is off to a great start.

Chapter 3

Justice

What do you say to the man who incinerated your heart when you see him for the first time in, I don't know, seven months?

Nothing, that's what.

I've had the you-were-the-biggest-mistake-of-my-life speech memorized since June, ready for the day our paths crossed. Well, today was that day, and I blew it. Terrence's cameo threw me off balance, and said speech went out the window. The words that had been desperate to escape wouldn't form, no matter how hard I willed myself to release them. Now I'm pacing around the hotel room like one of those cage fighters, ready to rip someone's head clean off.

Should it upset me this much to see him?

No.

Does it piss me off?

Hell yes, it does.

Em and I only got here thirty minutes ago, and there's "someone at the bar" for him? What's next, a proposal by the end of the week?

When did he book this trip? After our split? *Before*? How many singles' events does he go to? I guess the only people who care he's still married are the Lord Our God and the State of Texas.

One of us wanted to come here, and it wasn't me.

This reunion sent me to a place of rage. A ring of Hell that scorned wives vacation in, and I hate it.

Why? You left him, remember?

I traded our dream home for a top-floor studio on the other side of the city in the name of independence and self-respect. It adds twenty minutes to my work commute and faces a back alley, but there's a rooftop pool.

What other option did I have? Crawl back to Virginia? Terrence is the son my parents never had. Our split broke their hearts as much as it did mine.

But when your husband isn't there to love you through one of the darkest times of your life and makes you question his faithfulness, how can you stay?

The move to East Austin shielded me from any physical reminders of the man who triggers the tattered lockbox that's become my heart. I *want* to forget him. God knows I've tried. Yet all it took was a second—a single glance—for every memory to crash through me.

His touch.

The hypnotic cocktail of citrus and bergamot he calls a scent.

The way my name leaves his lips in a whisper before he takes me over the edge.

No matter how much I craved that man, there's no shaking the hurt that broke us. That broke me. And now, I'm back at square one.

Terrence Reyes doesn't need the six feet three inches he is to suffocate rooms with his presence. Between his megawatt smile and down-to-earth vibe, you lose all sense of time with a single step into his orbit. And that Spanish smooth talk? Dead on arrival.

My body went from zero to hot and bothered at the sight of him. He switched up his look with a trimmed goatee, his curly black hair shaved down on the sides. But his signature style is still there. Denim jeans. A Henley shirt that rests over his sculpted chest. A thin gold chain.

Taming hungry hyenas is easier than taming my treacherous vagina. Whose side is it on, anyway?

The one that gets us laid.

Our separation severed our marriage, but there's still a gravitational force that pulls us together—like at a singles' retreat a thousand miles away from Austin, in the middle of nowhere. It took everything in me not to climb him like a flagpole. The mere smell of that man's aftershave awakened a part of me that's been hibernating.

Why the hell am I panting?

Stop it, Justice.

I collapse on the couch and put my head in my hands. This isn't good. This is so not good.

"Still dickmatized by your ex?" Emma smiles over the crystal tumbler at her lips with a quirked brow. The kitchen chandelier casts a halo over her mop of mahogany hair, which is in a high ponytail she'll soon transform into a fancy top knot.

How long has she been there?

"I'm not here for him or his parts," I say with a sigh and an eye roll for good measure.

Fool yourself all you want. You're the one breathing like you sprinted from the desert to get to the center of his Tootsie Pop.

Her nail taps against a glass of clear liquid. My guess is vodka. She studies my face and smiles. "Lie to yourself all you want, sweetheart."

Oh, who am I kidding? Terrence has a face and body made for sin. Dirty, sweaty sin. He packed on more muscle since his college football days and could arouse the dead with a wink. Most men over six feet are lanky, but not this one. His thick thighs and that backside are juicy enough to bite. I speak from experience.

He has the abs, the biceps, the pecs, and—

"Wipe your vagina and go unpack! We have to leave in one hour."

Did this woman teleport through walls to yell at me? I swear she has vampires for ancestors the way she slips in and out of rooms.

After I unpack, I stand and take in the suite that will be our home away from home for the next seven days. Our bedrooms are on opposite sides but have the same French doors with wood blinds for privacy. Rich earth tones add an extra layer of warmth against the knotted wood flooring. There's a cozy fireplace and views of the valley from the balcony, which has a jacuzzi. This place looks like one of those destinations you bookmark that costs a kidney and a rib on the black market.

A pamphlet on the coffee table catches my eye. Tonight is the last chance to register for the week's events. A red streak snatches it before I get the chance to open it.

"Hey!" I shout to the trail of jasmine perfume.

Emma heads back to the kitchen, her robe a cape of silk fluttering through the air. Her thick mane is now in an updo that looks like it took more than the minutes I spent fantasizing about my ex to craft. "It's handled." The ghost of a smile lifts her crimson lips. "We didn't come all this way for you to toast s'mores. At least, I didn't."

Here we go. I fold my arms over my chest. "Okay, Mom. What events are on my schedule for this week? Do you need to sign a permission slip?" I swear to goodness, if this resort has a see-through sex room...

"Relax. I didn't sign you up for anything that will require smelling salts to revive you. Your virtue will remain intact, Sister, Sister."

Ha. Ha. I *hate* that nickname, and she knows it. Wear a few bucket hats and overalls in high school, and it's a license to poke fun at my "incorruptible character" for a lifetime. Is it a crime to look like Tia and Tamera and love a good Hallmark story? Christmas movies are addictive, damn it!

Emma exudes seduction, a pheromone that brings men to their knees—and a few women in college. That kind of sorcery isn't one of my factory settings, no matter how much she tries to take me under her wing.

But don't let this good girl fool you. I let my hair down during my marriage. A sister can bend.

I glance into her room, and my eyes land on sheer black fabric. The thing is the size of a prayer cloth, with a plunging neckline that stretches down to the belly button.

Emma is on the hunt tonight.

She appears from the bathroom with a cocktail in hand. Amber skin bronzed from years of California sun glows against ivory silk, exposing hints of lacy black lingerie I'd pop two ribs trying to fit into. "You're welcome to wear one of my dresses if you can handle the attention that comes with it," she says with a grin.

I stifle a snort. Target boy shorts are more my speed. Comfort over style for under thirty bucks. "You know that's not me."

"It could be." Her arm wraps around my shoulders. "Jay, I love you as you are, but you need to stop holding yourself back."

Am I such a prude?

It's not like I grew up in a convent or wear ruffled blouses up to my neck. Okay, I do own a couple. The point is, my version of sexy is under a few layers of cotton and nerves. I can be seductive if I want.

You organize your panty drawer by color and giggle when you wear sheer bras. The Golden Girls are less vanilla.

Fine. I'm an erotic killjoy.

What the heck *am* I doing? I played by the rules, and where did it get me? A first-class ticket to a singles' retreat with my estranged husband. And future legal fees.

"I'm thirty-freaking-four!" The look on Emma's face questions if my outburst is the start of a nervous breakdown. Maybe it is. "I haven't lived. I can wear something"—I motion to the dress on the door—"like that." I won't be able to sneeze, cough, or bend over, but I'll look good standing.

Her lips curl as if we're about to steal all the presents from Whoville. I gulp down the contents of her glass for liquid courage and gag.

Vodka. Yuck.

That's okay. New year, new experiences. Some savory, and others pure evil. Like this drink. "Here comes the new Justice!" I call over my shoulder on the way to her closet. Hangers scrape against the rod on my quest for the perfect look.

Too short.

Too sheer.

Too little fabric.

Defeat pats me on the back and hands me a participation trophy. "I can't do this," I say through an exhausted breath.

"I know, dear. Here you go." Emma reaches around to hand me an outfit from my closet.

"Oh, thank God!"

"Hurry up. We don't want to be late."

Chapter 4

Justice

Self-care Sundays are a coveted weekly tradition. They're also an excuse to ignore the outside world in favor of laundry, deep-conditioning my hair, and reading a book that doesn't include the words "emotional healing" or "divorce." It takes an act of God for me to give up a low-key night with shrimp and broccoli. Yet, here I am. On cloud nine with a buzz, headed to the main ballroom.

Em's talents at the bar cart gave me the courage not to ditch my best friend for an evening with room service and Nick at Nite reruns. Who knew vodka tasted so good after the third cocktail?

A figure in a sleeveless lace blouse catches my eye. She looks elegant and confident, ready for an evening with other singles without the urge to vomit in one of the fancy potted plants. I stop and smile at my reflection in the mirror. My top looks like it's part of a stuffy suit until I turn to look over my shoulder. There's some backless action that stops right above the top of my winter-white slacks. I don't have a huge rack—it's a good handful—but these cheeks more than compensate for it. With my hair pinned in a messy high bun and this red lip stain, I look like a librarian in search of trouble. The tortoiseshell glasses don't hurt, either.

Call me a good girl gone bad...at least for the next hour. I make no promises after that.

Emma gives me the once-over and winks in delight. Her walk is more of a skate, one that defies gravity and would land me in the hospital with two broken ankles and a bruised ego. Her hips sway with every step. It's a miracle her dress hasn't crept above the toned stems she calls legs, as short as the thing is, but that's part of her magic.

We step into a ballroom that makes elegant look underdressed. On the left is a wall of floor-to-ceiling windows with French doors. Rows of crystals drip from the ceiling and hover above cocktail tables set with white linen and bouquets of red roses. Couples form in a sea of singles. Some gather at tables, deep in conversation. Others steal a private moment in a corner with a drink in hand.

"Oh, dear God, they have name tags." Emma frowns at the registration table in complete disgust at the "tacky" sticky labels that await us. I choke back a laugh. If I have to mingle with strangers, she can wear a name tag.

After check-in, we head toward the bar. Em's diamond heels wink in the light as she floats across the room without effort. She passes a man who swallows so hard after one glance at her cleavage, I say a silent prayer he doesn't have a stroke and die on this marble floor.

Her steps slow when her eyes land on the corner of the room. "You'll be good by yourself." It's more of a statement than a question. She's not coming back to the suite tonight.

I reach for her hand and give it a squeeze. "Be safe, lady."

Emma turns to me and smiles. "Always am, love. Try to enjoy your night. Don't leave to order room service upstairs as soon as I'm gone." She disappears into the crowd.

And then there was one.

Em hooking up on our girls' trips isn't uncommon. She doesn't turn up her nose at my need for a hotel with a soaking tub, and I don't judge her for prioritizing dick over turndown service. Hell, I had both when Terrence would pop in for marital relations if we were in the same city as his layover.

I get it, and I got *it*.

Don't leave to order room service upstairs as soon as I'm gone. Please. I can smile and chitchat without a chaperone, and I will prove it tonight. I do it during work conferences—like the time Olivia, my assistant, ate a taco with a five-o'clock shadow and spent our entire trip laid up in the hotel bathroom. I walked the whole expo floor by myself and only got the bubble guts twice, thank you very much. I just...need a drink first.

A lone stool at the bar wedged between two groups opens up. At least there's more than one bartender to make the service faster. This is fine. I'm fine. I'll grab a drink or two and check some people out.

Then I'll go upstairs and spend the night with room service.

I order a classic manhattan and swivel the barstool to face the room. The women on either side of me curl into their prospective lovers. Based on their giggles and their hand placement over their breasts, it's only a matter of time before they disappear into the night.

"Here you go, beautiful," a voice says from behind.

I turn and lock eyes with the bartender in a black vest, who has my drink. The rolled sleeves of his white shirt reveal a series of tats on his forearm. Our fingers graze when I take the tumbler.

"Thank you. That was fast." I shoot him a smile.

He leans in with an infectious grin and lowers his voice. "I would never make someone like you wait."

Someone like me? *Oh, he's good.*

A man like this has zero trouble with the ladies. I know it, and so does he. It wouldn't surprise me if women slapped their panties on the bar as a tip or lined up to play with his. He has to model on the side, with that styled golden hair and chiseled jawline. Those blue eyes must sparkle on camera.

Brad Pitt. He reminds me of a young Brad Pitt. Hints of ash brown hair dust his chin. My eyes track the glide of his tongue from one corner of his mouth to the other. He's still staring at me, and based on the hunger in his eyes, he hasn't eaten in days.

"Penny for your thoughts?" God, why am I blushing?

His eyes drop to my lips. "Thinking about what I want to do to you."

My eyes widen when they meet his. Oh, he's serious. Is this how people talk now? *Hey, how are you? Bend over.* I need to phone a friend for dating advice. I'm so out of practice.

He watches my attempt at another sip with an intensity that makes my hands tremble.

"You—you're very forward." I swallow to force out the words. "I bet you say this to all the ladies."

That's right, play it cool.

Ten bucks says he puts women in the hospital with his bedroom antics, gives them carpal tunnel from gripping the sheets too hard, and knocks them through the headboard and into next week. They end up in the ER, and he's onto his next victim by breakfast.

Silence lingers before he shrugs. "I could bullshit you and say no, but you're too smart for that."

I nod.

His eyes drop to my mouth. "I like to fuck. No strings, no commitments." He leans into my ear and whispers, "I promise you a night of orgasms you'll never forget."

It takes a silent pep talk to wrap my hands around my glass and not fan my face with cocktail napkins.

Jesus.

Part of me wants to throw caution to the wind for once in my life. To say eff it and let someone worship me, even if it's for my body and for only one night. To be *wanted* again.

He's now inches from my face. His eyes drift down to my lips, and is it me, or does the room start to spin? "Um...wow." A clumsy laugh falls out. "As tempting as the offer is—"

"West."

"One-night stands aren't my thing, West." That, and my heart is still in knots over my ex even though I pretend it's not. Hot mess central right here. "I'm sure you'll find someone who will take you up on your offer."

"Okay then. Had to try." He stands up straight and taps the counter with his knuckles. "If you change your mind while you're here, I'll be at most of these events." *How convenient.* I smile with a nod before he heads to the other side of the bar.

If this is what's in store for me this week, *I* might have a stroke.

A hand squeezes my shoulder when I move to get off the stool. My eyes follow the hairy paw attached to a man on a phone. He has salt-and-pepper hair and wears a suit that makes him look like he'll sell you a Cutlass Supreme and a carton of cigarettes. I suspect the Gordon Gekko comb-over is an attempt to hide the fact that some of his hair went off to be with the Lord. He's not unattractive, but he gives creepy-uncle vibes.

"You look like you need another drink." My nose wrinkles at his greasy smile. "What are you having?"

"A manhattan, but I'm good, thanks." I lift my glass to swirl the contents still inside.

He pauses. "A manhattan? That's a man's drink, sweetheart."

My face tightens. What era is this asshat from?

This drink holds a special place in my heart. It reminds me of my grandfather and the nightcap he and my dad would have during his visits. I fell asleep to the clink of ice in tumblers and the laughter that reached my bedroom from my dad's study. The tradition continued with Terrence after Grandpa passed, and it's my cocktail of choice to keep his memory alive.

I stand to my full five-feet-six-inch height—six feet with these heels squeezing my toes for dear life—and slam my glass on the counter. "There's no such thing as a 'man's drink.'" Every ounce of disgust I feel wraps itself in my tone, the same way these shoes are mummifying my feet. I need to leave, for the sake of my circulation and not making a scene.

He grins and stretches out his hand. "I'm Warner, and you are?"

Not interested. I roll my eyes. "Justice."

A brow lifts. His eyes take their sweet time to travel from my open-toed pumps and stall at my hips. "This must be fate, Justice." He licks his lips. "I'm an attorney, and your name sounds like a case I can close."

I fold my arms over my chest. What a line. The will to mask how much Warner repulses me disappears with my patience.

Intrigue settles in his gaze. He's all but drooling when he takes a step into my personal space. It's clear Warner the Creep wants a conquest, and I would rather run into oncoming traffic and do the Wobble.

Warner rattles off his life story like it's a bio on an online-dating profile. He's forty-five, never married, no kids—thank God for favors—and isn't into committed relationships.

I interrupt his monologue. "You know, I need to get back to my husband." Ancient forms of torture would be more enjoyable than chatting with this man. Let Jigsaw ride across this bar on his tricycle to play a game and see how fast I offer a pound of flesh.

His eyes go wide. "I'm sorry, what?"

"Yup. Still married." I feign innocence and shrug. "I really shouldn't be here, but what can I say? Open bar." I hide my left hand to dodge questions about my lack of a wedding ring. As lust would have it, he spots a raven-haired woman and moves on.

Crisis averted.

Now for another drink.

"Well played."

The tiny hairs on the back of my neck stand at full attention. A rush of heat courses through my veins. I turn to the voice behind me, a smooth timbre that's commanded my body on more than one occasion. Terrence leans against the bar with his head tilted and a smirk I want to slap off his beautiful face.

I shake my head and groan. *Not tonight.* "Don't you have some woman to try to bed?"

His eyes narrow, and a brow raises. "You make it sound like that would be hard."

I'm done. He reaches for me when I try to leave. His hand grips my waist, and I swear time stands still. A familiar arousal spreads between my thighs and quickens my pulse. We're inches apart. Close enough for the hand at my waist to dip below my panties. Panties that are no longer dry, courtesy of his touch.

Terrence is hard to read when one of his go-to grins isn't in rotation. Like right now. I *think* that's concern on his face, but who knows? He frowns and shakes his empty glass. "Relax, princess. I'm not here to mess up your night. Need a refill."

A swift motion gets the bartender's attention. Terrence's eyes never leave mine, and neither do the fingers splayed across my belly. His gaze is hypnotic, because I'm now back on my stool with quivering hands, an uncontrollable heart rate, and coochie tingles.

This is too much.

He nods in approval and drops his hand to lift my glass for a sniff. "Manhattan? Some things never change."

"Guess they don't." My voice comes out small.

We stare at each other in silence. No words, no smart remarks. Just memories. His gaze drops to my mouth, and I lick my lips. Sweet Christ. How does this man still have this effect on me?

My eyes run over his body. If I'm a naughty librarian, Terrence is a college professor who could spread me wide for an A and play with my back door for extra credit. His white collared shirt peeks out from the navy pullover sweater hugging his frame. Classic denim rests over his muscular thighs and leads down to walnut oxford shoes. He's the Afro-Dominican Clark Kent in his black-rimmed glasses, and dang it if I don't want to run to the nearest phone booth and feel his superpowers.

The aroma of his cologne mixed with aftershave sends my senses into such a frenzy I don't realize I'm leaning closer for a whiff. The perceptive bastard laughs. He gestures in appreciation to the bartender who drops off our drinks, and I'm thankful it's not West.

No more close encounters of the awkward kind tonight.

Terrence straightens to hold out two manhattans. Electricity passes between us when our fingers touch. West might make me hot for a moment, but Terrence could make me wet for a lifetime.

I bite my lip and look up at him from under my eyelashes. *Stop flirting.* "Thank you."

What's with the Toni Braxton tone? Maybe I do need an intervention.

He gazes down and takes his time exploring my lips on the glass and my throat when I swallow. His eyes darken, and my legs threaten to buckle under the weight of his stare until he clears his throat.

What the hell was that?

"It's funny to see you use our marriage to get out of conversations," he says with a chuckle into his drink. "Classic."

My smile dissolves when a brunette behind him drapes her arm over his shoulders. Elton John sneezed on her. That's the only explanation for the sequins on her halter top of a dress.

She traces his collar with her finger. "There you are. Thought I lost you." The woman, who goes by the name Ava based on her name tag, has long hair and sways on hot pink heels. "How long do I have to wait before we take this party somewhere more *private*?"

Terrence chokes, and whatever moment we shared leaves as quickly as it came. Those were old feelings, anyway. Remnants caked on a jar you wash out and recycle. He's moved on, and Malibu Ava wrapped around him like a drunken tie is all the proof I need.

I knock back the rest of my drink, stand, and give him the glare of a thousand scorned wives. He will not break me again.

He searches my face and grimaces when Ava breathes on his neck. How drunk is she?

Terrence gulps down his drink and stands. With his hands in his pockets, he says, "Ask her," before he leaves.

Ava stares at his back like she's been stood up at the altar. She spins to me with flared nostrils. "So, who are you, his sister?"

"I'm his wife."

Chapter 5

Terrence

Had I followed my gut, I'd be upstairs enjoying a porterhouse steak and cold beer. Now I have to miss the game because I chose to attend this mixer against my better judgment.

When I registered for events, I didn't see the disclaimer about free admission to a drunken mating ritual. There should be a banner that says, "Enter at your own risk," the way people are at it. Something is in the air or the liquor, which is why I'm at a table in the far corner of the room with a bottle of water.

And, yes, I checked the cap.

The brunette I left next to Justice—Amy, I think?—reeked of perfume and was way too eager to get back to my room. Before Amy was Tracy, a dental hygienist who pawed at my crotch with a promise to "drill" into me that sounded a lot like pegging. Not a chance or my butthole.

I had my fill of women the first two years of college. I was a starting linebacker with a "bad boy" reputation by default, as I'm a Jersey boy. I was the Afro-Dominican playboy with great instincts on the field and panties thrown in his face off of it. Not the kid from Newark who was on a plane every chance he got to spend time with his grandmother during her chemo treatments.

I indulged in every bodily pleasure a woman offered because I thought I missed out growing up as the man of the house. But temporary pleasure didn't cut it. I wanted substance over convenience, and I found it my junior year in the form of a shy freshman who made me prove I was worthy of her love. A woman who became one of my best friends and opened my heart in ways that terrified me.

Justice made me wait an entire semester before she said yes to a date, and six months after that to be my girlfriend in fear of the "groupie" label. Since our split, when I'm not in Austin, I've tried a handful of dinner dates to numb the pain. It's a lost cause at this point. My work schedule prevents me from anything too heavy right now anyway, and that's fine with me.

I used my love of sports and degrees—a bachelor's in business and a master's in sports science—to become a strength-and-conditioning specialist to athletes. It was a slow climb to build up a name for myself, but it pays to not be a dick and maintain good relationships. College connections led to working with teams across Los Angeles. By the time Justice and I moved to Austin for her job, I'd established a clientele that extended to Texas.

My services are for professional athletes and celebrities across the world on an exclusive basis. It keeps my calendar full and me out of the house that's become a shrine to the failure that was my marriage.

People thought I was nuts when I didn't want to go pro. As much as I love football, it was a means to get to college and have a real chance at a stable life. I had no desire to roll the dice on an opportunity to earn millions with the risk of CTE due to repeated head traumas.

Travel consumes my days now that I don't have anyone at home. Have a fighter in Brazil with an eight-week MMA training camp? No problem. A production company wants me in Australia to help some up-and-coming star for a few months? Sure, why not. After years of hard work, I get to live out my dream. Business couldn't be better, and I have enough passport adventures and money in the bank to last me a lifetime.

So why am I so damn empty?

"Terrence Reyes."

I look up at the person who knows my full name, which isn't on this god-awful name tag, and meet hazel eyes. The woman's curious stare morphs into a smile. Her thick hair is up, and the spaghetti-strap number she's in molds to her curves like a second skin.

Madison Monroe.

"I can't believe you're here! What a small world." Thick thighs and wide hips strut toward me in black come-get-me pumps.

I cough in a failed attempt to mask my shock. "What are you doing here?"

She takes me in, stalling at my lips. Even with heels on, her head stops at my chest. "I should ask you the same thing, but I know the answer. We're both here for the singles' retreat."

Like me, Madison took the entrepreneur path after college. She became a personal stylist who grew her brand to include some heavy hitters in the entertainment industry. We see each other sometimes because of work, which makes this reunion very odd.

I didn't mention the singles' retreat, and neither did she.

Unlike me, Madison never married, so she could dedicate her time to the successful company she built. The woman is tough as nails and doesn't wait to take what she wants.

"W-were you in the area?" This damn retreat will be the death of me.

"I had business in Denver and wasn't sure if my schedule would allow me to attend. Can't say I'm not happy to be here." Gold bracelets feather against my hand at her touch. "It might be fate, running into you."

Two exes at the same event? What are the odds?

We dated for a couple of months our sophomore year in college after a hookup at a party. She dumped me and went off to France on some study abroad trip that summer, months before I met Justice in the fall. My relationship with Madison, if you could call it that, was brief but electric.

She isn't shy about her pleasure, but physical chemistry isn't enough to sustain a relationship.

Madison leans over the table, giving me an unobstructed view of her heavy breasts in a dare not to look away. Her body is on full display in its natural glory. No enhancements necessary.

Fuck.

"Want to go somewhere quiet to catch up?" Her voice slides down my spine like velvet. She bites her lip.

Call it a night and head back to my room to catch the rest of the game? Or take her up on her offer? We're old friends, right?

"After you."

We find ourselves in a small booth near the bar in one of the resort's restaurants. The conversation is light, and I, for one, don't mind the company. No heavy topics. No disappointed looks. My breaths are lighter without the weight of resentment pressed against my chest.

I sink into the comfort of the plush cushion and rest my arms against the booth. "Gotta admit, I had my hesitations about this retreat. But it's good to skip the small talk." I tip my glass to her. "I'm glad we ran into each other."

Madison signals to the server for another round. "So, tell me, what do you hope to get out of this week?"

"Honestly, I don't know." *Fail.* I scratch the back of my head. "Stuff like this isn't my scene."

"Well, I'm glad to see you trying new things. Who knows, maybe you'll find your match here."

I laugh at that. "Here? Doubtful. Events like this are more about instant gratification than going the distance." God, I sound like a Hallmark movie.

Her eyes darken. She tilts her head and stares at me like she has the answer to all of my problems. "Is that what you want, to go the distance with someone?"

I shrug at the idea. "I'm not sure marriage is in the cards for me again. Look where I'm at now."

"Maybe you weren't with the right woman."

Madison has had it out for Justice ever since she came home from France and found out we were together. At first, I thought she had an issue with me dating a freshman. But then I realized, as the years went on, that she just doesn't like her. *At all.* Hell if I know why.

"Madison." My voice borders on a growl. That shit wasn't cool with me then, and it isn't now.

She raises her hands. "You're right. I'm sorry."

It's not like she wanted to settle down. Madison made that clear in college—not that I ever thought about us engaged. "Barefoot and pregnant" is not her thing. Her words.

Marriage and kids were something I looked forward to after college. I like consistency and wanted a life partner to start a family with. *A family.*

Pain lances through my chest. Images of an inconsolable Justice and sleepless nights flash in my mind. A nightmare I barely survived. I close my eyes and push the memories down to the place that allows me to forget. It takes everything in me to steel myself. "So what are you saying? You, Madison Monroe, *want* to get married?"

She doesn't hesitate. "Career always comes first. I could have a lover in an instant, but I want more than that. I want an equal. Someone who's my match, who I can't live without."

"You honestly think you'll find him here?"

Her face softens. "Maybe the person I should be with wasn't available until now," she says with a smile. "Have you ever thought of that?"

That catches me off guard. "I guess I haven't."

"Well, you should."

Chapter 6

Justice

Sunlight greets me through a large window. Even with the drapes pulled closed on either side of the four-poster bed, it's deceptively hot, given today's high will be a balmy ten degrees.

Yeah, no thanks.

I tug the duvet to my chin, wrap myself in the rare bliss of sleeping in on a Monday, and moan into the pillow. Last night's mixer couldn't end fast enough. Who knows when the thing was over. I hightailed it out of there after my run-in with Terrence and the brunette.

The thought of him with another woman in the same hotel turned my stomach. It still does. We're over, but that doesn't mean I need to watch him find my replacement in real time.

Emma was nowhere to be found when my nerves got the best of me, so I took it as a sign to head back to our suite. My "happy ending" included a bottle of Riesling, scallops in a white-wine sauce, and *Full House* reruns until I fell asleep.

No reality show holds a candle to last night's mixer. People chased each other like wild animals ready to mate in a Nat Geo special. Malibu Ava and her merry band of mean girls got into a shouting match over a guy who faded into a wall of plants, only to make his escape off the balcony. Thank God we were on the second floor.

Speaking of escapes, where's Emma?

Either the pleasures of the plushest bedding to ever grace my skin have thrown off my Spidey-sense, or she never came back to the room.

Me: *Hey. About to order room service for breakfast. Want any-thing?*

When I get a response, it's safe to say an egg-white omelet isn't on her mind.

Emma: *Hey, hon. Worked up an appetite last night the menu won't satisfy. See you at lunch. xo*

Someone had a good night.

At this rate, I'll be the neighborhood cat lady with a lifetime supply of knitted socks by my fortieth birthday—in six years. Nuns probably see more action than I do, and I refuse to go out like that. It's time to give dating a go.

After I eat.

I call room service and order breakfast for one. Today is a new day, and I plan to seize it. What the heck did Emma sign me up for again?

I sit upright to dull the tightness in my chest. We're here for seven days. *Seven.* Parts of last night—Terrence madness excluded—are a blur. I *thought* my registration was okay, but the vodka cranberries Em made before the mixer lowered my inhibitions. Add in those two manhattans, and I could've agreed to sell my cheeks on the street.

I peel myself from my king-size bed and head to the common area. It's ridiculous how beautiful this place is. My room is half the size of my apartment and deserves its own spread in *Architectural Digest*. There's a chandelier over my bed, for goodness' sake.

After a quick scan of the living area, I zero in on my registration packet on the coffee table. Please don't let anything insane be in there.

Get a grip and read the itinerary. It's not laced with anthrax.

Snowmobiling.

Horseback riding.

Spa day.

Whiskey tasting.

Private movie.

These aren't bad. Good whiskey hits the soul, I'm so-so on a horse, and I live for a movie night. Em knows my fear of crashing into a tree on skis, so a snowmobile is up my alley. There's even a '90s party tonight.

We can work with this.

Relief proves to be a tease when I flip the page and see two activities that will earn her a swift kick to the crotch. Speed dating *and* a private dinner.

No. No. No.

A knock at the door interrupts my anxiety and the urge to pack my bags. "Coming!"

My lips part when I open the door and see Terrence. He freezes, his eyebrows in full retreat to his hairline.

I swallow the strange desire to sniff the air that now smells like his aftershave. My words fumble. "W-what are you doing here?" It's a question I seem to have on repeat.

He opens his mouth but snaps it shut and scans me from head to toe. This man's gaze overwhelms me so much, I pat my stomach to make sure I have on clothes. *Stop undressing me with your eyes.*

Knee-length socks.

A black tank.

Flannel pajama shorts.

Yup, still dressed.

My hair is up in a messy bun, courtesy of an oversize scrunchie, and my face is makeup-free. I stand a little taller and wait for an explanation. He's not at my door to discuss fashion.

Based on his deer-in-headlights performance, it's clear he didn't mean to come here. He glances around as if the person he wants to see will appear.

"My bad. I thought you were someone else. I mean, I thought someone else would be here."

I fold my arms across my chest. *Hold it together. You knew this would happen.* "What's the room number?"

"734."

"This is *744*." I point to the door. "That room is down the hall."

He runs a hand through his bed hair of wild curls. Or is it sex hair? Either way, it's a tell that he's uncomfortable—the hair-rubbing, that is. There's no mistaking the woman's shawl in his hand. God only knows who it belongs to and what they did.

It does look like sex hair.

Stop it.

I gesture to his hand. "Seems like you made a connection last night."

His caramel skin turns a guilty shade of red. He shoots his arm behind his back like I didn't see the mystery woman's shawl. "I talked with someone last night. We got drinks at the bar, but that's all that happened." He coughs. "What about you? Long night?" His weight shifts from one foot to the other.

Single Terrence is dangerous. He's a guy with the body of a model who is nice—shy at times, like right now. A guy who will look at you like you're the only person in the room. A guy who will invest the time to learn more about you to make dates more memorable. A guy who will lick you into paralysis.

I could lie. Part of me wants to, at the thought of him with another woman, but for some reason, I don't. Call it my mother's voice in my head that yells, *You better not!* or the fact that it's too early for this nonsense. I don't want him to think I'm jealous. Because I'm not.

Really, I'm not.

I shake my head. "I left early."

Approval reflects in his eyes, which drop to the floor. A smile spreads. Is he nervous?

"I'm surprised. Then again, you do wake up early."

For a split second, I forget the man in front of me knows me so well. I am an early riser and like to start my day with quiet time and devotions before the chaos. Terrence would sleep in most mornings after one of his many business trips, exhausted from the travel and the welcome-home sex.

Sex.

Like his questionable sex hair.

Stop it.

"Still true, but there's something about this place that makes me want to relax. So I slept in."

He nods.

The clank of dishes echoes behind him. A room service attendant glances between us. "Hi, madam. Do you need another place setting for your breakfast?"

Terrence responds first. "That's not necessary. Enjoy your breakfast, Jay." He disappears down the hall.

How many times will we run into each other?

Chapter 7

Justice

"You look rested." Emma stands to greet me at our table for lunch. Her thick, mahogany hair falls on bare shoulders above her cream sweater. She's camera-ready in black vegan leather pants and camel-colored thigh-high boots.

I take my seat and transport to a café in France. People sip from little espresso cups at their bistro tables. Black and white tiles checker across the floor to a handcrafted black bar that spans the length of the back wall. We're still in Colorado, but this restaurant gives serious Parisian vibes. Paris is a beautiful city. One that holds lots of memories...with Terrence.

Our server comes by with coffee and takes our orders. My stomach gurgles with zero shame at visions of a sweet crêpe. I need to stuff my face and stop thinking about my ex.

"When did you have time to change? I didn't hear you come in last night." Emma doesn't have on the clothes she wore to the mixer. Unless she visited one of the boutiques this morning, it's one heck of a magic trick.

Her narrowed eyes suggest the answer is obvious. She looks down at the oversize designer bag beside her. "I always pack an overnight bag, in case the sex is good and I want seconds in the morning."

"And if it's not?"

She leans closer and grins. "Then the only walk of shame is not getting good dick."

It's hard not to laugh. Em should teach a master class in confidence, the sexual and self-esteem kind. She's blunt, knows what she wants, and gets what she deserves.

"Looks like things worked out for you last night." I nod to her black vegan leather bag.

She adjusts her bracelets and settles her gaze on me. The edges of her mouth rise, and I sigh. Let the interrogation begin. "Let me guess. You ran into Terrence and sprinted back to the room early?"

Bingo.

My eyes fall on my coffee cup. I take a long sip to delay the play-by-play I don't want to relive. Once was bad enough. "He came over, had a brunette following him, and left me with said brunette. Pass the croissants."

"How are you doing with Terrence here?"

"I don't know, Dr. Phil, how would you be if your estranged husband were here?"

She looks at me like I threatened to make her wear flats for the rest of her life. "Don't be foolish, Jay. I don't do relationships. There would be no exes to care about or consider."

Thirty-five minutes of nonstop questions pass before the server returns with our food. If the CIA ever tries to torture me for answers, I'll be ready. Blueberries splash across my tongue as I bite into my crêpe. The whipped cream is smooth and light.

I look up and roll my eyes.

Emma can stare at me while I stuff my face all she wants. We're not talking about this. "I'm fine." I stab my food for another bite. "Just like I was fine when he showed up at our door this morning looking for another woman."

Heads turn at the clang of her fork falling to her plate. My eyes sweep across the room. Anyone else want to get in my business? Pull up a chair.

Emma scrunches her face. "Who did he want to see?"

I wave my hands in the air to conjure up someone who knows. "He confused the room numbers and didn't say." I tilt my head. "Why do you care?"

"I don't!" More eyes land on us, and my hands cover my face to conceal my identity. Why are we like this? She clears her throat. "It's such a coincidence Terrence comes to your room, of all places. It's like you two can't escape each other if you try."

Uh-huh.

Emma regains the composure she lost and digs into her bag for a compact to reapply her lipstick. "It would appear this trip is full of surprises from your past," she says, her eyes fixed on the mirror.

What now? I sigh. "Why do you say that?"

"Because Madison Monroe is here, and she's coming this way."

You've got to be kidding me!

"Hello to you too, Justice." Madison approaches our table with a smirk.

Crap, did I say that out loud?

Yes, you did.

The mere sight of her makes me itch. I'm face-to-face with the thorn who's been in my side for over a decade. She's a dedicated roach dressed in Gucci who won't go away.

How convenient she's at the same retreat as Terrence—scratch that. It wouldn't surprise me if she found out his plans and decided to show up. Madison would suck him from the back with bedazzled kneepads on if it meant she could replace his shadow.

"What brings you to Vail?" Who gives a damn? Get out of my face and this hotel.

"The eligible bachelors. There are *so* many options here," she says with a sigh that oozes into a joker grin.

How much bail money would I need if I pushed her out a window?

She towers over me in her stilettos in a desperate attempt to get under my skin. *Not today, cankles.* I sit up straighter. "Of course there are. Well, have at it, and best of luck." With that, I rise to my feet and signal to Emma. It's time to leave.

"I see Terrence is here," Madison says to my back.

My body stills, and my lips purse. She wants me to be jealous. I don't need a reminder that we're at a *singles'* retreat. The odds of my ex with another woman are up there with snow in the forecast. What healthy, single man flies to Vail, Colorado, of all places, to invest seven days of his time and *not* see some action? He doesn't have a low drive, and I'm not stupid.

Terrence is free to see whoever he wants. But if that someone is Madison Monroe, I'll put them both six feet underground.

Anyone but her.

They dated their sophomore year of college for a few months—or so I heard—before she dumped him to study abroad in France. Terrence and I met in a history class, and when she came back, our relationship went from friends to lovers. Her desperate attempts to sink her hooks in him because she "had him first" were as appalling then as they are now.

It's not like I hung around the bleachers in deep prayer he would give me the time of day. I had no desire to be a notch on the bedpost of one of Bodie's most eligible football players. I was on his radar, but he wasn't on mine. That was, until we got to know each other and became friends. He was different from the playboy linebacker everyone expected him to be.

Terrence is compassionate and a true family man in every sense of the word. I fell in love with his heart. I never wanted his image.

Maybe Madison thinks I took her man, but that wasn't the case at all. Yet here we are, still wrapped up in the same college drama almost fifteen years later. The reason why is beyond me.

She's an attractive woman and a savvy entrepreneur. Her time in France inspired her to pursue fashion and become her own boss. The only reason I know so much about her is because we were cheerleaders when Terrence played football. Even then, I could see her lust for him in her eyes. The one who got away.

Despite my current disdain for the woman behind me, Madison's beauty is undeniable. She hasn't changed a bit since college, and she looks incredible. Her thick, cinnamon-brown hair covers the top of her ivory blazer, illuminating her pecan skin. The hourglass curves on this woman put her in a league of her own. Add a hint of a Louisiana accent thanks to her Creole roots, and she's a woman who can bend anyone to her will.

My pulse pounds in my ears when I turn around to face her. *Breathe in and out. We're not cutting a bitch today.* "Yes, he is. I'm sure that makes you happy."

Her smile widens. She laughs and steps closer. I try not to hate anyone, but she can go straight to Hell and enjoy the ride for all I care.

"Terrence is a good catch. I'm happy to see him back on the market. It was so nice to get drinks last night and...talk." She pauses to search my eyes. "He was even a gentleman and dropped off the shawl I left."

If I grind my teeth any harder, I'll crack a tooth and the vein bulging in my neck. Terrence wanted to see *Madison* this morning when he came to my room by mistake. That means she's on the same floor as me. My stomach drops at the thought of them together. Was this his plan the whole time, to be with her?

Don't think about that. It will take you to a dark place.

Too late.

It wasn't uncommon for Terrence to see Madison after he started working with high-profile clients. They didn't run into each other *all* the time, but it was enough to make me uncomfortable and insecure. To his credit, he was transparent. He never put himself in a situation where the two of them were alone, and he never proactively reached out. Or so he said.

I steel my spine and stare through Madison's eyes, straight into her soulless heart. "I'm glad he found your room after he came by mine."

That's right, witch. Two can play this game.

I don't need to emphasize *mine*. My little revelation catches her off guard. Her poker face folds, and her jaw tightens. *Didn't see that one coming, did ya?*

Who cares if it was a coincidence?

"Oh. I didn't realize."

The temptation to tell Madison her mother should've swallowed her grows with every second of this standoff. But I won't allow myself to sink into the gutter, no matter how much she tries to pull me down. She won't get that power over me. I want to choke Terrence, but I'll pocket the urge for now.

"You see, Madison"—I step closer, my hands in fists behind my back—"Terrence and I might be separated, but we *aren't* divorced." I save the *yet* to suffocate any hope. "He's still my husband. I know you're *so eager* to try and take him, but there's a reason you never had his last name. Desperation is not a good look on you and hasn't been for fifteen years. It's time to move on. We're too old for this."

Justice: 1. Madison: 0.

Emma folds over in laughter, oblivious to the icy stare aimed her way. Madison is now the one with a vein threatening to burst through her neck. "You of all people have the nerve!"

In true bestie fashion, Em doesn't miss a beat. "You're right." She raises her hands in surrender. "I'm just sad you missed lunch. No worries. Justice still has a few crumbs on her plate for you to make a meal. We all know how much you love her leftovers."

We link arms and exit the restaurant. This isn't the last time we'll face off on this trip, I'm sure of it.

"I'm so proud of you for sticking up for yourself, Jay."

We're back in our suite on the sectional near the fireplace, a bottle of merlot and two glasses between us. The Madison encounter replays in my head, along with Terrence's unexpected visit this morning.

"Did you know she was here?" The question comes out soft. Gone is the adrenaline. In its place, uncertainty lines the pit of my stomach. The answer terrifies me, but I need it.

Emma looks down at her glass and takes a breath. "There was someone last night who looked like her." She sips her wine. "I'm sorry, Justice. I wasn't sure, and the last thing I wanted was to put you on high alert with Terrence here. I know how much you questioned your marriage because of her, and I didn't want history to repeat itself."

I cut her a weak smile and sink back into the cushion. She'll do anything to protect me, and I'm not about to give my best friend the silent treatment for it.

Still, this hurts.

"I need to get used to him dating...even if it's her."

"Do you still love him? I know we swept this conversation under the rug, but now might be a good time to revisit it, given the circumstances."

I breathe out the air in my lungs to ease the pain straining against my chest. I loved that man with my soul. The hardest decision I ever made was to leave him. It's one I still question to this day, but I needed to do it for myself.

Terrence and I married right after college. We were young, in love, and naïve about the pressures that come with "I do" in the form of friends and family who bombarded our love life. *When are you having kids? Do you think you'll get pregnant on your honeymoon?*

Is it okay for me to enjoy his dick without strings?

Emma and Miles were the only people who didn't want play-by-play updates on my uterus. I always wanted to be a mom, but not at the expense of my career. So we packed up what little we had and moved to Austin for a job that was too good to refuse.

Terrence supported me without hesitation and worked on his business while I found my feet in the marketing world. The decision to hold off on kids was a no-brainer. He didn't want us to struggle like his mother did when he was little, and I had time to make a name for myself in my mid-twenties. But, despite our best efforts to stick to our timeline, life had other plans.

After the second miscarriage, I didn't want to try again. It felt like my body failed me every time we tried to bring life into this world. Couple that with two years in conception mode, and I was beyond repair. Wrecked. Broken.

Family gatherings morphed into pity parties. Between my parents' excitement about the prospect of their only child having babies and Terrence's family—with enough cousins to fill a CVS receipt—I shut down. We considered IVF and adoption, but all of that went out the window as his business became more successful. Terrence took every opportunity to get away from me. The constant reminder of why he wasn't a father.

Was I that much of a disappointment?

Toward the end of our marriage, Terrence became a memory of the man I loved. I lost the husband who wrapped me in his arms and told me it would be okay. The one who ended business trips early if he'd spent too much time away. He grew more distant at home but was a different person around others.

How could I *not* question if there was someone else?

I scrolled through endless photos of him with clients on social media, which put me in a dark place. He jet-setted across the world while I struggled to cope with the aftermath of our pregnancy losses. He popped up in posts with attractive women and celebrities.

It was too much.

We became strangers over time. Soon enough, I hit my breaking point. The ache to ease the pain outweighed the desire to stay. I saved up money for an apartment and new furniture, found a decent spot on the other side of the city, and moved gradually, when he was away on business trips.

By the time he noticed, it was too late.

Terrence lost it the night I left him. I've never seen him so angry. So cold. He couldn't look at me after I told him I had my own place.

His silence was my farewell gift. I loved him, but I did what I needed to do: I saved myself.

My body stills at the hand on my knee. I clench my fists and sob. "I'm so mad at him."

Emma wraps me in her arms and rests her chin on my shoulder. Through it all, she's been my rock. She refused to let me close up when my world caved in on all sides. Even with her busy schedule, she made time to fly to Austin. She loves Terrence but never pushed me to reconcile. To her, marriage is transactional. She scoffs at people who dedicate their lives to each other. But deep down, she rooted for us.

"Whatever you decide, I'm here for you," she says against my hair. "And if we need to get Madison out of the way, I'll push her off a mountain myself."

Laughter finds its way through my ragged breaths. She's such a good friend. A sister. "Love you."

"Love you back."

Chapter 8

Terrence

It's three in the afternoon by the time I wake up. Extra sleep does wonders, even if I missed lunch. A fifteen-hour flight from Japan is no joke.

My phone pings. Six missed calls and ten text messages from Miles. It takes two rings for him to answer.

"What's up?" I run a hand over my face and wait to hear about whatever mess he got himself in.

"What's *up* is you've been MIA since yesterday." Who needs an ex-wife when you have a pissed-off man-baby for a friend? So much for not needing a wingman. "Did you stay up all night with Madison?"

"Nah," I say through a yawn. "We left the mixer to grab drinks and catch up. Came back to my room right after."

He sucks his teeth. It scrapes my eardrum and my last nerve. The disapproval is loud and clear. In his mind, if I were really over Justice, I would've moved on by now. "Sounds like you blew your chance."

The only thing that matters to Miles is whose legs he's between, which is why he equates marriage to a terminal illness. I'm still hopeful my childhood friend will grow up one of these days. He's thirty-nine. It needs to happen soon.

But underneath his brash and offensive behavior is a guy you want in your corner. Besides Justice, Miles is one of the few constants in my life.

We grew up a few doors down from each other, in a dingy apartment complex in Newark with questionable water pressure and stained vinyl floors. Single moms raised us. He never knew his dad, and mine walked out on us when I was seven to play house with a woman in the Bronx who shared his Dominican roots. My mom couldn't raise three kids alone, so we moved in with my abuela—my only connection to my sperm donor—who watched us and every child on the block, much to the family's dismay.

Graciela Reyes embodied every part of the blessing her name signifies. Colorism is real, and it cuts deep in our community. She knew the family would push my mom to the side without a second thought. As the darkest of four children, Abuela Reyes understood being an outcast firsthand, and she opened her two-bedroom apartment and her heart to us.

I learned cleaning to Fernando Villalona is not up for discussion and not question my abuela when she said, "*Mira, coño,*" because that person probably deserved it. She's the reason I keep *Vivaporu* in my bag for ailments and eat *sancocho* on summer days.

Not once did her bastard of a son ever check on us or send her money. His own mother.

Seeing my mom go through the shit she did is one of the reasons I would never cheat on my wife or not provide for my family. Miles, on the other hand, decided to take a different path.

The streets claimed him by the time he was eleven. With his mother at the hospital on double shifts, he got into trouble left and right. My mother did her best to talk some sense into him. She made him stay with us most nights while his mom worked so he didn't get himself arrested—or worse.

He was the older brother I never had, the one who pushed me to do better than him. It's a miracle he turned his life around in high school. Miles had become a rising star on the football team by the time I came along as a freshman. He was Jersey royalty when Bodie University scooped him up, and I followed him out to California on a scholarship of my own two years later. I was a walking stereotype during my first two years of college. People treated us like kings on and off the field. We had endless women on tap and access to whatever we wanted.

But then I met Justice.

A knock on the door snaps me out of my thoughts. I look down at my phone to see the call has ended.

Shit.

I pull on sweats and bolt to the door. Miles only has one civilized knock in him before he'll reenact an FBI raid.

"Where the hell is your head at, man?"

"Come on in," I say to the back of his black tee and jeans. Our rooms are only five down from each other. The walk isn't far enough for him to complain, but he will.

He takes a seat on the leather sofa, which looks like an oversize chair under his frame. My room might be the size of a one-bedroom apartment, but it's still a dollhouse for guys built like us. I thought a suite was too much for me by myself, so this will have to work. It's not horrible for a standard room. There's a dinette and a minibar.

Speaking of which.

I grab water for us and sit on a barstool across from him.

"You need to get your head in the game, T." He guzzles down the bottle in three gulps and heads to the bar to make a drink. "We didn't come all this way for you to stay locked up in your room and sulk."

I swivel my stool to face him with crossed arms. "Did you not hear me say Madison and I went for drinks last night?"

"Did she come back to your room?"

"No."

"Did you go back to hers?"

"No."

He shakes his head and sips the scotch he poured. "You know, if you play your cards right, you'll have everything you want."

What the hell is he talking about now?

"And what exactly is *everything* I want?" My brow will fall off if I rub it any harder.

He gives me a look I interpret to mean *dumbass* and takes a sip. "To have Justice one last time *and* sink into Madison."

I shake my head and grab the tumbler. Alcohol it is. "You got it bad for her, bro."

"No, she's got it bad for *you*," he says with a pointed finger. "Why not give in? I know it's been months since you've had sex. I'm sure your hand is tired."

"And how do you know it's been a minute?" I put my right hand behind my back when it twitches in defiance. Traitor.

"I'm not blind, idiot. You haven't had that cheesy teenage grin on your face since Just—" His eyes narrow. "Do you want your wife back?"

I sigh. "I didn't say that."

"But you didn't deny it either." His stare hardens when he takes another sip from his glass. What is with him and this cross-examination? He acts like I ditched him for an entire week. He ignored my texts for the two hours I was out. You don't see me bitching about it.

Miles changed after Justice moved out. He'd never admit it, but he longs for a life partner of his own. It was in his gaze when he'd steal glances at us together. Call me crazy, but this push to get me in bed with other women is a mask for his disappointment because she left. Miles doesn't let too many people get close to him, which is why he treats them like they're expendable if they don't fall in line.

I motion to the room around us. "I'm here, aren't I? I could've made up an excuse to go back to Austin, but I didn't." A ten-day business trip in Japan and a fifteen-hour flight to make it here on time were reason enough to stay home. It's a fight to keep my eyes open as it is. But here I am, under attack for sleeping in.

He's silent for a beat before he looks me over and nods.

Thank Christ.

Miles is like a brother to me, but I'm not about to open up to him, of all people. There's no point.

"Whatever, man. Look, I came over to make sure you aren't in this hotel room the entire trip. There's a pajama party tonight, so wash your balls, put on some silk drawers, and meet me at the main bar around nine."

"Bro, the only pajama party I plan to attend is the one in my bed." *Alone.* "The flight from Tokyo was fifteen hours."

He rolls his eyes and puts his empty tumbler on the bar. "Fine. You get a pass tonight. But don't make me drag your ass out of this room tomorrow. We hit the slopes at eleven."

I stand and yawn at the rush of jet lag ready to knock me on my ass again. "Yes, dear. Do me a favor, don't catch a case tonight. I won't be awake to bail your ass out of jail." I pat him on the back and walk him to the door.

With Miles out of my hair, I'm free to do what I want: call up room service, stuff my face, shower, and sleep like I'm in a coma.

My kind of night.

Chapter 9

Justice

Will Smith's "Gettin' Jiggy Wit It" thunders from loudspeakers. Beams of neon colors dance from wall to wall. Black-light party balloons and streamers hang from the ceiling, above a carpet of confetti on the ground. God bless the person in charge of cleanup.

Emma and I check in and pick up our complimentary fanny packs. Hers gets a one-way ticket to the trash. No surprise there. I secure mine across my oversize T-shirt and take two scrunchies off a table to tie over my curly pigtails.

I'm in '90s heaven.

"Could you look more childish?" Em scans me from head to my slouch socks.

Cotton pajama shorts hide underneath my shirt. Minus the high-top sneakers, if I weren't at this party, I'd be ready for bed.

I take a pair of plastic shutter shades off the tray of a server walking by. "Now I look like I'm in middle school again," I say with a smile. "Let's go."

We weave through the horde of singles on our way to the bar. Some wear their '90s finest, and others look like Victoria's Secret models in skimpy getups. It's no surprise Emma opted for door number two, with a red silk nightgown and a robe that touches above her knees.

"We meet again, beautiful." West grins from behind the bar. He matches me in a pair of blue plastic shutter shades, and he has his biceps on display in a neon-yellow sleeveless tank. His hair has a little gel in it to slick back the sides. Zack Morris in the flesh.

My smile fades when he takes in Emma. She's red-hot tonight, but his stare is familiar. Is he licking his lips?

She takes a seat. "I see you two met."

Um, *what?* Did they…?

"You slept with him?"

Didn't mean to blurt that out.

If it weren't for Busta Rhymes blaring in the background, everyone at the bar would know my best friend had sex with the hot bartender on our first night here. I know Emma moves fast, but damn.

West rubs the back of his neck and points to me. "She's your friend?"

Emma shrugs. "Justice, yes. How do you know her?"

I look between them and laugh. He eyes me like I'm an escapee from a psychiatric institution, but I don't care. What are the odds? It's not like West and I are an item. Hell, we never even kissed. He's just some guy who made me blush.

"Oh, please. Let's not make this weirder than it needs to be." I motion to the bar. "Make me something strong and fruity, West?"

He pauses and taps the bar with his knuckles. "Coming right up."

Emma presses the back of her hand to my forehead and examines my face. "What are you doing?" I swat her away and grab my drink to take a sip. Tequila sunrise. Good choice.

The intro to Montell Jordan's "This Is How We Do It" activates my running man. I'm itching to get on the dance floor, but my friend insists on staring at me like I have two heads.

"What?"

She shakes her head. "Nothing. Surprised you haven't flipped out—minus that psycho laugh." Her eyes turn serious. "Jay, I'm sorry. If I knew you had your eye on West—"

I raise a hand. "Stop. West gave me a little attention last night at the mixer. It was a nice tune-up, but I'm not naïve about what he wants." A grin tugs the corners of my lips. "Come on. We have a date with the dance floor."

Eight songs and three drinks later, I'm still at it. Emma tried her best to keep up but eventually threw in the towel. I'm in a circle with three other women who are as tipsy as me. Couldn't tell you their names if my life depended on it, but there's a weight off my shoulders tonight.

For the first time in a long time, I can breathe.

A cry rings through my ears at the start of Adina Howard's "Freak Like Me." It takes a second to sink in that I'm the source. My body sways to the beat on autopilot as the lyrics pour out of me like it's 1995. I had no business singing about a freak in the morning and a freak in the evening when I was seven—I was clueless what a freak *was*—but those were the days. Tootsie Rolling to songs for grown folks with a Kool-Aid Burst in one hand and Gushers in the other at one of many cookouts.

Large hands wrap around my waist and pull me against a hard body. I turn but freeze when a forearm snakes across my chest to keep me in place.

My captor presses his mouth against my ear. "Didn't mean to startle you but couldn't stay away." His arousal strains against my butt as he grinds against me. "You're perfect, you know that?"

Minus the fear in my eyes, we look like a couple caught in an embrace. The group I was with is nowhere in sight.

Great.

I push back on his thigh to put space between us. "Please let me go." He doesn't budge when I attempt to peel his arm off. "Let me go," I say again in panic. My body shakes at the threat of danger. I want to scream, but who would hear me over the music?

"Relax, baby. I won't hurt you." He tightens the hand around my waist and kisses my neck.

Nope, not happening. Adrenaline forces me to act. His hands drop when my foot collides with his. I turn and let my fists take over. "What part of *no* don't you understand?" The audacity.

I crane my neck to see his face and gulp when I reach his eyes.

I'm pretty tall, but this mystery assaulter towers over me. He's lanky—six foot five if I had to guess—and could pass for Adrien Brody's less attractive older brother. His bloodshot eyes make it hard to tell if he drank too much or is high. Either way, I'm out of here.

The creep holds his jaw and grabs my arm when I try to bolt for the door. "Stupid bitch. I see you like it rough." He pulls me close with a steel grip I'm sure will leave bruises. A slow smile forms. "That's not a problem for me."

"Get off!"

The music drowns my screams. I make another failed attempt to free myself when a dark hand the size of a bear paw connects with Faux Brody's face, sending him across the floor. Bodies freeze midmovement and take in the scene.

"Let's see if you have a problem with *that*, fucker."

Tears fall at the sound of Miles's voice. His eyes remain fixed on my assaulter's unconscious body. With clenched hands and a wide stance, he's ready to strike.

He peers down at me with hyperfocus. "You okay, kid?" I hate that nickname, but I welcome it with open arms tonight. He relaxes at my nod and keeps a hand on me like a shield. "I'm sorry I didn't get to you sooner. There are too many people in here."

Despite his ability to annoy me to no end, Miles is a good guy. He might run from commitment, but he's also loyal to a fault. Five years my senior, he's always treated me like his pesky little sister. With that comes protection from a guy whose build rivals a UFC heavyweight. He's a terrifying dude, but he has a soft side he tries to downplay.

"I'm fine," I say with a sigh. "Not thrilled with Sir Gropes-a-Lot, but I'll live."

We scoot to the side when security rushes to apprehend the motionless bastard on the floor. Blood leaks out of his now purple nose. It looks broken, and I'm jealous I didn't deliver the blow myself.

"I wish I'd knocked him out." My body tenses at the memory of his touch.

Miles brings me to his middle. We don't always see eye to eye—in life or with our height difference—but I take comfort in his embrace. "Easy there, Ali. Your shots popped his head back, but he was still a bigger guy."

"Justice! Are you okay?" Emma pushes through the gathered crowd in a frenzy and charges into me with a hug. She looks like she's seen a ghost. Her nails dig into my back. "I'm so sorry I left you. I thought you were okay with those girls." Her voice cracks. "Some friend I am."

I take her hands in mine. She's shaking, unable to meet my eyes. "Hey, none of that, okay? This isn't your fault." I pull her into a hug. "We've had enough of '90s night." I wrap my arm around her shoulder and turn to Miles. "Buy you a drink?"

He nods. "I'll never turn down a threesome."

Chapter 10

Justice

Agroup of men in suits gives us the once-over on their way to the bar. Minus the drunk monkey and the random baby, we look like extras from *The Hangover*—a hot mess of characters, and in pajamas, no less. Miles is Mike Tyson, Em's eyes are still puffy from crying, and me? Well, let's say I look how I feel: dazed and confused.

What a freaking night.

I finish my whiskey in four gulps.

"Easy, kid. You're still a lightweight." Miles shoots me the look of a big brother who doesn't want to deal with his younger sibling's crap. My nerves are still on high alert. It's either this or a pacemaker to take the edge off.

I tip my empty glass at him. "Guess things have changed since I last saw you." I'm not surprised he's here. Terrence and Miles are like Mario and Luigi looking for their next adventure.

"Yeah, no shit." He scratches his goatee with a chuckle. "The last thing I expected was to see some son of a bitch's hands all over you at a singles' retreat. Talk about a reunion."

Miles and his chocolate wall of muscles absorb one side of the table. With his pink cupid pajamas and slides, you'd never know he knocked a man unconscious ten minutes ago. He'd never hurt me, but he gives nightmares bad dreams.

"Trouble finding a woman to put up with you with the lights on?" I give him a playful nudge under the table. A guy just assaulted me on the dance floor, and my estranged husband is under the same roof, likely getting to know someone in the biblical sense. I need normal before I lose what's left of my mind.

His brow lifts. "Isn't it past your bedtime? The night is still young for me." He unleashes one of his million-dollar smiles and sits up. Thick veins flex when his large forearms hit the table. His gaze turns serious. "Had to make sure you were okay first."

Dang it, man.

You couldn't buy his devotion for the people he loves.

Miles graduated from Bodie University before my freshman year. We only spent time together when he came to check on Terrence—unannounced, of course, and fully expecting of a plate of food. He landed a gig in intelligence and cyber ops that allows him to travel and do God knows what to God knows who. The details of his job are "need to know," which keeps it a complete mystery. My guess is the mafia or the government.

I wave a hand to dismiss him and the subject. "I'm okay." I'm not, but I don't want to talk about this anymore. "So, what's new?"

The tiny booth creaks when he shifts his weight. His legs widen. "You know me. Work. Travel." He eyes Emma and scans her silk nightgown. "Women." Even with bloated eyes that make it look like she needs an allergy auto-injector, my friend is beautiful. "What's good, Em?"

She rolls her eyes. "Not on your best day."

"Ouch." He grips his heart. "Why do you deny the inevitable?" Another grin flashes. "It's only a matter of time, kitten."

Kitten?

My eyes ping-pong between Miles and Emma's staredown. Since when do these two have pet names for each other? They never spend time together, and they barely like each other. Sure, they're both attractive and enjoy wild sex that requires marathon stamina and stable knees. But Miles is...Miles, and Em has a zero-tolerance policy for cavemen.

Her gaze stays locked on its target. "I don't have time for your little antics," she says over the rim of her glass.

He doesn't break eye contact. "Baby, there's nothing little about me." His voice drops a level, and his eyes burn with a heat that wasn't there before. *What the hell?* Miles stares down at me when I clear my throat. "So what brings you to a singles' retreat? Finally ready to pull the plug on your marriage?"

The question hits me like a punch in the gut. My hands curl into fists under the wooden table. Memories dance in my mind, threatening to pull me back to the dark place I fought so hard to escape.

Guess I will lose my mind at this retreat.

He needs to get his facts straight. *I* never wanted to "pull the plug." Terrence forced my hand. But this is not the time nor the place for that conversation, least of all with him.

Where the hell was Miles when I spent nights alone on the bathroom floor with no husband to comfort me because he was away?

Did he care about my marriage then, or when I mustered up enough strength to leave his best friend because the pain became too much to bear?

I close my eyes and count to ten.

Keep it together before you end up in a cell next to Faux Brody.

My eyes rise to meet his. I open my mouth to speak, but Emma beats me to it. "If the person you're with makes you question your worth, at some point..." She shrugs. "Their marriage was over before she walked out, so if you want to chastise anyone for 'pulling the plug,' go find your friend."

She squeezes my hand under the table. Happily ever afters are a waste of time for Em. But, like the man who sits across from us, she'll walk through the fire and back to keep the people she loves from pain.

Her response gets her a side-eye. Miles would protect me from a physical threat, but there's no question where his loyalties lie. "Uh-huh." He takes a drink and stares at me like I'm a complex equation he can't solve. His gaze fixes on something over my shoulder.

I turn to see a bombshell with jet-black hair in a red dress at the bar. Her hourglass shape leads to red pedicured toes in gold heels. She entertains my old friend with a cocktail cherry that twirls on her tongue and turns up the heat.

What does it mean again if you can tie a cherry stem with your tongue? You're a good kisser? Good at giving head? Is it a bad sign I can't? There was a daily deal for one of those pop-up blow job classes recently. Maybe I should enroll. You know, in case I ever decide to give love a try or want to flirt with a random stranger at a bar.

Miles licks his lips at the brown beauty and drains his glass in a single gulp. "It's been real." He stands and walks to my side. "You sure you're good, kid?"

"Yeah. Time to head back and get some sleep." He's an ass, but it is my bedtime.

"Then I guess this is see ya later," he says with a nod and a head pat, his attention on the woman he plans to bend over. He makes his way to her, but not before he says, "You know I have to tell him."

"No, you don't!"

"Yes, I do!"

Chapter 11

Terrence

Ten hours. The dead would be at peace with that amount of sleep, let alone someone who traveled over fifty-eight hundred miles. Not me. Not after the texts from last night. I'm on edge, too wired to go back to bed.

My grip tightens around my phone. A man with a death wish put his hands on Justice. The bastard should count it as a blessing that he's in a cell. Far away from my reach and my deep hunger to punt his dick through his throat.

I found myself in front of Jay's suite before I realized my feet had led me to her door. The urge to knock was there, but I stopped myself and headed back downstairs. She might be an early riser, but she's not awake at five in the morning.

What the hell would I say anyway? *Sorry I couldn't protect you* again *because my useless ass was asleep?*

I broke her trust, and I have no right to run to her aid a fucking day later.

A man can only pace around a room for so long. I glance at the kitchen clock for the third time. It's five past six. Gym it is. I storm back to the bed and rip my gym bag from under it. My heart hasn't slowed since Miles told me about Justice's attack, and I need a release.

A healthy one that won't land me behind bars.

It takes less than five minutes to slip on basketball shorts and a compression shirt and throw on my shoes at the front door. I always keep a pair of hand wraps in my bag, and I hope to God this place has something to punch other than a wall or someone's face.

My stride mimics thunder down the hall. I'm pretty laid-back, but I have no problem putting an asshole in the ground if he threatens the people I care about. *Especially her.* Fast steps turn to slow when I reach the third floor. I'll give myself an ulcer if I don't calm the hell down.

Studios with walls of mirrors and views of the valley appear on the opposite side of the hall. They must teach lots of classes here to need so many rooms. Further down on the right is a glass wall that overlooks a large pool with swimming lanes. I make a mental note to check it out later, along with the hot tubs off to the side. An open meditation room is next to a closed day spa when I round another corner. I question if the gym is on this floor until I see her.

Justice stands by herself. Her back is to me, and I don't have to look at her face to know she's deep in thought. Her shoulders are tense, and her hands are in fists by her sides. My approach is slow so that I don't startle her. It all goes to shit when I touch her.

"Justice."

She spins to hurl a punch I block. Her reaction is quick, but my reflexes are faster. "Easy there, princess." I hold up my hands. "Just saying hi."

Panic drains from her eyes when she takes me in. She lowers her shoulders and lets out a long breath. "You scared me."

It hurts to see how guarded she is after last night. If only I could get my hands on the prick who groped her. I swallow the urge to rip out his throat. This is the first time I've seen Justice since the night of the mixer. I want to comfort her, but I know she won't let me.

"Are you okay? I heard what happened." My eyes search hers.

"Yeah. I'm fine," she says with a high-pitched laugh, unable to make eye contact. It's a lie, but I won't press her. If I pile on too many questions, she'll get defensive.

"So, we meet again." It's my best attempt to lighten the mood, and it seems to work.

There's warmth in her laughter. She shakes her head. "So we do." God, her smile could heat the sun.

Our eyes linger on each other longer than I expected. I take in her purple tank and leggings that accentuate her Tinkerbell shape. Her racerback sports bra curves around the swell of her breasts, which are more than a handful. High-waisted bottoms hug her figure and give a peek of her stomach. This woman has a delicious peach of an ass and full hips that make a person drool.

"Are you waiting for a class to start?" The question comes through a cough. I'm hard and need a distraction.

She scans the studio. "I thought there was an early morning Pilates class in here. Guess I was wrong."

Unlike me, Justice doesn't believe in physical fitness unless it's tied to food. I tried to work her out—in and out of the bedroom—but she's not the best at taking instructions when they come from me and don't include a sexual command.

A glance around the room reveals some resistance bands on the back wall next to medicine balls and yoga mats. We can work with this. I stuff my hands into my pockets. "I could train you."

She stares at me like I shot her and asked for bail money. "You want to train *me*?"

My brow arches. "You remember I do this for a living. There's no need to let this hour go to waste."

The trapped look in her gaze tells me her mind is at war. She eyes the exit but turns to me with a smirk. "Yeah, sure. Don't expect me to pay you."

I walk closer, until I'm inches from her face, and smile. "You couldn't afford me, princess." I would never charge her, but it's fun to remind her I'm good at what I do. Damn good.

Once I have the equipment set up, I give her the ten-pound resistance band and motion for her to go to her mat. "Let's start with a warm-up in a high plank position to get ready for push-ups."

"Push-ups?" She frowns and moves at the pace of a slug.

"Yes, princess, push-ups. I know you can do them. Get on your knees if you want." I lower myself to the mat and grin. "It wouldn't be the first time you dropped to them."

She tries to mask her smile and checks me with her shoulder. "I see you've matured."

After we finish our planks, I place her hands over the resistance band's handles and put the latex tube on her shoulders for push-ups. To her credit, Justice keeps my pace. I slowed down for her, but it's still impressive. We crank out fifteen and go into twenty squats, fifteen bent-over rows, twelve shoulder presses, and twenty sit-ups with the bands and minimal rest between the exercises.

"That was good," Justice says in a pant. Sweat glistens her skin and coils her natural hair. "Welp"—she stands and wipes her brow—"this was fun."

Her cluelessness is adorable. "Oh, princess, you should know better. That was the first round of our circuit training. We have four more to go."

Color drains from her face. She puts her hands on her hips and huffs. "*Four* more rounds? You want me dead that bad, Terrence?"

Four rounds were child's play the way we went at it when we were together. She'd never bat an eye if I wrapped her legs around me for another endurance activity. I push the memories away and chuckle at her melodrama. It's not like I strapped a weighted backpack to her and told her to run outside in the snow.

"I could add a few sprints if you think I'm not going easy on you. I thought I was fair, but—"

Her eyes widen. "Nope. That won't be necessary." She claps her hands together like a contestant ready to take on the *American Ninja Warrior* course. "You'll do this with me, right?"

I bite back a grin and nod. How can I say no to that face?

We finish forty-five minutes later. I used two extra resistance bands for intensity, which has me shirtless in a pool of sweat. "Ready to cool down?" I grab the two bottles of water I keep in my gym bag and hand her one.

She takes a moment to catch her breath before she takes a long sip. "That would be nice."

My directions happen without a second thought. I tell Justice to lie on her back, and I take a knee beside her. One hand holds her right ankle, and the other braces her thigh to straighten her leg against my chest. She tenses. "Just breathe. Don't fight me. I won't hurt you."

Her body relaxes on an exhale long enough for me to move her leg. I switch sides after thirty seconds and repeat the same process.

"Your groin is tight. Here, let's try this." I put her left leg down and kneel in front of her. "This might look weird, but it will help open you up, okay?"

At her nod, I diamond her legs by placing the soles of her feet together between my knees. Her muscles tense at the pressure I apply to hold the position. Assisted stretches are no big deal to me. I've done them thousands of times with clients. But this is intimate.

Focus, T.

Now is not the time to freak her out or cross any lines. "You okay, princess?"

The change in her breathing has my eyes on her face. Her throat muscles stiffen. I question if she's in pain until I see her nipples pebble against her sports bra. She's turned on.

"Justice?" My voice comes out hoarse, and our eyes connect. She's not the only one aroused.

I look down at my hands and realize they're now on her thighs, rubbing small circles against her leggings. "Shit. I'm sorry, Jay." I stumble back to give her space and run my hands through my hair. Feeling her up the day after her assault was not on my agenda.

I'm an idiot.

When she raises onto her elbows and pants, my wayward dick rises in full salute. Even with baggy shorts on, I can't cover the tent between my legs. Her eyes trail down to my erection, and she licks her lips.

Is she—

My lips crash to hers on impulse. Her breath catches at the weight of my body between her legs, and I swallow her moan through my ragged breaths. Her lips part, and our tongues mix with a desire fifteen years in the making and the longing of two people separated for months. I prop myself on my elbows to keep from crushing her and rest her head against my forearm.

Her soft moans rip the air from my lungs that would knock me to my knees if I wasn't already on them. My fingers tremble to hold her again, to caress curves I've worshipped for what feels like a lifetime.

My dick aches with need, tensing every muscle in my body. I grind into her center through the thin material of my basketball shorts and her leggings and groan. "*Fuck*, princess."

She digs her nails into my back and skims her full lips across my shoulder, trailing her tongue from my collarbone to the side of my neck. I reclaim her lips and thrust deeper, edging us closer to our breaking point.

A noise outside of the studio startles us apart. Neither of us moves or dares to break eye contact. "This was some workout," Justice says in a murmur. With her guard down, she's more relaxed than I've seen her in a long time.

"Yeah, it was." I have a goofy teenage grin, and fuck if I care.

She opens her mouth to speak but bites her lip. Pink dusts her cheeks when she says, "You really know how to give your clients the five-star treatment."

"Not clients, baby. You," I say without hesitation. My eyes meet hers in hope it's enough for her to believe me. No one comes close to her, and I doubt anyone ever will.

Her face presses into my forearm to hide a smile. "Come on, Romeo. The gorgeous women in your world are endless."

"You *are* my world," I say against her lips and kiss her again. God, I want her. "No one else matters."

She rolls her eyes with a smirk. "Not even movie stars?"

"Not even movie stars."

"Instagram models?"

My face twists at that. "I don't train them, but the answer is still no."

A brow raises. "Not even Madison?"

"Not even Madison."

"Okay," she says with a laugh. "It's not like you're stretching her out."

My smile falters.

Shit. Shit. Shit.

The walls of the room converge. I'm going to hurt her, but I can't lie. "Actually, that's not entirely true."

Her breath hitches like I punched her. "What?"

"She asked me for pointers to try during her business trips. And—"

"*And?*"

"It led to some in-person training sessions."

The force of Justice's shove leaves no room for interpretation. I fucked up. She rolls to her side to get up, the blush of arousal replaced by one of anger. "You've got to be kidding me!"

I stand and put my hands in my pockets. I can't bear to look at the pain in her eyes. Pain I caused yet again.

"How long, Terrence?"

Tell the truth. "On and off for five months."

"So you mean to tell me for more than half of our separation, you've been training a woman who's wanted your dick since before we met? A woman who *coincidentally* showed up at the same singles' retreat you're at, who *you* spent the night 'talking' to?" She looks to the ceiling. "God, I'm such an idiot."

I want to touch her but stop myself. Nothing I say will lower her guard. She's tenser than she was when I found her before we started fooling around. Justice is not the idiot. I am.

How did I mess this up so fast?

I run a hand through my hair. "Justice, I know how this looks, but I promise it's not like that. My business became my life after we separated. Madison is someone I know who's a client. That's it. I've never crossed the line professionally and would never."

In hindsight, it was a bonehead move for me to train Madison. I wasn't thinking when I agreed to do it. It's not like I see her every week. Maybe once a month, but nothing too frequent.

Her laugh mimics the Joker about to go on a killing spree when she pierces me with her gaze. "You know what, Terrence? I watched you fill your calendar with work and said nothing. I watched you smile your butt off with other women on business trips and said nothing. The only thing I believe is you'll hurt me if I let you, and that stops now." She grabs her stuff. "Enjoy the retreat."

My teeth and fists clench. "Fuck!" I didn't think things could get any worse.

Chapter 12

Justice

I told myself I wouldn't let him get to me, and what did I do? Run off like some schoolgirl pissed her crush didn't ask her to prom.

The hall distorts into a mix of shapes from the tears that are desperate to fall again. I can't reach my room fast enough.

How stupid do I have to be to allow myself to get hurt *again*? I should've left the moment I noticed Terrence. We keep finding each other, and it needs to stop before I lose what's left of my sanity on this trip. I will commit myself if I have any more thoughts about that man.

I make a beeline for the shower when I get back to my room. It's almost eight o'clock, which means Emma isn't up, and I don't want to wake her.

Liar.

Jerk-off.

Butthole.

I should be more mature than this. But right now, I'm stabby. *Really* stabby.

Hot water batters my skin. It comforts the tension in my muscles but not the pain in my heart. Terrence has been spending time with

Madison since our separation. *Before* I found out they're both here. At a singles' retreat.

My knees buckle at the weight of the betrayal. I steady my hands on the white subway-tiled wall for support and lean under the spray.

Thoughts of Terrence's mouth on mine force my eyes closed. His possessive touch made it impossible for me to control my response to his hands navigating my body. It was over the second he took off his shirt and put that chest and those abs on display like the caramel Adonis he is.

He had me under his spell, filled with the sudden desire to run my tongue from the base of his stomach to the rod between his thighs. Had we not heard someone in the hall, there's a good chance we would still be inside that studio. Planking on each other's private parts.

My teeth sink into my lip at the way he commanded my body. The man is a specialist who knows every spot and every way to make me erupt. Terrence might be easygoing, but in the bedroom—or inside some random studio, in this case—I'm at his mercy. Pleasure builds between my thighs as moans crash from wall to wall. My hand finds its way to my center and strokes my clit with a greedy force.

God help me with this man and his sexual powers.

I say a silent curse, finish my shower, and head back to bed. If Terrence thinks he can come here to meet whoever and do whatever with other women—*and* use me in the process—he's in for a rude awakening.

The rest of the morning was a blur. I ate, went snowmobiling with Emma, ate some more, and tried my hardest not to think about my ex who shall remain nameless. It's now day number three, and I refuse to spend the rest of my time in deep thought about...him.

Half the day comes and goes in the spa.

A deep-tissue massage here.

A HydraFacial there.

A wax downstairs no one will see.

After an hour in the salt cave, my mind is at peace. If Heaven is like this, take me now. I'm on my way to the lockers after four savory hours of self-care. There's a whiskey tasting tonight that has my name on it.

I pad across the marble floor in monogrammed slippers that are the coziest spa apparel to ever grace my skin. Second to this fluffy robe that caresses me like a cloud. The hotel will get these back over my dead, pampered body.

Signs for the locker rooms lead me past a sauna and a room that sounds like it needs a plumber. I've heard of those spa situations where water pours from the ceiling but have never been inside of one. Should I? The answer comes with a pull on the handle. It's unlocked. Why not?

The only light source inside is what I assume are flameless candles around the perimeter. It's hard to make out what's in here with such soft lighting. There's a few chairs, loungers, and a naked man.

A naked man?

Water rolls down his muscular physique. His backside thrusts into what looks like a wall. No, that can't be right. Why in the world would anyone pound his dick into the wall for fun?

Low, guttural moans seize my attention. I should leave, but, like I said, curiosity and all that. The patter of droplets against the tiled floor masks my steps. Rams-a-Lot's pace quickens. With a hand braced on the wall, he grabs something, or, rather, *someone.*

I rub my eyes. This isn't happening. There's no way a naked man is getting sucked off in here. My hands jump to my lips to stifle a gasp, but it's too late. He looks over his shoulder and zeroes in on me.

"What the fu—*Justice*? Is that you?"

Sweet Christmas. It's Miles.

My legs move faster than I can process. I fall over a lounger, sending me into the air and onto the slate floor with a thud. My robe falls open. *Shit.* I fumble with the cotton belt to retie it.

Miles's laughter echoes around the room. Glad one of us finds this funny. "What are you doing here, kid?" He reaches down to help me up.

I stretch out my hand to take his but snatch it back to shield my eyes.

Dick alert! Dick alert!

"Can you put some clothes on, *please*?" My knees scrape against the floor. I'm soaked and need to get out of here—far, far away from Miles and his peen. With one hand on the ground and the other covering my eyes, I make the painful journey to the door. At least that's where I think I'm headed. Sandra Bullock could come to reenact *Bird Box* and I wouldn't be out of place.

Arms snake around my middle and lift me in the air without effort. "You're such a kid," Miles says.

I suck my teeth while this nasty man carries me like a duffel bag. My hands are still covering my eyes—and now my mouth in fear of the weapon he just used to spear someone inches from my face.

He laughs in a roar. "Relax, I have a towel on. I won't smack you in the face with my dick." My feet touch the ground outside the room he used as his personal sex chamber.

"What the hell are you doing, Miles?" I brush down my robe to make sure I'm decent, unlike some people I know, who seem to get off in water rooms. Pun intended.

He shrugs and flashes a smile. "Thought it was obvious." My eyes can't roll any further. "I would say it's been a pleasure bumping into you again, but you interrupted my happy ending." He motions toward the lockers and gives me a nudge. "Now be a good little girl and go back to your suite."

I shake my head. "You're disgusting."

"Coming from you, Mother Teresa, I take that as a compliment." He winks and disappears back into the room.

Miles's words replay in my head while I dress. I'm not Mother Teresa, not even close. Maybe I don't have sex with strangers or slurp down someone in a day spa, but I know how to live on the wild side.

It's a miracle you wear lingerie without giggling. Who are you kidding?

Okay, I may have prudish tendencies on occasion, but I can be adventurous.

It's possible.

I'll admit *vixen* and *Justice* in the same sentence is uncommon. I still question to this day why Terrence chose me. He's sex on a stick. I'm the goofy girl who can't watch a love scene without squirming if others are around.

When we got together, I lacked experience in every sense of the word. But I was enough, even when I doubted myself. We earned gold stars in the frequency department, but I took baby steps when it came to freakiness.

The bench whines at my weight. *Same, buddy. Same.*

I really am a nun.

Like Mother Teresa.

Terrence is probably in his own spa room deep-throating someone right now. He has a crazy-high sex drive and even wilder stories from his early college years. Miles makes him look like a choir boy, but he still had his share of encounters with women who threw themselves at the football team.

His tongue alone threatened to put me in a coma on more than one occasion. The way he works his jackhammer should be illegal in every state and US territory. You don't learn what he mastered from watching tutorials on YouTube.

Now that he's single again, there's nothing to stop him from pursuing a woman who satisfies his kinks without a pep talk before and an aspirin afterward.

Like Madison.

I'm not like her or Emma. I can't compete.

The next man I date will look average, have an everyday job, and maybe a little fluff. Like an accountant or something.

I gather my purse to head for the door but stop at the full-size mirror. In front of me is a woman who doubts herself. One day she'll see her worth without second-guessing her value. At least, I hope. "You're more than enough," I say in a whisper.

"Yes, you are." I lock eyes with Emma in the reflection. She leans against the wall with her arms folded over the towel tucked into her cleavage. "Is this the day you'll finally stop questioning yourself?"

"Maybe?" The jury is still out. I turn to face her. "Where have you been?" I haven't seen her all day, and I thought we'd do these treatments together.

"Had some business come up. My session ended, so I'll go back to the room with you if you're headed that way."

"Are you coming to the whiskey tasting tonight?"

Her face scrunches. "Hard pass, ladybug. Vodka tasting? Yes. Whiskey? That's all you." I roll my eyes. She acts like I asked her to knock back cough syrup for the hell of it.

We leave arm in arm. "Guess I'll be out of my shell tonight." I'll die of shock later. Speaking of shock. "Em, you won't believe it, but I caught Miles mouth-banging someone in one of the spa rooms. It's the freakiest thing!"

She snorts. "Oh, Justice. You really are too innocent for your own good. Have you learned nothing after all these years?"

Chapter 13

Justice

We spend the next three hours in the bistro. I haven't laughed this hard in a long time. I'm talking full tears. I miss my friend, and I cherish the moments we have together. We text daily, but it's not enough.

There are no thoughts of my ex, what he's doing, or *who* he's doing. Day blends into night, and by nine o'clock, we're ready to go our separate ways.

"Holy shit, Jay!" Emma's voice bounces through the common area of our suite. I give her a sultry twirl in my black silk dress and peep-toe booties. My natural curls are on full display, courtesy of a wash-and-go. I'm ready to hit the whiskey tasting solo.

"Do you think it's too much?" I smooth the sides of my dress. It's not skintight but holds my curves in the right places.

"Honey, if I didn't love dick so much, I would take you home with me tonight. You look *amazing!*"

I steal a final glance in the mirror, apply my red lip stain, and put it in my clutch. "Thanks, babe. You know how to make a girl feel special," I say with a wink. If I get a compliment from Emma, I know I look good. "Where are you off to tonight?"

Her eyes avert mine to fix her bracelet. "You know, a little bit of this and a little bit of that," she says in a jumble. "There's a poker game on one of the upper levels I want to check out."

Emma at a poker table isn't unusual. As a little girl, she watched her father play other congressmen, and she has skills. Men who sit across from her soon learn she's more than a beautiful face in a designer dress. She's an ice queen who will steal your heart and the pink slip to your car if you underestimate her.

I smile at memories of her cleaning house on fraternity row in college. Em was Robin Hood. She'd take rich boys' money and their most expensive possessions with a royal flush or a four of a kind and give it all to the women they scorned. To see her work is to watch an artist create a masterpiece.

"I pity anyone who tries to take you on. Don't hurt them too much."

She pouts. "Where is the fun in that?"

I find my name on the attendees' list at the check-in table. There's a very good chance Terrence will be here tonight, but I don't care. I refuse to hold space for him in my thoughts any longer.

Tonight, I will enjoy myself.

I march into the tasting area with renewed purpose. A bar made of reclaimed wood stretches across the back of the room. Industrial light fixtures and greenery hang from the black ceiling. People chat at tabletops with wine-barrel bases. Whoever the decorator is deserves a raise and a show on HGTV.

A guy in a suit approaches me wearing the biggest grin. "Welcome to the tasting room," he says, like we've been friends for years. "There are whiskey flights for your pleasure at the bar. Enjoy."

I give a smile and a quick nod. Tons of people are here, but I shake off my nerves and keep my head held high. A seat opens up on the right-hand corner of the bar. I try not to squirm at its warmth and look at the menu.

"Hello again, beautiful," a smooth and familiar voice says in welcome.

I lift my eyes to smile at West. "Hi."

"Ready to try some whiskey?"

"Looks like you have the good stuff." With Glenmorangie, tonight will end on a tasty note.

"Sure do. And since I know how much you enjoy it, you get to choose your next flight on the house."

My brow raises. "Is this a ploy to spoil me because you slept with my best friend?" His smile falls. Shoot, he thinks I'm serious. "Calm down, Casanova," I say with a laugh. "No harm, no foul. I wouldn't sleep with you anyway, remember? No casual sex."

His eyes hold mine, and he nods. "I know that now. It's still on the house."

Who am I to stand in the way of free drinks from a gorgeous man?

West is attractive. Everything about him screams sex, but committing to the act with him—someone who slept with my best friend? That's a no for me. *Hard pass*. We discuss our favorite whiskeys before he goes off to tend to other guests.

An hour passes, and I must say I'm pretty darn proud of myself. I stay at the bar and talk to people about what brought them here and their favorite winter pastimes. The conversations come easy, which is a relief. It's a great time with total strangers and the drinks West supplies after I finish my flight.

I'm in the middle of a discussion when every ounce of air leaves my body in a rush. Terrence takes a seat at a small table, and he's not alone. Miles and Madison are with him. *Madison*. Tears prickle behind my eyes. I will not cry at the bar. It's a party sin, I know it is. My hands drop to my sides, and I force myself to take a breath.

You have to believe me, Justice. I'd never cheat on you, Justice.

Yeah, right.

Every promise this man ever made crashes into me at once. I close my eyes to center myself, which does nothing to calm my thundering heartbeat. I knew this would happen. I *knew*. That doesn't mean it hurts any less. If he thinks he'll play me for a fool, he picked the wrong one. Terrence hasn't spotted me yet, but I have an idea how to get his attention.

Game freaking on.

I interrupt West. "Hey, want to do me a favor?"

He follows my gaze to my ex and looks back at me. It doesn't take a PhD to see my intentions. "I'm game, beautiful," he says with a smile.

The edges of my mouth curve. "Perfect. Play along."

Chapter 14

Terrence

When I was a kid, my mom would tell me that God has a sense of humor. Now I get it. The joke is on me.

I chug every glass on my whiskey flight and pray the floor opens to swallow me whole. I'd rather be in a hell I don't know instead of the one I'm in now. Madison sits cramped between Miles and me at this small table. He's laughing his ass off at yet another random run-in with the second woman I can't avoid on this trip.

"How's the retreat for you?" he asks her. Our next flight arrives, and I waste no time drinking those. Miles gives me a look out of the corner of his eye, and I send it right back. *Eat shit.*

"It could be more eventful," she says. I choke on my drink at her hand on my thigh. "I hope to see more excitement." She turns to me. "Don't you agree, Terrence?"

Miles rolls his lips to suppress a laugh. I stare at the bastard, daring him to keep it up. My eyes lock on Justice before I have a chance to respond. She's leaning against the bar and in deep conversation with the guy behind it. Her black dress creeps up the back of her thighs as she bends over, and fuck me if the sight doesn't make me hard. The bartender leans down to whisper something in her ear that makes her giggle, and my fists clench when she bites her lower lip.

What the hell is so damn funny?

"Yo, T. You okay, bro?"

"Just peachy," I say, unable to look away from the show. I shake my head. This isn't like her at all. Surely she fell down a flight of stairs and lost consciousness before she came to this event in a skimpy dress I've never seen before to flirt with a guy. She doesn't act like this.

If I could take away the pain I caused her, I would. But this display right here will land me in handcuffs if I react to it. I'd never throw another woman in her face. Yet she thinks it's okay? Fuck that.

If you wanted to get a rise out of me, princess, mission accomplished.

A tiny hand grips my chin to break my gaze. "I had fun the other night. Are you speed dating tomorrow?" Madison's voice isn't the only thing that steals my attention. Her breasts are on full display in that tight white dress. She leans forward with victory in her eyes. Her hand creeps up my thigh. "I would really like to see more of you," she says in a whisper. Her words linger in the air. Heat and desire pour from her body.

Tempting.

Miles shatters my trance. "*Please* tell me that's not Justice about to walk off with a bartender. I've seen it all on this trip."

My gaze flits back to the bar to see her gather her pocketbook. The bartender takes her hand and smiles before they make their way toward a back hallway.

I'm on my feet and after them. It takes a minute to weave through the maze of people and reach the hall. The corridor is dimly lit, with a series of rooms on either side. So help me God if I walk in on them having sex.

She wouldn't do that, right?

The thought lengthens my stride. Justice can run, but she can't hide.

Laughter greets me when I turn the corner. Her voice becomes clearer through an opening on the right. I prepare myself to find Justice wrapped in the arms of the bartender and release a breath, a silent prayer of thanks. She on top of a wine barrel while the bartender searches through open cases. Her back is to me, but I can hear her smile.

Jail it is.

"And what the fuck is going on in here?" The roar in my voice silences the room. The bartender turns to me with a blank look and stands to square his shoulders. It takes me two steps to be so close our shoes touch. I tower the asshole with my wife by half a foot, and I have at least forty pounds on him.

"You're not supposed to be back here." He wants to be assertive but can't mask the fear that flashes in his eyes. It's the same look I'd get on the field before I knocked any man who tried to get by me onto his ass.

I point to Justice and say, "Well, neither is she," without breaking my stare. "Tell me something, do you often take other men's wives to the back room on your shift? I doubt this resort pays you for that kind of service."

Eyes wide, he holds his hands up and shakes his head. "*Wife?*" His tone suggests someone forgot to clue him in on that detail before they walked down here hand in fucking hand. He looks to Justice. "You never told me you were married. Listen"—he faces me—"I didn't know. Nothing happened between us." He looks to Justice, whose eyes remain fixed on the floor. "Why didn't you tell me you're married?" His gaze returns to me with a silent apology, and with the shake of his head, he makes his exit.

My eyes track his movement to make sure he's gone before I turn to Justice. She stares at me with her lips parted and gets off the barrel once my anger registers. I'm on her in one swift motion, caging her against a wine tower with my hands on either side of her head.

Her breath hitches, not because she's afraid I'll hurt her—I would never put hands on a woman like that—but because she knows what she did is low. We stay like this until she swallows and finally looks at me. "Terrence—"

"Save it." My jaw ticks. The fucking nerve of this woman. "There is no excuse for this bullshit. Want to get back at me for this morning? I've got news for you, princess. Nothing you say or do will hurt me more than the night you walked out—so cut the shit." I push off the wall to put some space between us. "If you want to go after another man, so be it. But sign the fucking divorce papers first. The ones *you* filed. And don't you ever disrespect me like that again!"

Her tone rises to meet mine. "You have no right to talk to me about disrespect when *you're* the one who broke our marriage!"

Did she smoke crack before she came in here?

"*What*? I never did anything this low to you. I never cheated, and I sure as hell never tried to hook up with someone behind your back *or* in front of you."

"Says the person who walked in here with Madison."

"Madison came by herself!" My voice is a shriek. "I didn't invite her, and I don't dictate where she goes. Jesus, Justice, you need to get off of it." I look away and run my fingers through my hair. If no one calls the cops to report two maniacs yelling at each other next to vintage merlot, it will be a good day.

"Don't you tell me what to get over, you son of a bitch!" She jabs a finger into my chest. "I can't 'get off of it'"—*jab*—"because *you* make her relevant." *Jab*. "You always made her relevant, which is why you couldn't wait to be with her after we split. I had to worry about her and whatever other women you were with on your trips."

I close my eyes to steady my breathing. I want to find the right words to say but come up short. Nothing works, and I'm losing my patience. "Your insecurities are your own issue to deal with." I pinch the bridge of my nose. "I can't make you see the truth if you don't want to. I've never been unfaithful to you."

She rolls her eyes and nods in a huff. "Yeah, you were doing your job."

"That's right."

"All that time you spent away from home when I needed you the most."

We both go quiet. Every emotion I thought I extinguished rushes through me with a force that makes me stumble back. I'm not proud of my workload after our pregnancy losses. God knows I would go back and fix it, but I can't. I didn't know what to do, so I channeled everything into my business as a way to cope. And it cost me everything.

I take in the pain now etched on Justice's face and walk toward her. Her eyes plead with me before they flicker. Her shield is back. "Don't," she says in a low voice.

My features soften to mimic the caress I yearn to give her. "Justice."

"I said don't!" Her scream breaks my heart all over again. "I told myself you wouldn't break me, Terrence." Tears spill. She wipes them and lifts her chin to hold my gaze. "You're right. The games stop here, because we're over."

I blink a few times before it hits me. "You want to see other people? Like, for good?" The lump in my throat refuses to go down. How the hell did we get here?

Her eyes burn into mine. They're cold now, void of any warmth or love. "We're broken, and I want off of this ride."

Don't let it end this way.

I turn my back to Justice, unable to face her or the reality of what she wants. A blow to the ribs with a knife, I could survive. It crushed me when I lost her the first time. I'm not sure I'll recover from a second. "If you do this, we're really over. I'll sign the divorce papers, and that's it." I turn around to face the woman who's held my heart and is ready to toss it out. Again. "Is that what you want?"

Her lips tremble. More tears fall, but she nods.

Fifteen years. *Fifteen years* together, and that's all I get? A fucking nod?

I'm shaking. Hurt turns into betrayal, hope into fury. What the hell am I doing here? This song and dance went on for seven months.

I'll be damned if I let her drag me along and accuse me of something I didn't do.

She deserves better, and so do I.

"I'll have the paperwork sent to your attorney in the next forty-eight hours." I walk past her, my eyes focused on the hallway. I don't want to look at her, let alone be in the same room. But I can't help it. I glance over my shoulder when I reach the doorframe.

Justice stares at the ground with her arms wrapped around her middle.

"I won't interfere the next time I see you with someone," I say. She looks up at me like she wants to speak but stops herself. So I continue. "You're right. It's time we both move on. I hope you find happiness, Jay."

Her face falls, and I walk away.

I will my feet to keep moving. She's not the only one hurt.

Chapter 15

Justice

"This might be the best idea you've had in a long time." Emma's voice glides through the phone.

I sink into the warmth of the lavender bubble bath and adjust the cucumber slices over my eyes. The hot water is a welcome embrace.

My marriage is officially over, or it will be once I receive the signed divorce papers. I spent thirty minutes staring at a wall of wine cases after Terrence left, as if they held the secret to life and why mine is in shambles. Things went too far with West, farther than I intended. But something inside of me snapped when I saw Madison and Terrence after his confession this morning. Every fear, every memory, crashed into focus, and I wanted him to hurt as much as I did.

As much as I still do.

"Do I need to come over there?"

This suite is so big Em and I can call each other from our bathrooms. She had a less than stellar night too. So here we are, soaking in our tubs with dessert trays, because why not?

I shake my head as if she'll see my reaction through the phone. "That's okay, love. We both need this. How's your chocolate cake?"

"It would taste better if it could erase the memories of a certain dick," she says.

"A person or an organ?"

"Both." Her reply is instant, and in a tone that makes it clear someone discovered a chink in her armor. Did she get too close to a man who is more than a good time in bed? I know it's not West. I've never heard her so unsettled.

She changes the subject. Guess I hit a nerve. "I'm surprised I didn't find you with our suitcases ready to go when I came back."

You almost did.

I blow out a long breath. "I thought about it, but what good would that do? You should've seen how much I hurt him tonight. Terrence was as mad as the night I left him."

"You two spent close to a year not talking. It was only a matter of time before things erupted. You're hurt. He's hurt. You both lost so much, and you haven't properly healed."

My fingers find the mute button right before a sob charges up my throat. I put the phone down to wrap my hands around my legs; my head is too heavy to bear the weight of her words. *You both lost so much, and you haven't properly healed.* How foolish am I that my friend who despises relationships has better sense than I do?

"You there, Jay?"

I unmute. "Yeah. You know, you have some pretty good instincts for someone who hates relationships." I take a bite of my strawberry cheesecake and let the flavors dance across my tongue.

"I'm not sure I'd know how to be in a relationship if I tried." Her voice is quiet.

Um, what? That's a first.

"Maybe we should switch places. I'll try to be more comfortable dating, and you'll settle down with someone." Dead silence. Water sloshes when I sit up. "Em, you okay?" Seriously, what is going on with her?

"Never better," she says dryly. "Are you ready to get out? I'm a prune, and it's not a good look."

We meet in the common area fifteen minutes later, both in robes with hot chocolate. It's like we're back in high school, only I'm not crying over Jared Franklin for asking Emily Johnson to the dance instead of me. This state of grief holding me captive to recycled thoughts is courtesy of my husband, a man I bet is en route to Madison's room for a nightcap.

I shift on the couch to put my feet underneath me. "So, what's on the agenda tomorrow?"

"Speed dating. Go figure, right?"

I snort. "I guess there's no better way to deal with the reality of a divorce than with a bunch of single people."

She reaches over to give my hand a squeeze. "Let's skip it. We'll stay in or go somewhere else. There's no need to put yourself through that."

I squeeze back and shake my head. "Nope," I say with a sigh. "I'm not leaving this retreat early. I need to get used to Terrence with other women...even if one of them is Madison." My eyes close to channel an inner strength that has yet to manifest. Am I okay right now? No, but I will be. I turn to Emma. "What do you say we stay up and watch *Girlfriends* reruns? We can sleep in."

She puts a manicured nail under her chin like she actually needs to think about it. "I say order the drinks, Joan."

My smile widens. "Get the TV ready, Toni."

Chapter 16

Justice

5:35 p.m.

Not a minute has passed since my third glance at the clock. Time is at a standstill. It's now or never.

I take a deep breath and look at myself in the bathroom mirror. *This is speed dating, Justice. Not an arranged marriage.* Horror stories from Lifetime movies do laps in my mind. Call me foolish, but they don't say "based on real events" for nothing. I don't need a stalker, a man after money I don't have, or a kidnapper tying me up in the woods.

The questions doing backflips in my mind won't let up, but only one makes my palms sweat. *What if the only person I match with is Terrence, and he wants Madison?* I close my eyes to push down the thought. With a clutch in my hand, my determination wills me to the door...right before panic forces a detour to the kitchen for liquid courage.

"Oh no you don't." Emma swoops in to peel the bottle from my hands. Vodka wasn't my first choice, but you work with what you have. "I need you alert, so you don't end up with some guy with halitosis and enough body hair to start a forest fire."

"You're right. This is no big deal." I hear the words come out of my mouth, but my heart still beats like I'm in cardiac arrest. This is my first time back on the dating scene since Terrence, and I'm scared.

My last first date was my freshman year in college, when he took me out for a movie and pizza at the mall. To get me to agree to go, he promised to pull out all the stops, and I couldn't stop laughing when he handed me a ticket for *The Break-Up*, of all films. Em just about died when she found out how cheap our first date was, but it was perfect. Terrence knew I was hesitant to be with a college football player, one three years older and with a colorful reputation at that. He kept our initial outings casual, so I would be comfortable, and he took the time to show how much he cared.

Now, I don't know what the heck to expect.

"Justice, look at me." Emma puts a hand on my shoulders. "I know this is out of your comfort zone, sweetheart, but it will be good for you. Just take a deep breath and try to have fun. That's all that's expected of you."

My exhale is slow, to ease the air that constricts my lungs. She's right. I need to loosen up. I can do that.

How come I'm not doing that?

You need to breathe first.

Right.

She grabs her purse and takes a final glance at herself in the mirror. Emma is stunning in her signature little black dress. It has a very noticeable piece of fabric missing from under the side of her right breast to the top of her belly. If looks could kill, whoever pissed her off yesterday is a dead man walking.

My look is business casual with a sexy twist. I have on a black blazer, but instead of a blouse, I opted for lacy black shapewear that looks like a bra. The peach of a backside I inherited from my mama is on full display in black ankle pants that lead to a strappy pair of heels. My hair is in an updo to accentuate my neck.

A figure at the end of the hallway catches my eye on our way to the elevator.

Madison.

"Here we go," I say under my breath, prompting Emma to look up. My lips twist at her curves, which are pressed against the short, off-the-shoulder lace dress that clings to her body. Is it see-through? The amount of lace I have on has nothing on her. It's clear she's dressed to kill, and knowing her intended target gives me a brief bout of acid reflux.

She stares at me with daggers in her eyes. A twisted smile forms. "Justice. I had no idea we were on the same floor."

"I take it you're going to speed dating too?" She won't get the satisfaction of seeing me bothered.

"Sure am." She takes in my outfit. "You look...professional."

"And you look eager." The elevator opens. "After you."

Tension rises as the floors count down. This will be fine. Great. Wonderful. We can be in the same room while she makes a love connection with my ex. Happens all the time, like on one of those reality shows. Not a big deal.

Madison saunters away as soon as the elevator opens, leaving me with anxiety that greets me with a death grip and refuses to let go. My eyes land on the entrance, and I swallow a breath.

Easy, Jay. This isn't that hard.

It's all good. Everything is fine.

"Do you want to give yourself that pep talk any louder? I don't think the women in the corner heard you," Emma says with a raised eyebrow.

Crap, did I say that out loud?

"Yes, you did. Now stop talking to yourself before you scare people off." She yanks my hand into hers and pulls me inside the restaurant.

Red rose petals form a pathway to a long row of white chairs and tables with scattered candles. Lights from town twinkle to illuminate the valley through the floor-to-ceiling windows.

"Champagne, madam?"

I give a quick curtsy and knock back two glasses on the waiter's tray. He gapes at me like he hasn't seen a woman about to lose her shit in front of a bunch of strangers. That's right, buddy. I don't give a flip tonight. *Piss off.* He dips his head and leaves after a brief staredown.

"Come on, let's find our seats," I say to Emma, who can't stop laughing. I guess my pre-midlife crisis is funny.

The heavens bless me with Madison seven chairs away from mine. I would do a high kick if Emma wasn't just as far. Looks like I'm on my own tonight. Another waiter comes by with more champagne. From what I understand, we get refills every time a "prospect" moves in front of us, like an adult version of musical chairs.

During registration, we filled out cards with a range of gender identities and sexual orientations. There are a series of speed dating events tonight based on how we identified and our ideal matches. Everyone wears a name tag noting their preferred pronouns and identities. My tag has "she/her" and "cishet woman," and Emma wears one that says "she/her" and "cisheteroflexible woman." She primarily desires cishet men but has the occasional same-sex attraction, though she's never fully acted on the desire and doesn't identify as bisexual.

A lady appears and explains what comes next. We'll have five minutes with each person. If there's a "spark," you mark it on your scorecard. Should you match with someone, you'll both go on a private date, with a formal invitation sent to your room that morning.

No pressure at all.

"Does anyone have any questions about tonight's event?" the coordinator asks the fifteen of us who are seated. "We will have short breaks throughout, so please refrain from leaving your seat unless it's an emergency."

Does a nervous breakdown count?

"The government practices mind control through tap water."

Five minutes seem like an eternity listening to Brian, a forty-something-year-old man who works at a zoo and is all about conspiracy theories. He has yet to ask me a single question, but I know everything about him. Let's see, he spends his vacation time trekking God knows where to find Bigfoot, lives one door down from his mother, and has a piece of lettuce in his teeth so big it waves at me every time he speaks.

He has to sense there's no chemistry. I lost all interest in the conversation four and a half minutes ago, but here we are. Deep in the bowels of purgatory.

"That's time. Please move to the next person."

Thank you, Jesus.

I glance Emma's way when Brian gets up to move to his next victim. A man with olive skin and a million-dollar haircut in an all-black suit sits before her. Her lips part when they make eye contact, and I know the game is over before it starts.

Don't hurt him too much, Em.

My eyes find Terrence. He's on his way to Madison with a huge smile on his face. She waits in anticipation with eyes that track his every move. I try to suppress visions of them in a hotel room with his tongue down her throat or between her legs but come up short. So I wave the waiter over to ask for three fingers of whiskey. When it reaches my hand, it's gone in less than four gulps.

Keep it together. You knew this would happen.

I did, but I didn't think I would have a front-row seat to their love connection.

Sweat trickles down my back, and I scan the room for the closest exit. The desire to make a run for it and get on the next flight out of here grows with each glance I steal of the two of them. But no matter how much it hurts, I know running away won't solve anything. So I stay in my seat like the big girl I think I am, smooth the wrinkles out of my pants, and steel my spine.

Terrence and I are over, but that doesn't mean life is.

"Switching to the hard stuff already?"

I jump at Miles's voice. How long has he been here? "Champagne isn't gonna cut it for this event."

His laugh is deep. "Okay, Justice, I see you." He wiggles his eyebrows and takes a seat.

"Five minutes start now," the event coordinator says to the room. Brian was an unbearable person to have in front of me, but I think Miles will take the award for most uncomfortable.

He cuts me off when I try to speak. "Now, before you get any ideas, I don't mess with my friends' exes. *Especially* wives."

I sit back and cross my arms over my chest. "As if you would have a chance. You're worse than a yeast infection."

Silence weighs between us before we erupt in laughter. He chuckles into his glass. "Never a dull moment with you, kid."

I rest my elbows on the table. "Any new adventures? Outside of getting head in the day spa." I'm loud enough that the people next to us stop and stare. In true Miles fashion, he shrugs, leans back, and puts his arm over the back of the chair. He couldn't care less.

"Now, now, Justice. You're still too young to hear about how grown-ups satisfy their urges." He pauses to scan my face. "You look wound up, by the way. Like you need a release. You and someone else I know." The last part comes out in a mumble.

Wait. Is he saying Terrence *hasn't* been with anyone since we split? Beautiful women—actresses, professional cheerleaders, and the occasional model—with more confidence and experience in the bedroom than I have surround him on any given day.

This can't be true, can it?

I glance over at my ex, who's in deep conversation with Madison. Pain spreads through my chest with every stroke of her hand on his. He's not stopping her.

"Your little stunt was his breaking point." I look up to see Miles's eyes on them. He turns back to me. There's an apology in his gaze that twists my heart. "I thought you two would go the distance," he says with a head shake.

I still at his words. Miles doesn't believe in commitment, let alone for life. He yearned to have his friend back so they could tag team women like they were back in college. I know he did.

"Don't act like you aren't happy he's single again. You probably have women lined up for him." I nod over to Exhibit A. "Starting with her."

"I'll admit I egged him on, but only to stop him from moping around like a Keyshia Cole song on repeat. You and I both know he's not into casual sex. Not since you."

"Sometimes the fairy tale doesn't turn out how you expect," I say with a weak laugh.

He stares at me for longer than I expect. "Uh-huh."

I slap his bicep. The thing is the size of a human head. "Don't tell me you're getting soft on me now. Since when do you care? You have your wingman back. Do a flip or something."

Miles rises at the sound of the buzzer. Our time is up. "Some people aren't meant to be single their whole lives, kid." His voice trails off when he moves to the next seat.

I spend the next thirty minutes in a silent prayer I'll somehow transport back to my room. A soak in the freestanding tub with a good book and bubbles sounds perfect. The bandwidth to track Terrence's love connections or decipher Miles's cryptic message is long gone. This entire night is a disaster. It's next to impossible for me to keep up with different conversations and smile at people I have no interest in pursuing.

The end of another round has my eyes back on the clock. Less than ten minutes left. "Thank God," I say to myself in a whisper. Only I'm not as quiet as I thought.

"Come again?"

My body startles, uncertain whether to soften or tense at the familiar voice. Terrence stares at me, his brows drawn together.

I sigh. "It's nothing. I'm ready for this to be over."

He takes a beat before he sits in front of me with a look on his face I can't decipher. "You're not having a good time?" His concern is so confusing. Why can't estranged husbands come with some type of manual?

My mouth opens to respond but snaps shut when I take him in. Is it too much to ask for him to look awful for one day? I'm two seconds from crisis, and he looks ready for a night on the town collecting women's panties.

His navy button-down shirt rests against his broad chest and dark denim jeans. The top two buttons are undone to reveal the gold chain his mother gave him when he turned sixteen. It's subtle, but it doesn't fail to make a statement.

How is this fair?

"It's so hard being the life of the party." I fan myself and roll my eyes.

He chuckles at the joke and scoots closer. "So what's new?" Terrence's voice crashes into me and crumbles my guard. Oh, hell. I miss this. Our talks. How easy it is to connect.

It takes a second to push down the emotions and answer. "Well, I got a promotion. I'm now the vice president of marketing."

His eyes go wide. I see the urge to pick me up and spin me. "That's great, Jay!" He slaps the table. "I know how hard you worked for that. It was only a matter of time." Pride sparkles in his eyes.

Terrence was there from the beginning. He encouraged me to take the job in Austin that uprooted us from Los Angeles. It was a bit of an adjustment since all of his business contacts were still in California at the time. But he never complained or made me second-guess my decision—our decision.

We stare into each other's eyes in silence, a habit that seems hard to break. The air crackles between us, and it's too much to bear.

Damn it. Do not cry.

"What about you?" I cough. "I'm sure you're living it up internationally."

He gives a slight nod. "Business is good. There's a lot of work, and you know me." He rubs the back of his neck, a tell he's uncomfortable. He doesn't like to talk about his success, but what he's accomplished is no small feat.

Terrence created a company that aligns with his passion and allows him to reach so many goals. He bought the house on the corner of my favorite block, the one that always caught my eye on our strolls. He moved his mother out of the small apartment he grew up in and into her very first home. She's now retired and spends her days traveling, courtesy of her loving son. Sadly, Abuela Reyes passed while Terrence was in college, but I know she would be proud of him. She always was.

"So we're both workaholics," I say, making us both laugh. We might come from different backgrounds, but Terrence and I are no strangers to hard work. We see what we want and go after it.

I reach for his hand out of habit. "Regardless of what this retreat brings, I really hope you find happiness outside of your job." Look at that. My courage kicked in. A few glasses of champagne and whiskey did the trick. "I mean it. I know we didn't work out, but—"

"Justice." His hand covers mine. There's more he wants to say but can't find the words. So I continue.

"We don't have to talk about it. I know you and Madison are... If she's the one you want"—I swallow and look him in the eyes—"I truly hope you're happy. Things haven't been the best between us." That's putting it lightly. "I don't want that anymore. Like you said, it's time for us to both move on. God knows it's been a while." The last part comes out in an unassured laugh.

Holy crap. I did *not* expect to say all of that.

Something changed in me tonight. I didn't think I could stomach the sight of him as a bachelor, but I remembered an important lesson:

I'm still alive.

Do I spend the rest of my years in tears over my failed marriage and the man I loved? Or do I pick myself up and pour into *me*?

At the buzzer, the event coordinator signals for the next move. Terrence takes one look at me before he gets up to leave.

"Goodbye, Justice."

"Goodbye."

Chapter 17

Justice

As expected, Emma didn't come back to our room last night. Out with the suit, is my guess. She did stroll in around noon, just in time for us to order lunch and exchange notes about speed dating. I gave myself a gold star in the form of a croissant the size of a boulder for not bringing up Terrence.

Today is a new day, one with a stomach full of carbs and horseback riding in the snow.

I'm sifting through my closet for an outfit to wear when it hits me. There's not a panty in my suitcase that won't hibernate in my crack. *Emma.* I lean back on my heels to yell at my considerate best friend, "Remind me to kill you later for only packing thongs!"

Is there such a thing as third-degree burn from thong chafing?

She shouts back from her room, "Thank me after a man helps you take them off!"

———eee———

We're behind the resort by three o'clock. The snow on the trees glitters in the sun's rays. The valley is gorgeous. Cold, but gorgeous.

Here's hoping I still feel my legs after I spread these thighs over a horse for the next ninety minutes in jeans and a thong.

Terrence and Madison aren't part of the small group forming, and that's fine by me. As much as I try not to care about their inevitable hookup, it will take an act of God to block it from my mind.

When it's time for instructions, a man I've never seen before makes his way to the center of our group. His name is Preston, a moniker that doesn't match a person who works with horses for a living. I don't know many Prestons, but I imagine someone behind a desk in a corner office, or a guy with a pompous attitude and a closet full of navy blazers and brown boat shoes. Like that Thurston Howell III from *Gilligan's Island*, which my grandma loved to watch.

This Preston is nothing like that.

He's tall, with olive skin and a muscular frame that's fit but not bulky. The confidence in his voice pulls you in to listen and take note. After his speech, he and the staff assign singles to horses. Preston walks my way with a purposeful stride.

"Hey, I'm—" My thoughts sputter like an overheating engine. Good God, the man is *fine* up close.

His cognac gaze locks me in a trance, one that starts with heart eyes and ends with *yes, Daddy*. The corner of his lips quirk to reveal another surprise. Hello, dimples.

"Ride me."

Nope. Not what I wanted to say.

My eyes dart to the ground in search of an emergency exit. Do I yell "April Fools!" in the middle of January? My gaze rises to his broad chest, which is wrapped in black-and-white plaid, then drops to his muscular legs pressed against rugged jeans.

I wipe my mouth as a precaution. If I'm not drooling now, I will be. "I mean, I'm ready to ride a horse." His eyes are still on me when I look up again. Back to the ground mine go. "My name is Justice." At your service and ready to faint.

He keeps his cool for a man with a bumbling idiot in front of him. "Justice." My eyes meet his, and he smiles. "Nice to meet you. I'm Preston." Soft hands enclose mine when we shake. No calluses. Huh. The pine scent is there in its woodsy glory. "Have you ridden before?" His voice is a soft lullaby, coaxing me to stare into his gaze. The dimples are back. "A horse, that is."

Oh my.

At least he has a good sense of humor. It's been a while, and this hotel should not let men like this out among single people unless we have the thumbs-up to straddle their saddles. Look at me. Thirty seconds in front of Preston, and I morph into Emma. He must have a degree in the dark arts of sexual wizardry.

Hocus pocus, coochie focus.

Preston leads me to my horse, a gray beauty named Stella. Her size proves to be a challenge in my failed attempts to mount her. Even at five foot six, I'm no match.

Lucky for me, my knight in shining plaid doesn't miss a beat. "May I?" Preston waits for permission to touch me.

"Yes, please," I say in a pant. A flutter builds in my stomach and stretches to my chest. His eyes sharpen and trail down my body, causing my breath to quicken. I tighten my grip on Stella's reins in fear my knees will give out.

Don't fall, don't fall.

"Stand behind the stirrup. Keep one hand on the rein and the other on the horn. Yes, the pointy part," he says with a smile. "Now put your foot in the saddle."

Preston crouches down, his chocolate hair ablaze in the sun's glow. He wraps a hand around my calf in a soft yet powerful grip and pushes me up with a burst of energy. My leg propels over Stella and finds the other stirrup. "Good girl," he says in a whisper that skates through his hand, which is now moving from my thigh and up my back.

If I stick around this man much longer, I'm going to need more than a thong to catch the arousal between my legs. Holy praise kink.

He looks me over. "Better?" His gaze settles on my mouth.

I bite my lip, overwhelmed and breathless. "For now."

Who am I?

He smiles. "Let's go, Justice."

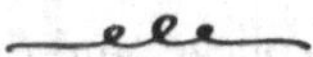

Forty minutes into our session, I'm in love. The view of snowcapped peaks surrounding endless trees is an experience I'll never forget. The sun is on my face, and the air has a bite to it but brings peaceful blue skies. The pain of my thong riding my crack no longer registers.

A win is a win.

I spot Emma trotting next to a man with a beard. His red cap keeps his light camel hair tame underneath. Sharp jawline. Full lower lip. Blue eyes.

She's found her Chris Evans mountain man. Guess you can manifest your desires.

"So, what brings you here?" A voice in front calls my attention. Preston slows his pace to ride next to me.

I shrug. "The singles' retreat, I guess."

"Really? You don't strike me as someone who takes joy in that." His eyes linger in wait for an answer.

Gosh, he makes me blush. "You're right. I wouldn't sign up for something like this on my own. Don't get me wrong, the resort is beautiful, but I'm more of an introvert when it comes to finding love again."

"Again?" He doesn't miss anything.

It's a struggle to muster up the courage to open up to a stranger. A handsome one, but still a stranger. I sigh and look into his eyes. "I was married. Technically still am."

"Oh?"

"We got married after college, and our relationship hit a snag almost a year ago. With divorce inevitable, my friend signed us up to get me back in the saddle." I look down at mine. "So here I am."

He goes quiet. Just when I think he'll tell his horse to speed up and leave the lady with the baggage in a trail of snow, he cracks a half smile. "Well, I'm glad you're here."

We continue our ride in silence until it's time to head back to the resort. I'm grateful for the quiet and the chance to commit these incredible views to memory.

A hand presses against my shoulder as I hand off Stella to a staff member. "Hey. I don't want to take up all of your time, but I was wondering if you plan to go to the movie tonight?"

Seems Preston also enjoyed our time together. He wants to go on a date. *Squee!* It's a date, right?

I toss a smile and mask the urge to do a high kick. Let me think about it. Hell yes!

"Emma, my friend, signed me up. I kinda have to go."

Those dang dimples peek out again when he nods. "Great, I'll see you there." He smiles and turns to take away our horses.

What is happening?

Chapter 18

Terrence

The elevator does a double bounce before the doors open to the scent of buttered popcorn. A group crowds around a vintage machine with red and white bags in their hands and anticipation in their eyes. Rectangular tables wrapped in red cloth line the entrance with every snack imaginable on display and for the taking.

Movies were more of a treat back in the day. I saved what I could and took my younger sister when my mom worked at the hospital, which was pretty much around the clock. When I didn't have it, my boy Leandro would let us slip in during his shift to make life easier on my wallet. A packed theater with sticky floors and candy from the corner store was the life. Now I enjoy the big screen from the comforts of my home theater. No long lines. No knee checks with the people next to you. No overpriced concession food. One of the perks of my job is being able to screen the occasional film before it hits theaters.

I scan the basement for Miles and a clue about the movie but come up short on both fronts. My fingers twitch in my pocket to hit the elevator button and go back upstairs for another night holed up with ESPN and whatever I order from room service. But I made a promise to put myself out there, which is why I threw on a gray thermal, a pair of jeans, and got my ass down here.

A hotel employee opens the double doors to reveal *Fifty Shades of Grey* posters taped to the center. A tickle flick with strangers while the main characters go at it? Not happening.

I turn back to the elevator and text Miles not to come when I run into a familiar face. "Hey. Did you know they were playing this?" I thumb back to the glossy image of a guy ready to choke a woman into submission.

Madison steps closer with a smirk. She bats her long eyelashes and runs her tongue over her red lips. "What's the matter, Terrence, can't handle a little kink?"

I huff out a laugh. "If you think this is kinky, no one has tied you up properly. Watching people moan in a public theater isn't how I spend my Friday nights." Most include a late gym session and takeout, but she doesn't need to know that.

Madison—who's wearing black leather leggings and a tight cream sweater—stares back in silence until I fold. "You want to watch *Fifty Shades of Grey*?"

She smiles and pulls me toward the entrance.

Guess she does.

We find two seats in the back of the screening room. It's big enough to fit seven rows and spacious enough not to feel claustrophobic while fake orgasms play out on the screen. The crowd has thinned out to a handful of couples. My guess is people took one look at the movie posters, grabbed their popcorn and wine, and got the hell out of Dodge.

At least we have the entire back row to ourselves. The oversize armchairs won't crush my nuts, either, so that's a plus. Red and gold are the colors of choice, some type of Old Hollywood vibe. This would be the perfect setup if the seats reclined.

Oh, wait. Found the button.

I hand Madison her small popcorn and pop the top on my Milk Duds.

"Have you seen this movie?"

"Hell no!" I clear my throat. That came out louder than expected. "Justice tried to get me to watch it because 'the love story evolves,'" I say with air quotes, "but I couldn't do it." I shake my head with a faint smile, lost in the memories of wrestling for the remote. On the couch. The bed. The kitchen counter. "God knows she tortured me enough with Hallmark and Lifetime movies."

Madison's face deflates at mention of Justice.

Idiot.

"Sorry about that." I didn't mean to bring her up. The thought just came out.

Her mouth turns up at the corners. "It's okay." She nods. "There's history there." What she really means is it's not, but we'll pretend it is. She shifts closer to me and crosses her legs. Gold flecks in her eye makeup sparkle. "I hope one day we'll make some of our own again."

The lights dim. I snake my arm around Madison and sink further into the chair. Without a divider between us, her body nestles against my chest, the perfect fit. Being with Madison is easy. There's no guilt or reminders of past mistakes. No condemnation. I can just be, and without Justice on my mind.

Until she walks in with another man.

The hell?

They don't hold hands, but, judging by the view, it's a date. To watch *Fifty* fucking *Shades of Grey*, no less.

She's not with the bartender I almost beat down two nights ago. Call it a hunch, but she only flirted with him to throw it in my face after I told her I train Madison. Miles said he heard the guy—West, I think—slept with Emma. No way he gets the time of day.

But this is different. She has no idea I'm here.

This guy has dark hair and a weightlifter's frame. He's got on jeans and a button-down that would look casual if it weren't for the yacht of a watch on his right wrist. It's hard to tell if it's a Rolex or a Patek Philippe, but it's clear he didn't get it from the mall. I'm around enough millionaire clients to know the difference.

I don't need night vision to see the stupid grin on his face. The way he looks down at her is the same gaze I had when I was with her, and fuck if this doesn't hurt. Fancy Watch has his palm on the back of Justice's shirt dress to guide her to two empty seats in my line of sight.

Fucking great.

My hands fist, and I sit up taller, shifting Madison off my chest.

"Everything okay?"

Nope.

"Yup." My jaw won't unclench. What right do I have to care? I'm the one who pushed her away. She's free to date whoever she wants, but that doesn't mean it's not a kick to the dick to see her out with another man.

Justice crosses her legs, exposing knee-high boots and an extra inch of her thigh. She slides closer to Fancy Watch, and he puts his arm around her. My Milk Duds box groans in my grip when I spot a large popcorn between them.

So this is a *date* date.

What next, a soda with two straws?

"Terrence?" I turn at the clipped tone in Madison's whisper. Crap. Was she talking? "Are you okay? We can leave if you're this uncomfortable."

I run a hand over my goatee and sigh. *Don't drag her into your shit.* "It's fine." I give her shoulder a squeeze and reassure her with a smile that doesn't reach my eyes. She searches them and nods before she's back against my chest.

The movie shines on the screen, but my eyes are on the scene playing out in front of me. The PDA between Justice and Fancy Watch is a slow burn. I should look away, but I can't.

Losing Justice left me with an emptiness I couldn't face. Did I go on dates after she walked out of my life? Yeah, but only the occasional dinner date that never got to dessert. It didn't fill the void, not that I wanted to replace her. I wanted to ease the pain.

Jay isn't a casual dater, or so I thought until tonight. This *date* doesn't look like a chance outing. There's a spark in the glances they steal at each other.

Did I lose her for good?

She's moved on, so why the hell shouldn't you?

I doze off halfway through the movie but wake to my dick straining against my jeans. I peek through my hand at Madison. Her eyes are on the screen with as much focus as her grip on my thigh. My dick jumps at the small circles her snake charmer's thumb traces.

What can I say? It's been a minute.

I fight back a grin when I glance at Justice. As expected, her head is down at a flogging scene. She has no idea how sexy she is without trying. Like right now. Her quick breaths and her lip between her teeth are a shit attempt at masking her arousal. I had quite the time breaking her shell. My curious princess is shy, but when she's in the moment, her inhibition melts away with every moan.

Madison's hand creeps higher up my thigh. I hold in a breath and close my eyes. A weight in my chest keeps my hands to myself and my attention on the screen. Justice is feet away from me, within my grasp, but still out of reach.

Is this how we both move on?

My wayward dick is now at full mast, ready for a salute. I turn toward Madison, my hand still on my face. "Guess you aren't into the movie?"

She looks at the screen, then back at me with an intensity that makes my pulse pound in my ears. "I found something else that has my attention."

Well, fuck.

Time stops. Justice and her date are two seconds from chasing the popcorn down each other's throats with their tongues. She made it crystal clear she wants to end our marriage. On the day she left me, and days ago, when she said it was over. Again.

At what point do I let go of the past?

When you sign the divorce papers like you said.

I turn back to Madison and let out a *tsk-tsk* when her fingers graze my shaft. If nothing else, the woman knows what she wants. "Did this movie turn you into a bad girl?"

Her touch lingers, and a slow smile builds. "Honey, *Fifty Shades of Grey* has nothing on me."

I'm not thinking with my right head when I grab her by the sweater and pull her to my lap. She whimpers, and I claim her mouth.

Don't tempt the bull, sweetheart. You'll get the horns every time.

Soft lips part for me to slip my tongue inside. My fingers wrap around her hips with an ache to pull her closer. Heavy breasts push against my chest as she wraps her hands around the back of my neck. I groan at the slow drag of her nails on my skin.

Our kiss falls into the rhythm of teenagers going at it before curfew. Madison wraps every touch in a plea for more. The hand she had on my thigh now has my dick in a death grip.

Shit.

I moan, and I don't give a damn who hears. Miles was right. My hand is tired, and so am I. Minutes weave from one into the next. At some point, I slow us down and hold her face in my hands. "That was nice," I say against her lips.

When we turn back to watch the movie, I peek at Justice and stiffen. It's not her glare that frightens me—make no mistake, it's terrifying. But what scares me is the etch of her brows and the way her lips tremble as she glances between me and Madison. They tell me I went too far.

She's on her feet the moment the recessed lights awaken and rushes out the door.

Fuck.

I close my eyes to swallow the guilt that reminds me I'm an asshole. There's a pull to run after her, but I stay frozen in place.

I hurt her after I vowed never to again.

No wonder she lashed out with the bartender. Who in their right mind would blame her for it? In her eyes, I was unfaithful in our marriage *and* had a secret affair with Madison. Someone whose face I just sucked on feet away from her.

And how did I handle things? Caged her in some random back room and threatened to sign the divorce papers. I couldn't be a bigger dick if I tried.

"Ready to get out of here?" Madison waits for a response. Her face is flush, her lips swollen. It doesn't take a mind reader to know what she wants.

"Actually, I need to turn in early," I say with a sigh. "I have a call with a client in another time zone tomorrow morning."

It's a dick move to lie, but my dick has done enough tonight. I'm a coward and can't bring myself to sleep with her. The horror on Justice's face tonight shattered something in me. I won't make another mistake in the heat of the moment.

The walk back to Madison's room is silent. We avert each other's gaze, except for a few darting glances. "Is everything okay?" Hesitation lines her question.

It takes seconds before I can look her in the eye. What the hell am I doing? I'm not a guy who leads a woman on or hops into her bed as a distraction.

"Madison."

She places a finger over my lips. "Don't. You don't have to explain." Her voice softens. "I like you, Terrence, and don't think I ever stopped since college. You're a great guy who happens to be going through a divorce. I won't pretend I know how that feels, but I believe in fate. There's a reason we're both here, and I think it's for us to have a second chance. You just have to be willing to try." She brushes her hand across my cheek. "At what point will you two realize it's over so you can both move on?"

Justice and I aren't together anymore, so it's true we're both fair game. I never expected her to move on, and if I'm honest with myself, I never expected to, either. Yet, here we are.

I wrap her in a hug and kiss her forehead. "You deserve to be happy."

That earns me one of her beautiful smiles. "And so do you."

Our eyes linger, searching for an answer that has yet to reveal itself. As much as it hurts, I don't want to hold Justice back.

We're broken, and I want off of this ride.

Her words play on an endless loop. She made it clear she doesn't want me.

My good night kiss with Madison reignites something buried deep inside. I miss feeling wanted, and the way her body leans into mine satisfies a craving.

Maybe it is time to walk away.

Chapter 19

Justice

A sharp mix of pain, rage, and betrayal fills my body. Terrence kissed Madison like she's the only woman he ever wanted. Maybe she is.

I didn't know they were a few rows behind us until I heard him moan. When you spend fifteen years with someone, you know their every sound, especially when it comes to pleasure.

Were there no other places in this big-ass resort to tongue down a woman he's likely tongued down for years? I didn't want to make a scene or alert Preston to the fact that my ex was behind us. It took everything in me—prayer, failed meditation, and silently chanting a kill list like Arya Stark's—to finish this movie.

Who the heck chooses *Fifty Shades of Grey* for movie night anyway?

I jump to my feet when the lights come on. "Can we go? I need some air," I say over my shoulder to Preston without waiting for an answer.

He comes up behind me and places a hand on the small of my back. "Is everything alright?" We might not know each other well, but thank the saints for a man who pays attention.

Outside the screening room, I scan for the nearest exit. A staircase. Fire escape. Open window. Somewhere I *won't* run into Terrence and Madison.

Images of him thrusting into her pull me back to a state of rage. Terrence is a damn specialist in the bedroom, and I want to kick him in his special dick.

"Unfaithful son of a bitch," I say between breaths. A regular workout routine is on the to-do list, after I become a widow.

I spin to see the ballroom and bolt for its entrance. The door flies open with a thud. Who knows where I'm going? Anywhere is better than here.

"Justice. What's going on?" Preston calls from behind me.

My eyes land on a series of doors that lead to a balcony. Looks like I'm freezing to death tonight, just like Jack Nicholson in *The Shining*.

The terror twins still have time to take me out.

"Justice! Are you okay?" This poor man thought he would spend a quiet evening on a date, only to find himself smack in the middle of a Tyler Perry movie without the bad wigs.

My steps refuse to waver. "Just need some air, that's all." And a punching bag and a stun gun, but one thing at a time.

The midnight air presses into my face at the push of a French door. Scattered lights blink against the valley's darkness, but they're no match for the black void in my heart. I close my eyes and take deep breaths. I shouldn't care about Terrence and Madison, but I do.

Why does it hurt so much?

You know the answer.

Preston spins me around to face him. "Justice. What's going on? You're freaking me out." His hands hold my face, and his breath is unsteady from his high-speed chase to calm me down. Even in my moment of weakness, he's still here.

"Kiss me."

His face scrunches. "What?"

I fuse my mouth to his. Let's hope he doesn't think I'm some killer who wants to assault him in the moonlight. I need this. I need him.

Please don't let him file a lawsuit.

Preston pauses at first, but then he pulls me into his arms with a possessiveness like he'll never let me go. There is nothing slow or soft about this man's kisses. Each one is hard as the muscle underneath his button-down shirt. I shiver under his touch, lost in our embrace. He wraps my hair into his fist, forcing my gaze to the sky. I moan at the tug-of-war between discomfort and pleasure.

Jesus. What did I get myself into?

His tongue glides up my neck until his lips hover over mine. "I don't know what's going on, but I've wanted to kiss this pretty mouth since I first laid eyes on you." His lips capture mine with a force that almost knocks me off my feet.

Hands trail down my back and lift me into the air. I hold on for dear life when he grinds my hips into his arousal.

"Oh, God." He's the one deadlifting me, and I'm out of breath.

Preston is so relaxed, I question if he dry humps women for exercise. If this is any indication of his stamina, I'm in deep trouble.

I don't know where this man comes from, but he wields his tongue like a sword to bend you into submission.

A chill from the cold night air creeps up my back that gets his attention. Preston breaks us apart. "You're cold. Let's get you inside." He sets me down on shaky feet and takes my hand to lead us into the empty ballroom.

Inside?

What does that mean? Like *inside*, where he comes to my suite or vice versa?

Sweat crawls over my body. This is too fast. I don't kiss on the first date, and I certainly do not hump in the moonlight.

Except I did.

My lungs gasp for air. I need to control my breathing or I'll pass out on this polished marble floor. Oh God, what am I doing? I'm alone with a complete stranger. He could knit scarves and stuff women's heads inside his freezer as a hobby.

Preston senses my hesitation. "Hey, hey." His voice softens. "We don't have to rush anything. I just want to make sure you don't freeze out here." His thumb rubs over my hand with a tender touch.

I close my eyes and exhale. Long gone is the confidence I had to kiss him with abandon. The self-conscious Justice is back, and I'm way over my head with this man. Everything about him, the way he commands a room, how he talks, how he kisses, proves he's out of my league—

"Justice. It's okay." He interrupts my thoughts. "I know you're in a complicated situation. I'm not here to force you into something you're not ready for, even if you bring me outside to stick your tongue down my throat." He winks, and I snort.

"Thank you for understanding."

And for not running away from the emotional woman in heat who tried to tackle you after one date.

He nods and grabs two chairs. The ballroom is eerie with just us in it. The only light in the room comes from sconces on the walls. Large crystal chandeliers loom over us from the high ceiling.

Preston lowers himself into the chair he put in front of me. He rests his forearms on his knees and leans forward, stretching fabric over his hard muscles. "Now, can you tell me why you ran out of the movie like a bat out of hell? *Fifty Shades of Grey...*"

I get lost in his scent. The pine has faded since our time outdoors, but the hints of nutmeg are still there. A five-o'clock shadow dusts his sharp jawline. Preston's thin lips move his trimmed mustache that brushed against my neck with each kiss.

"Did you hear me?"

Crap.

"Huh?" I blink. "Sorry. What did you say?" He really is a beautiful distraction.

A dimple peeks out when his lips twitch. "Something freaked you out, and I want to understand."

I run my fingers through my hair. How the heck do I explain this? "It's a long story."

"Unless you have a bedtime, that doesn't matter to me."

I smile at his reaction. *Guess we're doing this.* "Okay," I say with a sigh. "I told you I separated from my ex, but one thing I didn't tell you is that he's here at the singles' retreat. This is the first time we've seen each other in seven months. It's a shock, to say the least."

He frowns. "Sounds like it."

I nod. "Not only did we run into each other, but the woman who dated him in college before me—and still wants him after fifteen years—is also here. He says there was never anything between them while we were together, but tonight...they were in the theater, a few rows behind us, going at it."

My life is a bad drama, and I'm the star of the show.

Everything fell into perspective tonight. All of the hurt I've carried since our split. Madison. It's too much.

I squeeze my eyes shut. How do you heal when the wounds won't stop?

Preston places his hand over mine. "That is a lot for anyone to handle, and I'm sorry you have to deal with this. But I have to ask, are you ready to move on, or are you pushing yourself because your ex is with another woman?"

His question is fair. It's a reality check. I don't want to be anyone's rebound or make him mine. I'll admit seeing Terrence with Madison triggered my jealousy. Who *wouldn't* want someone to make them forget after seeing that? But there's something about Preston that goes beyond physical attraction. At least, I think.

"I won't lie and say I'm not emotional after catching them together." Even with a laugh, my voice shakes, but I push through. "Terrence swore he was faithful during our marriage, and seeing him now with the very person I questioned makes me wonder if he ever was." I take Preston's hand. "But our time together today opened me up for the first time in months. All I wanted tonight was to kiss you without thinking about anything or anybody else."

His thumb slides over my cheek in a soft caress. "It sounds like you still have to figure some things out. I'm no relationship expert, but it might be good to sort out how you feel."

Crap, here comes the rejection. I've had enough to last two lifetimes and stand before he continues. "Understood. Sorry to send mixed signals. Good night, Preston."

He grabs my hand. His eyes search mine. "I never said I don't want to see you. Why are you leaving?"

Running forces me to protect my heart when I want to stay.

I take in his words. My gaze lands on our joined hands. He's not pushing me away? "I thought that would be best?" Our eyes meet. "I'm honestly out of my element with this whole dating thing."

He stands and pulls me into his strong chest. Sandalwood and nutmeg wrap me in an embrace. The man smells good. "So we take it slow," he says in a whisper against my ear. "We get to know each other and see if this goes beyond the retreat." The kiss to my cheek is soft and assuring. Can I trust him with my heart when I'm still healing from my ex? "Come on. Let's get you home."

We walk back to my room with unspoken words and uncertainty as a chaperone between us. My life is a mess—a hot-ass mess, if I'm being honest. But for once, I have zero expectations. I want to live in the moment without thinking about my ex, our divorce, or what will happen a month from now.

When we reach my door, Preston lifts my chin to meet his eyes. God, he's so intense. "I had a good time tonight."

"So did I," I say in a quiet voice.

"Can I see you tomorrow?"

"That depends on whether or not you dance."

His brow lifts before realization sets in. "Oh yes, the salsa lessons for the singles' retreat. I take it you're going?"

"Actually, Emma signed us up."

"Then I'll be there. Maybe we could do lunch before?"

I smile at the thought. "I'd like that."

His eyes drop to my lips. He leans in for a kiss that gets interrupted when the door swings open.

"Well, well, well. What do we have here?" Emma leans against the frame in one of her silk robes. This one is lilac and actually reaches her knees. How the heck did she hear us?

She won't leave until I make an introduction, and I don't need any more embarrassment tonight. "Emma, Preston. Preston, Emma," I say, motioning between them.

"The pleasure is all mine." She shakes his hand. "Now, what were you doing with Justice to have her out past one o'clock?"

One? I never stay out this late.

He answers without hesitation. "We went outdoors to enjoy the stars after the movie." Minus the breakdown and me humping his erection, it's partially true.

Em takes one look at my face and rolls her eyes. "Yeah. I doubt that's all you did based on Justice's sex hair, but I do respect your ability to be discreet."

Do I have sex hair? Preston grabbed it a couple of times, but I didn't think it was that bad—

Forget this.

Why am I acting like Emma is my mother and I'm out past curfew? I *am* a grown woman.

I push her back into our suite and look over my shoulder with a smile. "Emma has to go, but thank you for tonight. I had fun."

He offers me a smile in return. There go those dimples. "So did I. Have a good night." He waves. "It was lovely to meet you, Emma."

I wait a beat before I turn and face my friend. Her arms cross in front of her chest as she scans me from head to toe. "Tell me *everything.*"

Chapter 20

Terrence

"You must really be in hell to call me."

After some soul-searching and groveling last night, Emma agreed to meet me in my room this morning to talk. I thought about a restaurant or one of those studio rooms, but I didn't want eyes on us.

Em sits at my dining room table with her arms crossed and her black manicured nails on display. She's ready for war. I pissed her off with this request to meet, but it's important.

"Hey, Em."

"Why am I here, Terrence?"

"Are you hungry?" I point to the menus on the table. "I can order room service if you want food." Her eyes cut through me. *Damn.* Straight to the point it is. I join her at the table to discuss the person who still consumes my every thought. The one my heart refuses to forget. I let out a sigh. "I wanted to check in to see if she's...okay."

"Who, sweetie? Because from what I hear, you like to put your tongue in women's mouths during kinky movies. You need to be a bit more specific."

I deserve that. If there's one trait about Emma I can't fault, it's her loyalty. She's a good friend to Justice—a sister—who will protect her from all enemies foreign and domestic. Estranged husbands included.

"You sent her into the arms of another man," she says in a huff. I flinch. Clearly, I didn't hear her right. How in the world did I push Justice into another man's arms? She came into the movie with one.

I sit back and cross my arms to mirror her stance. "Back up. She arrived with another guy. I'm sorry that I hurt her and broke her trust"—my stare becomes pained—"but I saw Justice on a date and lost it."

It hits me. Emma isn't talking about what happened before the movie. She's talking about *after*. Justice wouldn't have a one-night stand, but given her reaction in the theater, maybe I shouldn't put it past her.

My chest tightens. "She didn't..." The words to form the question scrape against my throat. If the answer is yes, it will wreck me beyond repair.

Emma puts up her hand. "It's not my style to disclose any intimate details about my best friend. But you look like you might have a heart attack. Justice and Preston did not have sex last night."

Thank God. Also, good to know this guy has a name.

She reveals parts of what happened. It's not ideal, but it's something I can live with. "She ran out of the theater, damn near had an anxiety attack, went outside for fresh air, and kissed him. Believe me when I say it shocked me. This is Justice. She doesn't stay out past midnight to slurp down men."

That visual will live rent free in my head.

After what you put her through, it's the least of what you deserve.

"I haven't seen this guy since we got here," I say, running faces in my head. The retreat isn't that big. I can't place a Preston, and that bothers me. "He just showed up out of nowhere?"

Her cheeks flush at the question. Did nobody stop and question who he is and where he came from?

She tries to reel in her emotions but stammers. "W-we met him Thursday afternoon, horseback riding. He gave instructions and worked with hotel staff, so we assumed he's an employee."

Not good enough.

I lean forward to put my forearms on the table. "But no one *actually* verified it. And now he not only has his eyes set on Justice but knows the room you're in?"

Her tone sharpens. "Look, Terrence, it's nice to hear you're concerned, but she's a big girl. She can take care of herself." *Bullshit.* Emma is replaying every piece of information Justice told her about this guy in her head. I want her safe. I want...

"I still love her." The words spill out on their own.

Her eyes widen. "Come again?"

"You heard me. I love Justice. I love my wife." The use of *wife* gives her pause. She will never admit it, but she's still Team T. At least, I hope.

Emma's lips curl at the edges. She leans in closer. "Well, what are you going to do about it?"

"First, I'll find out who the hell this Preston is. He might be a stand-up guy, but I need to make sure Justice doesn't put herself in danger. Then, I'll win her trust back."

I stayed up thinking about the last few years. Our marriage suffered because I refused to see the warning signs. I threw myself into work to cope with the pain of pregnancy loss and my failure to protect Justice from the hurt. My workload made days bearable for me but came at the expense of the woman I love.

It wasn't my intention to push her away, and I refuse to let that happen again. A future without my wife is a future I don't want. No amount of success or women will fill the void in my heart. I can't live without her.

I just hope I'm not too late.

"Is there no third goal?" Emma's brow quirks.

"Yeah, there is. After this is all said and done, I'm taking her home. She'll never question again whether she's loved."

"Well." Her grin widens. "I suggest you get started."

I hit up Miles's room after an early lunch to do what he calls "recon" on Preston. I don't know who he is, and I really don't want him cozied up against Justice—but one problem at a time.

"Bro, where did you get all this stuff?" I ask. He glances up from a makeshift command center but doesn't answer. Four full-size monitors surround him. There are two laptops by his side and what looks like black towers in the background. No way in hell he rolled up on a commercial flight with this equipment.

I walk behind him. "Is there anything else you found?"

"Give me a minute to work my magic, man."

I didn't have to twist his arm to help. Miles hates relationships, but he loves Justice—no matter how much he loathes the idea of love and marriage. He gives me shit about being whipped, but deep down, he's lonely.

His fingers fly across the keyboard to confirm Preston is *not* part of the singles' retreat. "No registration. No room number under his name. There's not even a restaurant bill for him."

The hairs on my neck stand on end. Justice, what did you get yourself into?

"Is there any way we can hack into the hotel's video surveillance? I'm not sure if there were any in the theater, but maybe the cameras picked something up that's useful?"

Miles swings his chair around and looks at me like I asked him for baby's blood. "You want me to go to prison so you can get back with your wife? I see how it is." He folds his arms in front of his chest, suffocating the gray sweater over his frame.

"No, that's not—"

He laughs. "Relax, bro. I'm messing with you. God, you're whipped." He turns back to face his monitors. "It's cute, though."

The clack of his keyboard is the only sound in the room. After fifteen minutes, he claps his hands together when he pulls up all of the surveillance cameras in the hotel. "You're lucky I'm good at what I do."

I slap my hand on his shoulder. "You're a genius, man." I give him a ballpark time to search for any footage with Preston. Miles scans a screenshot of Preston's face from a video of him walking to the screening room on one computer and uses another to run the image through some kind of database.

"I added search parameters to narrow down Preston's time here." He points at the second monitor. "I'll have all the footage he's in soon."

"Bro, how in the hell do you know how to do all of this?" This can't be legal.

He shrugs like hacking into a resort's computer system is child's play. "The less you know, the better."

We scroll through the results once the search finishes but come up short. Preston is only in a few videos. Either he knows where the cameras are and dodges them, or he hasn't been here long.

Either way, I don't like it.

"Wait, here's something." Miles enlarges a video taken after the movie. Justice storms out of the theater with Preston close behind her.

Memories of that night hit me like a brick wall.

I messed up, baby, but I'm gonna fix it.

The camera picks up Justice and Preston in what looks to be a ballroom. She's inconsolable and walks outside to the balcony with a complete stranger, isolating herself from help if she needs it. The thought of her in danger fills me with dread until I see what happens next.

"No shit."

I hear Miles but can't concentrate. Justice, *my* Justice, throws herself at a man—a trafficker, for all we know—who proceeds to try and fuck her with clothes on. She kisses him with a yearning that rips me to my core.

God, what have I done?

"Turn it off now," I say in a bark. I can't watch anymore.

How did we get here?

Miles stands and puts his hand on my shoulder. "Everything will work itself out. You two have been through hell and back. You'll get your wife, bro."

I scoff. "I'm not so sure anymore. I think I pushed her too far."

"Oh, please. It's clear as day you two still love each other. You burned her with Madison, and she burned you with that guy. You're even. So go heal together, or whatever the hell it is you married people do." He bumps my arm with his. "I've never seen you give up when you want something, and we both know Justice is worth the fight."

I twist to face him and raise a brow. "When the hell did you get so sentimental?"

He shrugs off the question and puts his hands in his pockets. "I'm a bastard when it comes to love, but you two are my family. There's nothing I wouldn't do for the both of you."

Miles's third monitor beeps with an alert on the screen. I point to it. "What's that?"

His fingers are frantic against the keyboard. He brings up what looks like code from *The Matrix* on his fourth monitor. Seriously, what the hell does he do for a living? I doubt he learned this in college.

"That would be the answer to who Preston is. I searched a few databases with facial recognition technology."

I frown. "A few databases?"

He nods but never takes his eyes off the monitors. "FBI. CIA. DMV."

"Jeez, Miles. What the hell do you do?" He turns to me with a *why are you still asking about my job?* look. I raise my hands. "The less I know, the better. Got it."

He pulls up a report on Preston and scrolls through the results. "At least he's not a murderer."

"Maybe he knows how to scrub his past or is looking for his first victim."

His head shakes. "Man, I told you to stop with those Lifetime movies. They'll keep you paranoid. Trust me, I know."

We look through his family connections and educational background and get to what he does for a living. That's when our eyes go wide.

It all makes sense why he's here.

"No shit," we both say.

Chapter 21

Justice

It's past nine by the time I wake up. I smile and roll over. These sheets really do wonders.

It takes forty-five minutes for me to get out of bed and run through my morning routine. My steps falter when I close my bedroom door and see Emma in the common area. She's dressed in a V-neck sweater blouse and—am I seeing straight? Jeans?

"It's rude to stare, Jay."

"You're in *jeans*. What do you always say? Oh yes, 'over my dead body.'" She's also not an early riser. It's a miracle to see her dressed before ten. "Going somewhere?"

There's a slight pause before she glances down at her phone and slides it into her pocket. "Something work-related came up. Had to slip out to the business center to take care of it." She walks into the kitchen. "What's on your agenda for today?"

"I'm meeting Preston for lunch." Another date with the charming horseback instructor.

Last night didn't have to end the way it did. An alternate ending would've had me curled up in the corner with my red eyes, a sore throat from crying, and enough chocolate wrappers to craft an area rug. For all I know, Terrence and Madison went back to one of their rooms, tore each other's clothes off, and had fifteen years' worth of sex in one night. I've shed enough tears on my ex and am ready to move on.

"Be careful, Jay. We don't know him. Text me when you arrive and leave, wherever you're headed."

I roll my eyes and grab an apple. "Yes, Mom."

Her stare catches me off guard. Oh, she's serious.

"I mean it. I want to know you're okay. Last I checked, dating isn't a level of expertise for you."

She's not wrong, but what's up with this mood swing? Wasn't the point of this trip for me to meet someone? "*Okay.* Thanks for looking out, Em." It's lunch. Not a rendezvous in a dark alley for some tickle play.

"Always, honey. I have to go, and I won't be back before you leave. I'll see you later this afternoon for dance lessons." She grabs a bottle of water and does a *toodles* wave on her way out.

What the heck was that?

Paranoia aside, her concern is cute. Annoying, but cute.

Two hours to myself before I need to head down to the restaurant.

What to do, what to do.

Back to bed it is.

I flip from channel to channel with no success. Nothing catches my eye until I see *Indecent Proposal.* Laugh all you want, but this movie makes me cry at the end. I crossed my fingers Diana and David would find their way back to each other. And they did. After a million-dollar proposition that cost them their marriage and dream home. Took some soul-searching and a hippo, but they did it.

Terrence and I spent many nights in each other's arms, pretending our life was a movie through our own words.

"Did I tell you I love you today?"

"No."

"It's true."

"Even now?"

"Forever."

Here come the tears. I watched *Indecent Proposal* more than I'll admit after Terrence and I separated. We don't have a go-to spot on a pier in California, but part of me hoped we could fix what was broken and start fresh. It wasn't in the cards for us. Time might be able to heal some wounds, but not ours.

My eyes well again. *Damn it.* This time, I allow them to fall, to mourn my failed marriage. To mourn the part of me who misses him and wishes he'd fought for us. I bury my face in my knees and let every emotion I've tried to suppress rise to the surface.

"It's time to let go."

The night I told Terrence I wanted a divorce torments my senses on an endless loop. My pulse raced at the heat from his glare, a silent figure who stood before me in our living room. A stranger in place of my loving husband.

Did we do everything in our power to fight for us? No, we didn't.

He was always away on a work trip, sometimes for weeks at a time. The void in my heart swelled after we decided to put a family on pause. After two miscarriages, my mind and body were beyond repair. I disappointed Terrence. He never admitted it, but why else would he travel more for work?

Job demands from my end picked up the same years we tried for a baby. Couple that with Terrence's hectic business travel, and, well, it was hard to make time to get pregnant. We discussed IVF and adoption but became more distant with every mile between us.

The soundtrack during the *Indecent Proposal* end credits brings me back to David and Diana's love story. To the one I lived out with Terrence that lingers in every thought. Would I take him back if he slept with Madison?

Diana had sex with someone other than her husband, yet you still rooted for her and David. Why can't you do the same in your own life?

I can't go back. It's too painful.

Our separation broke parts of me that have yet to heal. I need to protect my heart, especially now that I've seen him with another woman. I don't know much about Preston, but he makes me laugh and seems like a good guy—company to keep as Mr. Right Now. It's not like we'll head back to Austin together and ride off into the sunset. I'm not that naïve, and I'm not sure I'd be ready for anything serious.

Now you sound like Emma.

Whatever happens, I promise myself to be present in the moment.

I glance at the clock and jump to my feet. Shoot, less than twenty minutes to get ready.

Where the heck did the time go?

Preston stands from the table he reserved for us. "Justice, you look—wow."

It's no designer outfit, but I appreciate his words. Who knew a strapless sweaterdress with Em's thigh-high boots would be such a head-turner?

I smile and drink him in. "You look good yourself." His navy suit fits him like body armor. He motions for me to sit down and unbuttons his blazer as he takes his seat.

"Any particular reason you look like a Wall Street banker today?" More like a CEO, which makes me question how much he makes at the resort. It's none of my business, but how does a man who gives horseback lessons buy what looks like a custom suit and diamond cuff links? Thrift store maybe? Either way, he's giving *Kingsman*, and I'm here for it.

He shoots a smile and shrugs off the inquiry with, "Training day." The way he looks, I hope his boss gives him a raise and a bonus. The waiter appears at our table on his signal. Watching Preston give his order—and mine, which takes me by surprise—is a master class in confidence. I, on the other hand, look like a toddler drooling over an ice-cream cone.

"You okay?"

Caught. "Yeah—yes, I am." I raise the back of my hand to my forehead to check my temperature. Anyone else hot in here?

He coughs into his fist, unable to hide his smirk. Hello, dimples. "Are you enjoying your day so far?"

"I am, but it just got better."

He winks, and we fall into easy conversation. As the minutes weave together, it dawns on me that we *only* talk about me. He's hiding something, and I don't like it.

"Enough about me; let's talk about you. What brings you to this resort? Do you work here?"

His reply is curt. "Business."

I frown. *Okay.* So he's not an hourly employee who works with horses. At least, I don't think he is. "You aren't part of the singles' retreat, are you?"

He takes another bite of his lamb and washes it down with a glass of wine—an expensive bottle he ordered for the table, might I add. Definitely not an employee. "You could say my business at the hotel opened the door for me to enjoy a little pleasure."

My fork punctures my salad harder than expected. Another vague response. It shouldn't be this difficult to learn more about a person. Preston acts like I asked him for his Social Security number, and it's pissing me off.

Who is this guy, Prince Harry's cousin?

"So what the heck do you do? You know so much about me, but I don't know anything about you." I lean closer and lower my voice. "Are you married or something?" My question catches him off guard, but it deserves an answer. One that better be no.

Yes, I still am—technically—but we separated seven months ago. If he's some businessman with a wife who's drowning in diapers at home, who wants a good time with whoever, doing whatever, that won't fly with me.

He shakes his head. "No, not married."

Fine, let's play twenty questions, Preston...I-Don't-Know-Your-Last-Name.

"Then what?" My voice softens in a last-ditch effort to get him to open up. Certain people like to hide their identities. Cheaters. The mafia. Undercover agents. Royalty. Professional thieves. Serial killers.

He takes a long look at me before he says something I don't expect. "I'm not married, Justice. No wife. No kids. Just my career. The reason I'm at this resort is because I own it."

Real estate tycoon. Huh. Wasn't on my bingo card of red flags. I guzzle down my wine and swallow hard. "You mean to tell me all of this," I say with a hand wave, "is yours?"

His eyes hold mine in a stare. "Yes, and several other properties too."

"In the state?" Now I'm curious.

"The state. The country. The world. Let's just say my portfolio is diverse."

"So what you're telling me is you're some bachelor billionaire who happened to show up at a singles' retreat?" I giggle into my glass. "Sounds like a Hallmark movie." What are the odds?

His face is expressionless when I look up. I don't think he's mad—at least I hope he isn't—but it's hard for me to read him. "I don't like to talk about money, but yes, something like that. Though I'm far from anything you see on Hallmark." He inhales with a discomfort that's not from the gourmet meal in front of him.

Way to go. Happy now?

God knows how many women target him because of his status. I wipe my mouth with a napkin and reach for his hand. "Hey, I'm sorry if I offended you. I didn't know and don't mean to pry. We don't have to talk about it."

My words chip away at his defensive wall. His face relaxes, along with his shoulders. "I should be the one apologizing, Justice. I'm sorry for being so secretive." He strokes my hand with his thumb. "Because of my company, my life is very...public. I like to lie low to dodge the 'bachelor billionaire' label. I grew up around horses, and I just wanted to be Preston for a day—not Preston Donnelley. So I asked if I could fill in for the instructor. You seem so genuine, and I enjoy getting to know you as me. Without all of the layers attached."

I smile. "I can respect that."

Warmth returns to his eyes. He smiles back at me. "Now, ask me anything."

"Other than running your business, what are your plans for the future? Do you see a wife and kids?" Emma's voice in my head curses me for such a question. I know things are complicated in my life, but I plan to remarry one day, and I definitely want children.

His eyes never waver from my face. "I don't think I'm built to be a husband or a father. Business and travel are a large part of who I am. I've never pictured myself slowing down enough to live in one place."

"Thank you for your honesty."

"With that said, you are different. You make me question if I should change course."

Sorry, what?

I got out of a marriage because my husband traveled too much for us to fix our relationship. If that was hard, Preston would be impossible. I don't want to think so far ahead that I miss out on the present. But that's worth noting.

Focus on the now.

Right.

A goofy grin crinkles my face when I remember this afternoon's dance lessons. It's been a minute since I went anywhere to salsa, and I'm dying to get back in action. I smile at Preston and the thought of us on the floor. "So, about those dance lessons."

His face twists, and I see the disappointment coming. "I would love to, but there's some business I have to tend to away from the resort. I won't be back in time."

Déjà vu.

"That's okay." I do my best to keep the mood light. It's not the end of the world. Look at me with this growth. "Next time."

His gaze turns serious. "I promise I will make it up to you."

You better, Preston Donnelley. You better.

Chapter 22

Justice

Sweat and tears scald my eyes. The pain doesn't register because of the laughter that comes in waves. Emma and her two left feet are entertainment in its purest form. If she weren't on the dance floor, people might call for help.

The woman couldn't find the beat if her life depended on it.

"Don't think this reflects my skills between the sheets." She fumbles another step when I try to lead.

I brace my hands over my knees and holler. My best friend, who usually moves like water, looks a mess. And I freaking love it. I struggle to catch my breath and reach up to wrap her in my arms. She's out of her element, and I'm horrible for my reaction.

"I-I'm sorry, Em." I press my lips to her cheek to keep from laughing in her face. That earns me an elbow to the shoulder on the way to our table. Hey, I tried. I hand her a water and take the chair next to hers.

We watch other guests in silence when a strange noise fills the air. I turn, thinking Emma is choking, only to find her in tears. "Em, you okay?" I look her over for the source of the pain. Crap, did I push her too hard?

"I really can't dance for shit." The words barely stumble out before she leans back and snorts with laughter.

I lean against her and bite my lips to stifle a giggle. "Guess we can't all be perfect." Here come the tears again. I haven't laughed this hard in a long time.

She wipes her eyes and looks at me. "It's good to see you like this, even if it's at my expense." She straightens. "How did lunch with Preston go?"

I fill her in on all the details—the billionaire part included—and how he couldn't make it because of work. Emma is quieter than usual. Surely she has some response to me with a *billionaire*, of all things. She looks like she wants to say something but hesitates.

"What is it?" I frown.

"I'm really happy to see the confident Justice surface. I really am."

"But?"

"*But* I'm afraid you're entertaining a man who doesn't want the same things as you. I don't want to see you hurt."

Not what I expected to hear. "I thought you approved of Preston."

She puts her hand over mine and smiles. "If you want to bang a billionaire, by all means, honey. But I know your heart, and settling for a guy because the one you *actually* want isn't available isn't your style. Sweetie, never change yourself for a man."

Em's words roll through me with the force of a freight train. She's right. Preston seems like a good guy, but he's not the one for me. No matter how hard I fight to block out my desires, someone else still has my heart.

My bottom lip trembles, and my vision starts to blur. Not again.

Hold it together. If you act like a baby, they will put you in the corner.

I exhale. "You're right. I guess I wanted to enjoy his company here since I can't..." My voice trails off.

"Since you can't have Terrence?"

I look down and nod.

"Oh, sweetie." She wraps her arms around me and rubs my back. "As long as you're honest with Preston about your intentions, I don't think a few dates are a big deal. But he deserves to know it won't continue once you leave this resort." She leans back to look me in the eyes. "With that said, you need to have a talk—*not* a shouting match—with Terrence. If he's the one you want, you need to tell him."

"What if I'm too late? What if he doesn't want me anymore?" What if I pushed him away so many times that he landed in Madison's arms and doesn't plan on coming back?

Emma huffs and waves a hand. "What happened to the confident Justice? You're an amazing woman. An amazing catch. Terrence is only acting out because men are idiots and don't know how to express themselves. Madison didn't have anything on you back then, and she doesn't now. If you want your husband, go get him and his dick back."

I chuckle. "Why, Emma Douglass, when did you get sentimental enough to root for love?"

"Let's just say I had a recent change of heart," she says with a wink. "You're my sister, and you deserve the fairy tale. I never believed in that happily ever after nonsense because of my parents. But you and Terrence have a real shot at it if that's what you want." Silence passes between us until Emma jumps to her feet. "I can't do any more of these *Full House* heart-to-hearts. They make me itch. I'm going to the bar. Want anything?"

I can't help but smile. "Yeah, I'll take a margarita."

After thirty minutes, a DJ moves into place behind a set of tables. The lights dim, and the sound of Celia Cruz consumes the room.

"'La Vida Es un Carnaval!' I love this song!" My hips sway in my seat to the trumpets.

"That's wonderful, sweetie. Want to scream that to anyone else?"

"Dance with me? The beat isn't too fast to follow." I motion to a small group practicing the steps we learned in our lesson. I stand, but she doesn't.

She shakes her head. "Sorry, girl. You're on your own. I need another drink."

"Oh, come on!" Why take dance lessons if not to *dance*? "What happened to living it up? I need a dance partner."

"I'll dance with you."

I still at the voice behind me.

Chapter 23

Terrence

"Justice?"

I take another step to close the distance between us. She stays silent, unable to face me. "Would you like to dance?"

Come on. Turn around, baby.

As if she senses my silent plea, Justice takes hesitated steps but finally turns. She's never looked more beautiful. Every part of me is at full attention. Her red V-neck dress has a slit up the thigh and hugs the curves of her breasts. It's long enough to cover her when she spins but short enough not to trip over. She's a natural beauty who still takes my breath away.

Damn, she looks good.

The song piping through the speakers isn't loud enough to mask my heartbeat. Only God knows if she'll let me dance with her or flip me off.

Justice swallows several times before she says, "Okay."

She doesn't trust me. Her eyes play out the conflict between her mind and body. Leaving the past behind her or molding it with the present. There's no reason for her to take a chance on me, but all of that will change.

The crowd dissolves when we reach the middle of the dance floor. Her rose-vanilla aroma saturates the air with anticipation. I gaze at her, take her hand, and wrap an arm around her waist like it's the first time I'm touching her.

I miss this.

Being half Dominican, you'd think I'd have a slight advantage in the dance department. Salsa. Merengue. Bachata. All were rites of passage with my grandmother. I took Justice to a salsa club on one of our first dates, expecting to show off my skills. But she surprised me with hers, courtesy of the weekly gatherings at her friend Carmen Rivera's house when she was in middle school. Dancing is one of many things we have in common, and I pray I can use it tonight to get my wife back.

Her face lights up when I hit her with a hammer lock.

"I forgot how good you are." She smiles like she did when we danced the night away so many years ago.

I pull her close and leave little space between us. "I'll never forget how good you are," I say against her ear.

We stare into each other's eyes, frozen in time. "Another one?" I'm not ready to let her go.

She fights another grin but gives in. "Lead the way."

An hour passes before either of us tires. It doesn't matter what the DJ throws our way. We're ready for it all. Hot as hell, but ready. I roll up the sleeves of my button-down. Justice's chest rises and falls, her hair frizzing from the heat. Droplets of sweat drip down her breasts, and damn it if I'm not hard again.

Settle down.

I'm ready for a break, and she says what I'm thinking before I get the words out. "Want a drink?" Her ability to read my mind never ceases to amaze me.

"Sounds good. I was going to ask you the same thing."

She flashes an irresistible smile and disappears to the bar. Who knows what the future holds, but tonight, I'm a blessed man.

Two hands wrap around my chest when I turn to make my way to the table. I look over my shoulder to see Madison's dark gaze.

"I didn't know you would be here." She nuzzles her head against my back.

This cannot happen now. Justice will lose it.

The plan was simple. Talk to Emma. Find out more about Preston. Lay my cards on the table with Justice. I had every intention of apologizing to Madison for last night so she wouldn't think there is an *us* and look at me the way she is right now. I told her I wouldn't be here to buy myself enough time to patch things over with Jay before lunch tomorrow.

Assuming she takes me back and this doesn't blow up in my face.

"It was a last-minute decision." I peel her hands off my body. The weight of my tone signals something is wrong. She attempts to process what happened between last night and today, and damn it if I'm not an asshole. I should've called her earlier, but all I thought about was Justice. She is and always will be my priority.

Madison deserves more, someone who will give her his full heart. I never meant for last night to happen or to lead her on. She needs more than a two-second brush-off, which is why I need to tell her we have to talk tomorrow.

But I never get the chance.

Justice looks between us in a pained stare. She closes her eyes to fight back tears, and when her gaze lands on me, I know the damage is done.

Shit.

She throws our drinks in the trash and makes a beeline for the exit. But I'm not about to lose her again.

As I run after Justice, I yell back to Madison, "I gotta go!" She and I will talk at some point, but now is not that time. I need to find my wife.

Justice is in front of the elevator when I catch up to her. Her foot taps the carpet, and her arms are crossed against her chest. My approach is cautious. I might tower her by more than half a foot, but I'm not stupid. This woman makes a black mamba look tame when she's upset.

"Justice," I say in a soft tone.

She spins in a fury. "I'm not doing this anymore."

I raise my hands in innocence. "I had no idea she would be here tonight. If I did, I wouldn't have shown up. That's God's honest truth."

She storms into the elevator when it arrives.

"Would you please talk to me?" I follow her in and press the button for the sixth floor out of habit. Fear creeps up the back of my neck at the thought of losing her for good.

"Why? What else is there to say, Terrence?" She wears the look of one of those women from *Snapped* who wants nothing more than to poison her lover and set his body on fire. I shift to the other side of the elevator to let her pace like she does when she's mad. But I never take my eyes off of her.

"I don't know what the hell to think anymore. I'm so stupid. I *knew* something would happen. It always does with us."

When the elevator doors open, she bolts down the hall, unaware we're not on her floor. Luckily, she's headed toward my room.

"Would you please slow down so I can talk to you?" I forgot how fast this woman is, even in heels. "Justice!" I do my best not to yell, but I would have an easier time talking to a brick wall at this point. I double my steps to catch up, and grab her by the arm.

"I said wait." I turn her to face me. "No more running. We'll talk about this—about everything—tonight." I look down at her in a dare to challenge me. "*Tonight*. There's no backing away from this conversation. It's long overdue." I pull my room key from my pocket with Justice's arm in my other hand. She'll sprint just to spite me if I let her go.

"Don't treat me like a child."

I shrug. "If the shoe fits, princess." I wave my key over the sensor and hold the door open for her to go inside. "After you."

She looks past me with a hardened expression and doesn't budge. Stubborn woman.

"Come on." I release her arm and motion for her to go in. "You can let me have it inside."

She struts in, but not before I catch an elbow. "Plan on it." The juiciness of her backside hypnotizes me when she walks by. What were we talking about?

I close the door, toss my key card and wallet on the kitchen counter, and walk to the middle of the living area where she is. Her attention is on the view of the valley twinkling through the windows. It keeps her quiet, but not for long.

When she realizes I'm close, Justice snaps out of her thoughts to face me head-on. "I'm so angry, I can't stand to look at you right now." She starts to pace around the room. Wisdom tells me to keep my mouth shut until she's had enough time to vent.

My eyes track her like a predator that has its sights on its prey. She refuses to look at me, but I expect nothing less. I cross my arms and lean against the wall next to the bar to wait it out.

Take your time, princess. We have all night.

"How long have you two been screwing?"

Not this again. I push off the wall. "There's nothing between Madison and me. There never was." I told myself to give Justice space to vent, but I refuse to let her work herself up with thoughts I was unfaithful in our marriage.

Fuck. That.

Her eyes roll. "Please. You two looked *so* cozy last night when you had your tongue in her mouth. Just tell me the truth."

"You want to know the truth?" I say through gritted teeth. My patience went out the window with her common sense. She takes two steps back on my approach. "There is *nothing* between Madison and me. I'll admit I was a bit dense during our marriage." Very fucking dense. "I didn't see the signs you did, but I *never* stepped out on you, and I resent the fact you think I did.

"Have I wondered during this trip what things would be like if she and I got together? Sure, I'll own up to that. But that's because I thought *you*"—I point at her—"wanted nothing to do with me. It felt good to be desired. I'm sorry, Jay. I wish I could take it back, but I can't. I'm human."

"I find it very hard to believe that in all the time we were together, and all the times you ran into Madison while you were away on 'business,' you two didn't hook up. You're both here—at a *singles' retreat*—popping up at the same events and going at it like teenagers in a movie theater."

"Jay, I fucked up! I'm sorry. I was lonely that night. I've been lonely for a long time, and she was there. We kissed, but we never had sex."

This woman, this fucking irritating woman, could star in the sequel to *Clueless* without an audition. She's the most gorgeous person I've ever met and has a heart of gold, and she *still* doesn't recognize her value. If I believed in reincarnation, I'd come back as her self-esteem.

Nothing I say will get through to her. Even the truth.

"You really expect me to believe you two are just friends? The way you fisted her hair last night is a special definition of *friendly*."

I couldn't look more dumbfounded if I tried. Does Justice not remember that *she* was out with another man last night? I mumble a quick prayer in Spanish to keep my composure. "I hit a breaking point last night. I snapped."

"Please, you wanted it!" She heads for the door.

Like hell she's running. "No, I wanted you!" I turn her to face me. "You want to know why I was there yesterday?" She stills when I hold her face. My touch is soft, to comfort, not intimidate. "Because I was looking for *you*. I didn't know Madison would be there until I ran into her."

For a moment, I think I did it. I finally got through to her. But the smile tugging at the corners of my mouth falters when she shrugs out of my embrace.

"Let me go, Terrence." She opens the door, but I push it shut.

"No."

I lean my forehead against hers and lower my voice for her heart to hear what her ears refuse. "I lost it when you walked into that theater with another man. That's what triggered me—what wrecked me." Her breath hitches. "The hurt I caused you is something I'll regret for the rest of my life. Not just last night." I close my eyes to push out what cuts into my throat like glass. "You had every right to leave me. I was too numb to recognize your pain. Please let me try to make things right."

"I thought you didn't care about me." Her voice is so low I have to strain to hear it. "I thought you moved on, and I figured it was time for me to do the same."

I frown. "Is that what you really think? I wasn't the one who wanted to end our marriage."

Her tear-filled eyes pierce mine. "I had no choice. You checked out a long time ago. All those business trips were an excuse to get far away from me."

"That's not true, Justice."

Her voice cracks through a sob. "I needed you after our losses." She shakes her head and steadies herself. "You weren't there for me." Months of hurt rip through her at once. The pain on her face is unbearable to see.

I caused this.

"Baby, I'm so sorry. I didn't know what to do back then."

She pushes me away when I try to hold her. "You hurt me." More tears stream down her cheeks, and it takes everything in me not to touch her.

I drop my head in shame. "Work was the only way I could cope." My hands slide up her arms. I press my lips against her cheek and whisper, "If I could go back and change things, I would. You mean the world to me, baby."

The room weighs heavy with silence. She wipes her eyes and lets out a ragged breath. "I don't know if I have the strength to go back."

Don't do this. "What does that mean? I love *you*, Justice. I never stopped loving you, and I will *never* stop loving you!"

I stare into her eyes in search of an answer. This can't be the end. It *can't* be. Behind the hurt in her gaze is a hunger she tries to mask. Her face is hard, determined to push me away. But her body betrays her.

A flush creeps up the smooth column of her neck, up her jaw, working overtime to swallow down the sharp breaths lifting her chest. Honey-soft breasts strain against the fabric of her dress. I want to trail a finger down her cleavage and tease her nipples with my tongue and fingers.

The thought of losing her for good moves me to action. My body presses against hers, and I take her mouth.

Chapter 24

Justice

It's happening. Oh, dear God. It's happening.

My skin heats in a slow burn, and my nipples tighten against the built-in cups of my dress. The friction of the fabric would be almost too much if it weren't for the man in front of me, igniting my body with hot, open-mouthed kisses. Everything in me yearns for Terrence, but my mind taps me on the shoulder with replays from our highlight reel as a reminder of why I left.

I pull hands that freed countless orgasms from my face and gaze up at him with heavy eyelids. How did we go from last night to this?

Terrence is breathing like he tried to outrun a car. The way he looks at me leaves zero room to question how much he wants me. Every inch of his desire presses against my stomach.

This is not the time to think with your head. Your coochie needs a tune-up, and he's the mechanic who knows what to do under your hood.

He devours my mouth again and says in a breathless whisper, "Don't think, baby. I need my wife." His lips curl around my tongue and suck.

My thighs clench together at the sensation flooding my center and the husky voice that calls for his *wife*. My arousal soaks through my panties. I want him.

Terrence presses his delicious weight into me, sending our bodies against the door with a thud. He pins me with a hand pressed into the curve of my hip. The other trails up my thigh to wrap my leg around him. I dig into his shoulder for balance and gasp at the glide of his fingers along my seam.

"Someone is ready for me." His mouth explores the side of my neck and sucks on the pulse point. It's a fight to keep my legs from giving out. I hiss at the steady thrum of rising pressure. I want to let go and get lost in him.

So I do.

I plunge my hands into his hair and let out a feral moan, all thoughts and logic be damned. Tonight, I need him—all of him. My hands claw at Terrence with only a need he can satisfy. Scattered buttons patter to the floor like raindrops when I rip open his shirt.

Our kiss becomes frantic. He picks me up and presses me back against the door. My dress now rests above my waist, exposing my red lace thong I grind into his belt. The friction of the metal buckle quickens my breath and floods my sex with pleasure.

"There's my naughty girl," he says in a groan between kisses.

We move from the foyer and into the hall, our tongues intertwined and our bodies aching with need. We're doing it. Us and *it*. The flutters in my stomach morph into uncontrollable trembles. I'm not ready. One, it's too soon. There are also too many questions that need answers.

"Wait, wait!" I'm out of breath but muster up enough strength to press my hands into his bedroom doorframe. Seven months' worth of emotions pummel into me, lifting my lust-filled haze for a dose of reality. I can't tell up from down, much less remember how to breathe.

Is it possible to have a panic attack before sex?

"I-I don't know if I can do this."

Terrence examines my face. His voice is soft when he answers. "What's wrong?" With the switch of a grip, wraps his hand around the back of my neck and waits for me to reveal whatever is freaking me out. I stare at him and try to say everything with my eyes. There's so much I want to tell him, but I blurt out the first thing that comes to mind. It surprises us both.

"I promised myself I would be celibate." Is there a way to teleport through hardwood?

He's biting his lip when I look up to meet his eyes. Did he just laugh in my face?

The corners of his eyes crinkle. "Did you forget we're still married, princess?" He flashes a grin big enough to make a woman in the Sahara Desert wet.

"But what about protection?" I don't want to catch anything.

He levels me with a look like I questioned his integrity. "I've only had sex with one person in the last fifteen years. I'm staring at her."

"No seven month itch?"

His gaze is full of so much love, it leaves me breathless.

"The only itch I have is to get my wife back. I want you and only you."

I lean in for a kiss. "Forget I said anything. I'm not thinking straight."

His lips brush the shell of my ear. "Baby, when we're done, you won't walk straight." He gives a sexy wink and kicks the door closed.

~ ell ~

Moonlight illuminates the room through open curtains. Terrence moves us to a large four-poster bed, and my heart races against my chest when he lays me down like I'm made of glass.

He appraises me and removes his torn shirt. Light from the winter night dances off his toned abs as he unbuckles his belt and eases out of his pants and boxer briefs in a single motion. The muscles in his thick thighs flex. My eyes glide down his body and lock on the steel rod between his legs.

Sweet Jesus.

He grins back at me and strokes himself. His thumbs glide my dress up my thighs when he reaches the bed. I shiver under the touch of his hands, inching closer to my center. He presses a thumb over my thong and slides it back and forth over my clit. My back arches, and I yelp when he pulls me to the edge of the bed.

Holding my gaze, he sinks between my legs to tug the flimsy lace material off. Once I'm spread open, he puts my legs on his shoulders and presses soft kisses inside of my thighs in a trail to his destination.

"It's been too long since I've tasted you." The raspiness of his voice mirrors the longing in his eyes. His tongue brushes up my lips and laps my dripping desire. One lick. Two licks. My breath catches at his deep inhale. He swallows hard and moans before latching onto my clit like it's his last supper.

What this man does with his mouth.

My body jolts at the fire Terrence stokes between my thighs. Ragged breaths morph into a chant at the orgasm that's desperate to erupt. I gasp and wiggle under his grip, but he stays the course.

Vibrations from his chuckles pulse through my core. Coarse hairs scrape against my slit, over and over until I see stars from our own galaxy. He's never shaving that goatee. "Hang on for me, princess."

I cry out when he plunges two thick fingers inside and moves his tongue back on my clit. His mouth is velvet on my skin. My legs convulse at the rhythm of his tongue that demands my orgasm. "Terrence!"

There's no time to recover. Absolutely zero.

"Arms up."

Bunched fabric skates up my body, grazing my nipples along the way. He keeps my dress over my eyes like a blindfold, the kinky bastard. The warmth of his breath on my breasts turns my nipples into diamonds. I squirm when he takes one between his teeth and switches to the other. I don't have the biggest chest, but that doesn't stop him from cupping them and sucking on the sensitive peaks until my body tingles from head to toe.

All concentration flies out the window when his fingers find their way back into my sex. Heat dampens my skin, and my toes curl at the start of another orgasm from his fingers pumping into me. "Ready to come again." It's a statement, not a question, and God help me.

They'll put *Death by Orgasms* on my tombstone, and that's fine by me. If I die tonight, what a way to go.

His mouth covers mine to muffle another scream, a mix between the sounds of Mariah Carey and a Jack Russell terrier. I taste myself on his lips. He pulls the dress from my eyes and drops to his forearms to kiss me with a softness that makes my heart melt.

"I missed you." His words linger against my lips.

This man paralyzed me with a tongue and two fingers. But those three words—and the way he looks at me after his whispered confession—are too much. His gaze answers every question I had.

I reach to caress his cheek, unable to blink back tears. "I missed you too, baby."

His eyes close. With a sharp inhale and a slow nod, he turns his head to kiss the inside of my hand. Terrence says he's not good with words, but he loves with his whole heart. We kiss each other with adoration. There's no urgency or desperation.

We're home.

The head of his shaft grazes my entrance. Hungry eyes peer through mine. "Are you sure?"

At my nod, he places his arm behind me to cradle my head and leans down for a deep kiss. His other hand holds my hip as he slides in. My head tips back, and my breath hitches at the burn, a mix of pain and pleasure.

Our moans intertwine with every inch I take. Beads of sweat freckle his forehead at his slow worship. He's holding back to keep from splitting me in two. "Just breathe, baby." A flurry of kisses coats my neck.

My body relaxes at his touch. He moves until he bottoms out and waits for me to adjust to the stretch. He leans in and kisses my forehead. "Te adoro," he says, his voice thick with emotion. *I adore you.* Spanish rolls from the lips planting slow kisses on a tour of my body.

"Eres mi vida." *You are my life.*

"Te quiero tanto." *I love you so much.*

He presses his mouth over my heart for a final declaration. "Eres la dueña de mi corazón." *You own my heart.*

The tenderness of his words in rhythm with his gentle strokes overwhelms my senses but soon becomes a dark craving for more.

"Terrence?"

He stills. "Am I hurting you?"

I shake my head and lick my lips. My hands wrap around his muscular globes to push him deeper as my hips lift to meet his center. *Give me your worst, Mr. Reyes.* In one swift motion, he pulls back and slams into me. I cry out and grip the sheets to hold on for dear life. He widens my legs and rolls his hips for harder thrusts, knocking the breath from my lungs. Our bodies clap together in a sound that rises to a crescendo.

"Oh, God!" I gasp for breath at the surge of heat that spreads through my body. My nails dig into his back as another orgasm rips through me and snatches my voice.

I collapse from my release, but he's far from done. Terrence moves off the bed and drags me to the edge. He stands between my legs, sinks his fingers into my hips, and slams into me again. My body goes limp at the force of his thrusts.

How is his breath steady when I sound like I'm having an asthma attack?

He smiles and winks. "Hold on, princess. I'm not done with you yet." I stare at him in confusion before he lifts my butt like he's curling a barbell to spear me on his dick.

My mouth is dry, and my vagina wants to put up an out-of-office sign. I try to tap out like an MMA fighter, which earns a laugh, of all things.

"Is my baby tired?" I whimper at his taunt.

His pace quickens. He's close, and with three hard thrusts, he empties himself inside of me. I stare at the wall, unable to lift my head. There aren't enough protein shakes and fitness routines to justify what happened. He broke my coochie, plain and simple.

Terrence puts me in the covers. I get a kiss on the forehead before he disappears into the bathroom and returns with a washcloth to clean me up. Then he wipes himself, tosses it to the side, and crawls into bed. "Are you okay?" He pulls me close.

"Mmm." It's all I can get out in this sex coma.

He shakes his head with a smile and takes my face in his hands for a kiss. "Such a drama queen." Terrence squeezes my ass and rolls onto his back. "Rest up, princess. Round two in ten minutes."

I'm not going to make it.

Chapter 25

Justice

After four hours and three—yes, *three*—rounds of make-up sex, we finally rest. My body aches in the best way possible. And those kisses? They were consuming, possessive. I came alive with each sweep of his tongue.

I also came hard. Multiple times.

Terrence stays in shape, but good damn, that man has the endurance of a horse.

I missed sleeping in his arms. It's safe, like nothing will touch me because he won't let it. I pull my phone off the nightstand and check the time. 8:33 p.m. Back to my room, I go.

Are you out of your mind leaving this beautiful naked man in the bed by himself?

I can't help but smile at the smirk on his face. Even in a deep sleep, he's at peace. Terrence has one hand tucked behind his head and the other on top of the covers over his crown jewels.

There are so many things we still need to fix. For starters, did he talk to Madison? Hell, the last time I spoke to Preston, we took a rain check on our date. Imagine his surprise when he finds out I reunited with my estranged husband, swapped buckets of bodily fluids, *and* spent most of the evening putting dents in one of his hotel beds.

I love Terrence, but I need a moment to myself to process my life. Without his beautiful penis as a distraction. I didn't expect to attend a singles' retreat, make out with a billionaire stranger, *and* make love to the husband I haven't seen in almost a year.

It's a lot.

I steal one last glance, put on my dress, grab my heels, and tippy-toe out the front door. There's a fifty-fifty chance Emma didn't come back to the suite after our dance lessons, so maybe she won't see my walk of shame—or whatever you call it when you have sex and sprint off like you're on an episode of *Cops*. Dick and dash?

I make it halfway to my room when her door swings open. "Surprised you're able to walk straight after getting your back blown out."

My skin heats at the memory. It's not my back that will land me in a wheelchair for the next couple of days. I face her with my bottom lip between my teeth to suppress the goofy grin that wants to break free. "What makes you think I did anything sexual?"

She saunters over in a silk robe. "For starters, your hair"—she gestures to the mess of curls on my head—"looks like it got stuck in a blender. You're also walking funny."

"Okay, you caught me." Why play innocent with a bloodhound? She sees right through me and the smile I can't contain.

"I know I did. Took you long enough to admit it." She rolls her eyes with a look I know all too well. One that begins with *dumb* and ends in *ass*.

Of course she knew.

"Madison put her arms around Terrence on the dance floor. Childbirth is probably less painful than your reaction was. But the way you two eyed each other before she came..." She shakes her head. "There's no way something *wouldn't* happen. Did you see yourself and how quickly you agreed to dance with a man who pissed you off only a day ago?"

Terrence chose me over Madison. It shouldn't come as a surprise, but it's a tiny spark of hope, and that has to be worth something.

I love you, Justice. I never stopped loving you, and I will never stop loving you.

"I surprised myself with that one. I don't know what came over me."

"You want your man back. Nothing wrong with that." She guides me to the sofa. Here comes the Danny Tanner speech. "We've been here for a few days now, and I don't need a mind reader to know you wish you were still with him."

"You *are* a mind reader," I say under my breath.

Emma checks my shoulder with hers. "Of course I am, dear. That's not the point." She laughs. "The point is, what you feel right now is what you used to feel with Terrence. I get why you decided to leave him—and I will always have your back no matter what—but I really think you shouldn't deny your heart because you're too caught up in your head."

I don't think I can sigh any louder. "It's not that easy, Em."

"Who says it has to be complicated? Did you two talk?"

"Yeah."

"And?"

I mutter something unintelligible.

"Sorry, what was that?"

"We, uh, had sex...three times."

Emma's eyes light up. She clasps her hands like I told her we won the lottery. "*Three* times? Praise the Lord, those cobwebs are gone!"

I shake my head and stand. Orgasms aside, there are a million and one ways why this second attempt at love won't end well. "Something will go wrong. I know it."

"No, Jay. You're *thinking* of all the ways things will go wrong instead of living your life. You have a chance to be happy again with the man you want. Don't sabotage your joy because of self-doubt."

I look to the ceiling in hopes I'll find the answers written on the wall. "You're right. I just need some time to think." I went from near divorce to reconciliation, and I need a minute.

She nods. "Fair enough."

The pep talk ends with a hug and a butt pinch for good measure. Preston and I need to speak. He deserves that much.

"Hey, Justice?"

"Yeah?" I say over my shoulder. Did we not just cover the bases? I have no idea what else there's left to say, but her face reads confused...or constipated.

"If you and Terrence kissed and made up...where is he?"

Here we go.

"He's still in bed. I came up here."

Her eyes go wide. "*Please* tell me that's a joke." She folds over with laughter. I see tears, actual tears.

My face scrunches. "What's so funny? I thought it was best to come back to my room to think without distractions."

More laughter.

My thumb hits my chest. "What?" *I left his room, not the state.*

Emma deadpans.

"Should I ask him for permission before I pee too?"

Silence.

"You act like we won't see each other as soon as he wakes up."

More silence.

I roll my eyes. "This is no big deal, Em. I need to shower."

The doors close behind me when I enter my room. She's right. This will start an argument.

"It's not a big deal," I say to myself as I turn on the shower tap. This place is amazing, but the water will give you second-degree burns if you aren't careful.

Terrence knows we can't just snap our fingers and erase our problems. I don't care how spectacular the sex is. It doesn't work like that. If we really want to give this a go, we can't run away from the problems that broke our marriage.

Like you ran away from his bed?

"It's not the same thing," I say to no one.

Or is it?

Chapter 26

Terrence

I wake to a door closing. My room is far from the front to hear the hallway, but I catch it. Damn I'm hungry. I wonder if Justice wants to order room service or go down to one of the restaurants for a late bite. Then I'll spread her legs for dessert.

Speaking of which, where is she?

Her side of the bed is nothing but wrinkled sheets with a few dents. She acts shy, but my wife is a vixen when she wants to be. I didn't expect us to have sex, at least not so soon, but I make no apologies for it. I missed her and every inch of her body.

My voice cracks when I attempt to call out to her. Nothing. There's no sign of her when I lift my head to scan the room. She's not in the bathroom because the light is off. *Where the hell is she?*

Now I'm awake.

"Justice?"

Still nothing.

I rip off the sheets and stand. Her clothes are gone.

She left.

Great.

It takes seconds to put on a pair of sweats and a shirt and reach the front door to grab my shoes.

"You're gonna get it, princess," I say in a huff.

I thought we were past the disappearing acts. Clearly, I was wrong. Justice goes into flight mode the second things get too hard or become uncomfortable, and her David Copperfield days are over.

With my key card and wallet in my pocket, a mint in my mouth, and an erection for all to see, I jog out of the room. Screw the elevator. The steps are faster.

It takes two knocks for Emma to open the door.

"Ready for round number four?" Looks like the gossip train beat me here.

"I need to talk to Justice."

She nods and steps aside.

The glimpse I had of this suite before doesn't scratch the surface. My spot is nice, but this place is *nice*. I thought about splurging but decided against it. If Justice and I had come here together, we would have had all this and more.

"Where is she?" I call over my shoulder.

"In her room, straight ahead. I suspect she's in the shower." I nod in thanks and make my way to the closed double doors. "I told her it was a bad idea to leave you. That she would have hell to pay for it."

I stop and turn with a hand on the door. "You're right about that. Also, sorry."

She frowns. "For what?"

"For the sounds that are about to come out of this room."

A grin spreads across her face. "No apologies needed. Go take care of our girl."

The shower is on when I step into her bedroom. Justice is singing what sounds like Al Green's "Let's Stay Together." Her cheerful but off-key rendition gets louder with each step I take toward the bathroom.

The urge to burst through the door with an over-the-top serenade and fuck her senseless builds with every lyric. But she won't get the pleasure, because she ran away from me.

Again.

I stand in the doorway and take in the showroom that is her bathroom. It's the size of our first apartment after college and has a huge soaking tub in the middle. Damn, I should've upgraded.

My smile spreads at the private performance. This woman still has no idea I'm here. The soft lines of her curves appear in silhouette against a curtain of fog that does nothing to conceal her body. My eyes sweep up her wide hips and stall at the slopes of her breasts I'm desperate to put in my mouth.

Fuck. I want her. To touch, devour, and make come multiple times on my face and dick.

Her allure hypnotizes my senses with the sway of her hips until she throws in a random James Brown spin. I stifle a laugh at her *heh!* for good measure.

My dick begs for her to sing into my mic. Seven months is too long, and I refuse to spend another minute without her. I want to watch her like this all day, but we have unfinished business. I lean against the doorframe with my arms crossed. "Nice to see you're still alive."

She jumps at the sound of my voice. "Jesus, Terrence!" The shower door opens, exposing her body from the neck up. "You scared me."

"Makes two of us, princess. Why did you sneak out like that?" I walk to her, my eyes fixed on the soapy target with track star tendencies.

She goes quiet. "I...got scared. I needed to think without distractions."

"Baby, there's nothing to be scared of. Do you want this as much as I do?"

"Of course I do." Her voice comes out in a whisper.

"So we make it work. We made it work before, and we can do it again. But you don't get to leave the second things get hard or if you're scared. I know I hurt you in the past and put distance between us. That will never happen again."

Her eyes rise to meet mine, and she nods.

"Now scoot over." I kick off my shoes and pull off my shirt.

Her eyes turn into saucers, like it's not obvious what comes next after I yank off these sweatpants. "Wha—"

"Do you know what it's like to want your wife back for seven months, finally get her, and wake up to an empty bed because she left? Hell no, that doesn't fly with me."

For once, the woman is speechless. I have to snap my fingers to pull her laser focus off my dick, but she eventually backs away from the frameless shower door so I can enter. After staring quietly—at my face this time—she opens her mouth. "I'm sorry."

"Didn't hear that. What did you say?"

"I said I'm sorry."

"No more running." I look down at her and lift her chin. "If things get hard, we work on them *together*. I'm not losing you again." Tension rolls off her in waves.

She smiles up at me and nods. Water trickles from her wet coils down her neck to her breasts. I plant a kiss on her lips and chuckle at her gasp when I push her against the shower wall. Her chest heaves with anticipation. My eyes flick to her nipples hardening under my gaze. Soap drips down her breasts, and fuck me if her body doesn't look like chestnut silk.

My dick strains against my stomach.

I need her. Now.

I lean in. My mouth is inches from hers. "Don't think you're off the hook. I'm your *husband*, and I don't give a damn how long we've been separated. From here on out, where you go, I go."

Her legs spread at the press of my knee between her thighs. The tips of my fingers tease her entrance. "I didn't hear a 'yes, Terrence.'" She bites her lip and lifts her chin. *God, I love this woman.* "Does my baby want to play?" Three fingers slip into her pussy. Her breath catches, and I use my other hand to hold her neck. One thumb traces the outline of her pulse, and the other makes slow circles on her clit. She can take it. "Alright, let's play."

Her eyes roll back. "Oh, God." *Fight all you want, princess. You won't win this battle.*

My tongue follows a trail of water from her neck down to her collarbone. "Is that a 'yes, Terrence?'" She bites her lip and clamps down on my fingers. The shower's steady flow drowns out the sounds of Justice's wet pussy when I pump my fingers in and out of her. I smile at her defiance and stroke her G-spot.

Her whimpers morph into a scream. "Yes, Terrence!"

Our mouths collide. Goosebumps break out over Justice's arms that wrap around my neck. "I want you," she says through a shiver.

Justice drops to her knees and drags her fingers up my thighs, watching me urge her further. I didn't expect her to go down there but sure as fuck won't complain about it. Hungry brown eyes appraise my shaft. Her tongue licks me from base to tip, swirling my crown before taking me deep. My head tips back at the steady motion of her mouth moving up and down my erection.

Well, shit. "You're going to kill me, woman," I say through a grunt.

Her eyes darken. She strokes harder and moves her mouth with more force. I try to distract myself to make this last but do a shit job. My balls tighten at the soft lips about to put me in a coma. A bench comes into view out of the corner of my eye, and I pull her up to move us. She presses into me for a kiss and runs her fingers through my hair. My teeth pull at her bottom lip before I spin her around and bend her over.

Two slaps have her ass in a blush.

"Terrence!"

"Don't 'Terrence' me now, princess. This is what you get for leaving me." I wrap her hair around my fist and waste no time driving into her. A moan slips, and Justice braces herself on the bench. "Take this dick, baby." I smack her ass again and thrust harder to match the rhythm of my beating heart. I pull her head back and expose the length of my tongue. She takes it into her mouth. *Good girl.* My hands roam her hips, and I pick up the pace. I break the union of our lips to hammer into her and almost come at the chorus of our moans mixing with the patter of water against the tiles. My grip tightens, and a wave of heat shoots up my spine.

Justice arches back with every forceful thrust; her pussy clenches my dick with an iron grip. "Terrence! Terrence!"

When her body convulses, I give in. Her name comes out in a chant when I empty myself in her, a promise to be the man she deserves. Aftershocks wane, and I lift her into my arms to sit us down. Laughter rumbles under my chin.

I pull back to look at Justice. "What's so funny?"

"I forgot how good making up is. Maybe I should leave more often," she says with a smirk.

A swat to the butt makes her jump. "Try it again and see what happens."

Chapter 27

Justice

J oy.

Indescribable joy.

It's what surges through my chest and takes my breath away. I want to pinch myself but resist the urge to wake up from this dream. One I prayed for with my heart but denied with my mind. A dream I never thought would happen because in life you wait for the other shoe to drop. Any minute now, I'll come to my senses and realize I'm tucked away in bed, not sitting on the edge of it, gazing at a man who continues to seal my heart with his.

Terrence stands in nothing but a white towel. His back is to me, showcasing muscles with complicated names that have become an obsession, along with his forearm veins and those juicy buns. My ovaries jump in a frenzy when he winks over his shoulder and rattles off our breakfast order to room service. The self-control I have not to lick him from his abs to his biceps is at a minimum.

Who am I?

He hangs up the phone and eyes me with a knowing look. "Ready for another round, Mrs. Reyes?" There's a playfulness in his tone.

Why, yes. Yes, I am.

My body hums at the promise of another orgasm. I have the biggest grin on my face and even bigger sex hair. *Mrs. Reyes*. The moniker radiates throughout my body and leaves me breathless. I want to bottle the yearning in his gaze and seal it to my heart forever. Terrence makes me come alive, unafraid and unashamed to let myself fall into the pleasures of our love.

The look I give him from under my lashes is one of innocence we both know is long gone. "Yes, Mr. Reyes." Inch by inch, I lower my robe to expose myself. He stares down at my breasts and rubs his jaw. God, I'm so hungry for this man. Last night was... Well, there are no words. But I want more.

His eyes darken in an appreciative scan of my body that starts at my toes and travels to my lips. "Put your hands on the headboard and spread wide for me."

Here we go again.

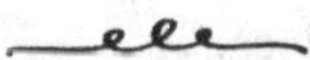

The rest of the morning came and went in a blur. I fell asleep after breakfast, which gave Terrence enough time to go back to his room for few items. I didn't think I was out for long, but I woke up next to him typing away on his laptop.

"Hey there, sleepyhead."

The towel is gone. In its place is a pair of gray sweats coupled with a white thermal and his gold chain. If there's one thing sexier than this man in a towel, it's watching him in his business element. I'm in no rush to move. Not on a Sunday morning on vacation, and not with him in my bed.

In *gray* sweatpants.

The scent of citrus and bergamot lures me to turn to its source. Heat pools between my legs. If I keep this up, I won't walk for a week. His computer will have to do as a distraction. "Work?"

He nods, deep in thought, with his eyes fixed on the screen. "Yeah. I'm closing a deal on a property and have to look over some contracts."

Property? That's news to me. I had no idea he was into real estate. Then again, we haven't spoken in seven months. "Sounds promising. What's it for?"

"A training facility in Austin so clients can come to me for a change. I'll still have to travel from time to time, but this will allow me to be home more. I also want to start an institute there for student athletes. Possibly some type of summer camp for kids who love sports but can't afford fees."

"That's amazing." I sit up and press my lips over his. "You're amazing." Another kiss. "I can't wait to see it come to life."

The smile he gives me grips my heart. "Thanks, Jay. That means a lot." He readjusts his laptop so I can snuggle against his broad chest. My own personal space heater. The smoothness of his skin evens out his rigid muscles pressed underneath his shirt.

"Is there a reason you want to cut down on travel?" He can't pack a suitcase to save his soul, and he hates airplane snacks but loves exotic destinations.

"There is."

"What?"

His eyes lock on mine. "You."

This man.

"I love you, baby."

"I love you more."

Room service gets another call by one o'clock. We spend half the day in bed. A little work. Lots of rustling sheets. And church. Oh yes. Saints we're not, but our faith is another vine that connects us. Terrence couldn't stop staring at me after we discovered my new church is the one he watches on his computer when he's out of town. What are the chances?

I muster up the strength to peel myself from bed in search of something to wear. An off-the-shoulder sweater and leggings will have to do. The doorbell rings. I let in the attendant with the food cart and notice a shiny gold envelope between the metal food domes. "What's that?"

"Ah, yes. That is your formal invitation to your private dinner tonight, madam." I must look dumb and lost, because he stares back at me and repeats himself. "The private dates from speed dating were last night." He points to the envelope. "There is a special request for your presence tonight."

Huh?

I smile at his frown to keep from looking like a bigger ditz but bare my teeth by accident. With a quick nod, he bolts through the door. The envelope weighs heavy in my hands when I catch a glimpse of Terrence on his way to the kitchen.

A special request?

"Want some wine?"

"Yeah, that would be great." I'll take the whole bottle.

He sits at the table with two glasses of white wine. "What's that?"

"It's an invitation...to a private date tonight."

"Private what?"

I hand it over for him to open. His face goes blank when he looks inside. "I forgot about this" is all I get before he sets down the envelope, picks up his fork and knife, and digs into his food.

"I don't understand why I have this. I didn't turn in my card after speed dating."

"Well." He points his fork at the envelope. "It looks like you have a date with Preston tonight. Seems he pulled some strings to make it happen since he wasn't there."

Sure enough, a peek inside reveals he requested my attendance at a restaurant tonight at seven. This must be his way of making up for the dance class he missed. Guess we were both busy yesterday. "Who did you blow off?" If the private dates were last night, did Terrence stand someone up? Was it Madison?

He mumbles something and spoons in another mouthful of spinach.

"Come again, Mr. Reyes?"

He mumbles again.

"Yeah, I still didn't hear that." I wave a hand in the air. "Must be the altitude."

He levels me with a stare and says with clarity, "No one."

My fork drops to my plate. Did I hear that correctly? Because it's not the answer I expected. "Wait. You mean to tell me, out of a sea of single women, you chose *not* to go on a date with anyone?"

"You know the answer to that, Justice." He wipes his mouth and eyes me with a look that says to knock it off.

Any woman would drop to her knees in front of this man. Terrence checks every box with his charm, heart of gold, and successful business. And that's *without* his sexual appetite. I always assumed he enjoyed life as a bachelor, including with Madison, who's done everything but throw her panties at his forehead. Hell, maybe she has.

Did he really hold out for us to get back together? That can't be true, because I've seen him with her. There's no way—

"You'll give yourself a headache thinking so hard, princess," he says with a chuckle. "If I did want a fresh start, it wouldn't be with someone I met at a singles' retreat. And before you ask me *again* about Madison, it wouldn't be with her either. Did I have a knee-jerk reaction when you were with someone else? Yeah, I did. But a relationship with her is a road I already traveled, and it's a dead end."

I cut into my salmon. "Well, that settles it. You need to take Madison out tonight, and I need to go to dinner with Preston."

Terrence opens his mouth to respond but snaps it shut. Based on that vein about to burst through his neck, I'd say he's somewhere between blowing a fuse and taking me to a psychiatrist to have my head examined.

"Why the hell would we do that?"

"For closure, or whatever you call it when you lead someone on but need to cut it off." I reach for his hand. "It's not fair to them to pretend like nothing happened."

Look at you being all mature.

"Justice..."

"I'm serious. Let's use tonight to tie up loose ends."

Brown eyes stare me down. "Loose ends." You'd think we ordered a hit on them the way he says it. His brows pull together, and he looks down at his plate. I'm ready to call the whole thing off until he says, "Okay. We'll play it your way, Jay." He shakes his head like I asked him to rob a bank. "This is the first time I'm going to call her on this trip."

What? "Time-out. You never called Madison on this trip?"

"I told you the truth, Jay."

This man.

I smile and take another bite of my salmon. "So that's our plan for tonight. We say goodbye to them and meet up tomorrow morning."

His face twists. "Tomorrow morning? Why then?"

I wipe my mouth and stand to close the distance. Strong hands find a home under my butt when I straddle his lap. I lean in, press my mouth to his ear, and roll my hips. "Because the next time we make love, I don't want to smell her on you."

Terrence stills. Without warning, he jumps to his feet and tosses me over his shoulder. "In that case, we'll spend the rest of the day doing what we can't tonight."

I squeal. "You're a nut!"

He smacks my ass. "And you're about to get mine."

Chapter 28

Justice

Terrence leaves my room at five thirty after taking me two more times. Clearly, rest is not an option. The stamina of that man is something researchers should study at a university. God knows I don't understand it, but I'm not about to complain.

The irony of us on *dates* with other people tonight isn't lost on me. But as long as we leave here together, that's all that matters.

"I gotta give it to you and Terrence. You two are handling this well," Emma says from a wingback chair in the corner of my room. She's yet to utter a word about her date last night. It's not like her to keep secrets, which leaves me with questions...lots of questions. If I weren't knee-deep in my own mess, I'd press her for answers.

"Preston is a good catch. He deserves the truth."

"While that might be true, I hope Madison hears it loud and clear that Terrence is off-limits."

She will tonight. Though Madison always discovers new ways to claw beneath my skin, hurt people hurt people. Under different circumstances—circumstances that don't involve her life quest to get my husband's dick—I see us as friends. Sure, she's conniving at times, but I won't pretend like Terrence didn't fuel her hope of reconciliation.

Time will tell how everything unfolds.

I'm down at the ballroom at six forty-five. Preston strikes me as someone who arrives early, and I want to be ready. As expected, he's outside the French doors, waiting for me. The man looks like the million bucks—sorry, the *billion* bucks—he's worth in a charcoal suit and white shirt with the top buttons loose. The ice-gray pocket square intensifies the cognac eyes now on me. My knees threaten to buckle on my approach. There's no question he's successful in business the way he wields his stare. It's unnerving.

I tense when he takes me into his arms. This is dumb. It's a *hug*, but I'm still a turd for the bomb I'm about to drop.

"You look great." His gaze traces a slow path from my eyes to my toes. My skin heats under his appraisal. If only he knew this black dress cost seven dollars at a thrift shop. I think it's nice, but designer it is not.

"Thanks." I try to mirror his smile. *Fail*. "You look great too."

With his hand on the small of my back, he guides us to a table near the floor-to-ceiling windows that frame the view of the valley. The ballroom is a far cry from the shell it was after movie night. Round tables with fancy cloths and rattan chairs fill the once-empty space. Servers with trays of wine and fine cuisine whisk by patrons who are deep in conversation. I told Preston about my problems with Terrence the last time we were here. After I dry humped and tongued him down on the balcony.

What a turn of events.

Votive candles illuminate our table in a soft glow. A small bouquet of roses sits in a vase at the center. Did he do all of this for us?

My heart beats like a war drum as Preston pulls out my chair. He unbuttons his jacket and takes a seat across from me. Candlelight dances across his eyes, which hold mine.

I'm going to the deepest pits of Hell.

Calm down. You're not breaking off an engagement.

He reaches for my hand. "Sorry I missed the dance lesson with you yesterday. A business meeting came up, and I had to attend."

My hand covers his. I'm not sure how I'll get through the night, but here goes nothing. "It's okay." I straighten in my seat and stare into his eyes. "Preston, I need to tell you something."

"That you and your ex are no longer estranged?" His calm tone grips my senses.

Does he?

No.

How?

What?

He looks unfazed, like he hasn't concocted a plan to chop me into pieces and sprinkle my remains in the bushes. I don't know him well, but I hope that's the case. A rich serial killer was only a thing in *American Psycho*, right?

Well, there are the Menendez brothers, John Du Pont, and Robert Alan Durst, to name a few.

That's it. No more true crime for me. I need something easy and joyful, like *House Hunters* with a hopeful homebuyer who massages goldfish for a living and has a $3 million budget.

My cheeks burn, and I let out a breath. "H-how do you know?"

Preston holds my gaze. "Video of you two on the dance floor. You both looked cozy."

My back hits my chair in a thump. I don't know if I should breathe a sigh of relief or bolt for the door.

And go where? He owns the resort.

"Were you spying on me?" My voice betrays any attempt to remain calm. Owning a hotel is not a license to monitor potential love interests. That can't be legal.

There better not be any cameras in our rooms. Oh God. What if there are?

He smirks as if he senses my discomfort. "Relax, Justice. I'm not a stalker. I wanted to see how you were. I hated that I had to leave yesterday." His face turns serious. "I assume things worked out the way you'd hoped?"

The dents in your comfy mattress prove they did.

I swallow hard and look him in the eye to say what's in my heart. What's been in my heart. "We found our way back to each other. It's something I brushed off because of past pain. But what can I say? When you find your soul mate, it's hard to let go."

An expression crosses his features. He said he isn't into commitments, but any frustration with me at this point is understandable. I never wanted to lead him on. It takes a few beats, but he nods. "I respect that."

Sorry, what?

He waves a hand and chuckles. "Honestly, I envy your situation."

So this is what it's like when one of the men on *Maury* find out they're the father. My mouth is open, and my eyes are wide. *He's* envious of *me*? I shake my head and squint in hopes his words will make sense. They don't, but the night is young. "I thought you said you don't do long-term relationships?"

We sit in silence until the waiter comes to take our order. Preston nods at the menus and waits for me to make my selection. I guess we're having dinner after all. When we're alone again, he searches my eyes. "I'm not opposed to anything long term, but part of the reason why I'm hesitant is I was once in love with someone who got away."

It's a good thing the wine has arrived, because I'm going to need it. Will this night bring any more turns? Scratch that. I don't want to know.

"Really?"

He leans forward, like he's about to tell me a secret, and clasps his hands together. Preston met a young woman in his late twenties. They dated for close to a year, and it was the most passionate relationship he's ever had. But something happened that made them lose touch, and he regrets it to this day.

"I was so young, just coming into the business. I didn't know what I had." He shakes his head, still lost in the memory. "I would marry her today if I ever found her."

I reach out to take his hand as he continues.

"I've had many women in my life, and I've wasted so much time trying to fill a void all of these years."

Emma told me Preston is forty-one, thanks to an extensive online search that would put Homeland Security to shame. This man has enough money in the bank to last lifetimes and enjoys nothing less than luxury. There's a good chance he has models on speed dial. A walking advertisement for confidence, this one is, but something tells me his willingness to be vulnerable tonight is a side of himself he doesn't often show.

"I don't know what to say. Thank you for trusting me with your story. I hope you're able to find love like that again."

He smiles and nods, in thought about the one who got away. "I know you're back with your husband, but your story—and the one-in-a-million chance you two found yourselves here, of all places—gives me hope. I haven't felt that in a long time."

I blink back tears. Whoever is lucky enough to get this man's heart will have it for a lifetime.

We ease in and out of conversation like old friends who haven't seen each other in years. Terrence walks in with Madison when the food arrives. He looks business casual in a black button-down and dark jeans. We lock eyes, and I give him a quick nod to let him know things are okay. He smiles before he and Madison go to the bar. Guess they aren't getting dinner.

Preston follows my line of sight and stares longer than expected.

"Hey. Is everything okay?" I ask. My eyes shift between Preston and the direction Terrence went.

"Yeah, I'm fine." He pushes a smile. "I take it that was Terrence and the woman he's about to let down."

"It is. Her name is Madison. They dated for a few months in college. She broke up with him, believe it or not. We met not too long after, and the rest is history. Anyway, we got married, and she...well, she's been pining after him all these years in a not-so-subtle way."

"Terrence must be a catch if that's the case."

I can't help but smile. "He is a great guy."

Our evening ends with a walk back to my room after dessert. We exchange a hug and well-wishes. Things went better than expected. Silence hangs in the air to let me know Emma isn't here. I kick off my shoes and pad over to my room for an evening in the soaking tub.

Chapter 29

Terrence

I step off the elevator at seven thirty to a small crowd gathering for the pop-up restaurant in front of the ballroom. The place is wall-to-wall people. The decision to grab a drink at the bar is proving to be a good idea. Sweat glistens my palms, which smooth over my shirt for the fourth time. I'm thankful I chose to wear dark colors that will conceal any stains if Madison throws a drink at me. Doubt it will happen, but you never know.

She arrives with a smile that fades once she meets my eyes. "Hey." I give her a quick hug. There's no reason to be more of an asshole than she already believes me to be. We haven't talked since I ran out on her, and I'm sure she wants answers.

"Hey yourself."

Dinner with Madison didn't sit right with me. Justice and Preston should. I trust her. Unlike Jay and the billionaire, Madison and I have history, years of it. A bar is more casual, and it gives us space to talk without waiting for each course to arrive.

I gesture for her to go inside. "I hope you don't mind, but I wanted to go to the bar tonight."

"Sure, that's fine," she says, though her face reads otherwise. Madison can't hide her disappointment.

We pass the hostess, and a sensation in my chest tugs me to look out the corner of my eye. I catch a glimpse of Justice near the window, beyond rows of tables. Madison remains by my side near the wall, unaware of my wife's presence or tonight's intentions. Justice has her hand on Preston's, but the gesture looks more like comfort than romance. We lock eyes briefly, and I smile at her when she nods she's okay.

Inside the bar, Madison and I grab a high table and scan the menus.

"Interested in a whiskey flight? You didn't finish yours at the tasting," she says.

My neck tenses at the memory. "I forgot about that." It's not a lie. I *did* forget about the whiskey tasting, because my focus was on my wife and the twist of betrayal that sliced through me at her decision to end our relationship. An awkward silence passes between us. I need to rip off the bandage in a way that doesn't do more damage. "We need to talk."

"We sure do," she snaps. *Here we go.* "What the hell happened last night, Terrence? You just up and left me on the dance floor to run after your ex-wife. Then I don't see you at the private dates." Madison sits back in her chair with her arms crossed. She deserves an explanation.

"I'm sorry about that, and I'm sorry for my behavior these last few days."

She frowns. "What are you talking about? I thought we were having a good time together? Did I miss something? And that kiss in the movie theater was...wow."

I reach for one of the glasses when the flight hits the table. "My separation from my wife has been rough, to say the least. I haven't been in a good headspace." I sigh. This next part will come with either understanding or a public scene. "When I kissed you, it was a reaction to seeing Justice with another man. I snapped."

Oh man, here it comes.

The anticipation of a slap, a fist, or a drink to the face lingers with each second. Aside from the kiss, I didn't lead Madison on. I never called her to go out or checked in to say hi. Our time together was by chance, not intention. Still, I have to own up to my part.

She stares back at me with a face that's hard to read before she knocks back a glass of whiskey. That's a good sign, right? "I guess I should've seen this coming. You weren't exactly banging down my door to be with me."

"I'm sorry if I led you on. I love Justice."

She winces at her name. Nothing fazes Madison, but this stings, I can tell. "Can I ask you a question, Terrence?"

"Shoot."

"What does she have that I don't? I know we weren't together long, but I still remember what we had. It was pretty amazing. At least, it was to me."

This is a loaded question. I don't want to answer, but I need to make sure that after tonight, whatever games Madison played in the past to make Justice jealous end. "She's my heartbeat."

The tear that falls catches me off guard. I've never seen her cry. She lets out a nervous laugh and wipes the corner of her eye with a napkin. "Part of me feels so dumb, but I'm thankful you told me the way you did. You didn't have to, and I appreciate it."

I reach for her hand and try to reassure her with a look that tells her whatever attachment she feels to me will fade. In all honesty, I'm not worthy of it, and I never was. "You're a good person. I know you're going to find someone who makes you come alive the way Justice does for me. I hope we can still be friendly whenever we run into each other, but I also need the games between you and my wife to stop."

Madison studies me and nods. "I'm sorry about that," she says with a sigh. "I really should apologize to her, but I am sorry. You're an amazing man, Terrence. You're so kind and so thoughtful. Only two men in my life have had my heart. You were the first."

"What do you say we forget all this romance talk and finish off this whiskey?"

Her shoulders relax. "I'd like that very much," she says with a smile.

We spend the next forty-five minutes talking before I pay the tab and walk Madison back to her room. Justice consumes my thoughts on the way back to mine. All I think about is the woman I adore, the one I can't live without.

Chapter 30

Justice

I blink up at the shadows dancing across my ceiling, unable to fall asleep. A long soak in the tub. A bottle and a half of wine. *Living Single* reruns. Nothing is enough to slow down my mind.

Is he still out with her?

Does he have second thoughts?

Did she put his head on a spike after he rejected her?

When the hell did I get this insecure?

Unsteady feet take me to the bathroom. Disheveled hair in a messy updo, sunken cheeks, and tired eyes greet me in the mirror. Tomorrow's hangover is imminent, but at least I'll feel good in this plush hotel robe.

"Go to bed, Justice," I tell my reflection. As if she'll listen. Why did I push for us to not see each other until tomorrow? It's not impossible to wait until morning. We endured seven months apart. This is light work in comparison, but still.

Forget this.

An idea pops into my wine-clouded mind. The dry-cleaning sack in the closet now doubles as an overnight bag for my clothes and toothbrush. After I'm certain I don't look or smell like a zombie, I grab what I need and strut out of the suite in hot-pink heels on a mission.

Time to bring my man to his knees.

It takes less than five minutes to reach his room. No small feat with tall heels on and the coordination of a baby seal on a tricycle. I didn't think I had *that* much to drink, but the slant of my steps says otherwise. All I know is, Terrence better be in his room. In bed, alone.

The door swings open. My hand is in midair, and at my new height, my fist almost collides with a face that looks very confused to see me.

What did room service put in my wine? I don't remember knocking.

Terrence squints at the light from the hallway. Aww, he was asleep.

"Is everything alright?"

My brain stalls at the sight of him shirtless and in a pair of sweats. *Gray sweatpants* that model the outline of that juicy dick I'd like to ride. The gold chain on his neck forces my eyes back up his body before they settle on his deep V-cut abs. I lick my lips to keep what little dignity I have left.

Who am I kidding? It's gone.

"You okay, princess?" His eyes watch me with amusement. Terrence is quite aware of the effect he has on me. Or the effect the wine had on me. I'm not sure which one.

I lean forward to put a hand on the doorframe but stumble before I can steady myself. "Yup, never been better."

He's laughing now. "You drunk, baby?"

I bite my lip and lean into the door, inches from his face. "I had a glass or two but am coherent," I say with a wave of my hand and the tone of a game show host.

Tell him what he's won, Johnny! A horny wife! Better than a top-of-the-line refrigerator, if you ask me. But maybe not a convertible.

Nope, I am.

His lips quirk. It appears my husband likes this unexpected visit. My breath catches when he leans in with his gaze locked on me. "I thought you said we wouldn't see each other until tomorrow. Yet, here you are"—he tugs at the knot in my robe and drops his voice—"at my door, in a robe and heels." His eyes drag down my body and take their sweet time to meet mine. The smirk on his face dares me to continue, so I rise to the occasion.

I don't break our stare as I toss my bag into his room. Thank God it made it. My aim is crap on a *good* day. "It's past midnight, so tomorrow is here." His eyes follow my hands as I slowly unravel the knot in my robe. It pools on the floor in the form of a clumped turd. Hey, it's cotton, not silk.

His eyes bulge. Someone's awake now. "Jesus, Justice." I lean into his touch, which becomes more of a drag when he pulls me inside. The door shuts with a thud.

I channel my inner supermodel with a sashay to his bedroom in nothing but pink heels and my birthday suit. I stop at the entrance and look over my shoulder. Terrence is still at the front door. He needs to stop the fantasy that's playing out in his eyes and come get the real thing.

"You gonna stand there and stare all night or handle your business, Mr. Reyes?"

He reaches me in three strides and throws me over his shoulder. The sting of the first smack to my ass registers before another lands and travels up my spine. "Like you need to question me." Another smack.

I expect him to toss me onto my back when we reach his bed, but he flips me in the air in some CrossFit motion and puts his head between my legs. I grip his thick trunks in fear of a face-plant and welcome the erection that's now in my face.

We meet again, old friend.

"You want to play games, princess?" My clit tingles against his breath. "Let's play."

Oh yes, please. I like games.

He tightens his hands around my thighs, spreads me wide, and latches onto my sex. Up. Down. All around. His tongue flattens to devour me in long strokes that build in pressure. He zeroes in on my clit to give it some figure-eight action with his tongue. This man is going to suck my soul through my vagina, and I'm more than okay with that.

With an arm around his lower back so I don't fall, I take him out of his sweatpants. His dick springs to life, and I brace myself to take him deep in my throat in this twisted Spider-Man position. I lick him from base to tip and swirl my tongue around his head for good measure.

Two can play this game, buddy.

Our groans mix with the scent of our desire. He places us on the bed and turns so I'm on top. His arms rest against my inner thighs so he can nestle into my sex. You'd think the man hasn't eaten in weeks the way he feasts on my body.

"Bet I'll make you come first." I swirl my tongue down his shaft, which makes a *pop* sound.

I whimper at the thrust of two fingers hooked on my G-spot. "Game on, princess."

Welp, I lost.

Mondays are the worst, but not this one. If someone had told me my estranged husband would press a red rose to my nose to tickle me awake—*in his hotel bed*—I'd have called you full of it. But here I am with the biggest grin on my face. Terrence is at the end of the stem and on the side of the bed with a smile.

"Good morning, sleepyhead." He kisses me.

My body purrs. "Morning, baby. What time is it?"

"Twenty minutes past nine."

I'm up in a scramble, on autopilot to find my robe and heels. The realization that my bits are jiggling proud and free doesn't hit until I see Terrence bent over in laughter. My cheeks flush, and a bout of giggles takes over. "Go ahead. Laugh it up."

His body convulses in his fight to contain himself. He coughs twice. "There's no rush to get up. You can relax, princess."

I don't remember the last time we laughed like this. It's nice, even if he's in tears at my expense. Terrence wraps me in his arms and kisses my forehead. "I love you. What do you want for breakfast?"

I run my lips over his chest. "I was thinking something Dominican, from Newark."

His eyes darken. "Dominican, huh?" He nods. "That's on the menu. It's a little hot, though. Think you can handle it?"

I take my place in the center of the bed on all fours, my appetite for food long gone and my sex in full view. "Not a problem," I say over my shoulder. The coochie tingles this man arouses. He makes me want all kinds of things. Nasty things.

The bed dips with his weight. He towers behind me and glides his hands up my thighs. My back arches at the electricity of his tongue. "Breakfast is served."

Chapter 31

Terrence

"Terrence, I—Oh, God." Justice whimpers and digs her nails into the couch. Our eyes lock over her shoulder. *That's right, baby. Let me take care of you.*

We've been at it for the better part of the morning and took a break to eat before fucking again. There were no fluids left to give, but when I caught a glimpse of Jay in one of my button-down shirts after a shower, I chased her from the bedroom to the living room.

Heat from her body shoots a chill up my back. I plant a foot on the sofa she's bent over and harden my grip to move with more force. Her breath hitches at the hard thrusts. I inhale and drive deeper into a tsunami of pleasure.

Her walls constrict around me as she screams my name. My balls rise, and I pump harder. Justice's body goes limp when I spread her cheeks. I'm not done with her.

"Terrence, I'm tired."

I chuckle and ease my grip. "You want me to stop, baby?" My pace relaxes, now a series of lazy strokes.

Her eyes open, and a slow smile curls the corners of her lips. "No."

Didn't think so.

My speed quickens. I slide one of my fingers through her back entrance. She clamps down on my dick, and fuck if I'll last much longer. The clap of her ass smacking against my thighs sends me into overdrive. I thrust harder and harder until her name leaves my lips in a cry.

I pull Justice down to the sofa and nestle her against my chest. I'll never get enough. My lips brush against hers. "I love you."

"I love you too."

There's a heaviness to Justice's gaze when I pick her up and head back to the bedroom. She's tired, and I need a nap. I put us in the sheets and pull her to my chest. As expected, she jolts to her feet after a peek at her clock.

My wife, ever the worrywart.

"It's eight minutes to noon! We have to check out. I'm not packed! Why are you laughing? This isn't funny, Terrence."

I wave a hand to will it away. Justice is cute when she turns frantic. "Relax, baby. I changed our flights to tomorrow and requested a later checkout time." I eye her. "Guess it pays for you to know the owner of this hotel."

She stares at me like she forgot how to speak. I roll my eyes and kiss her neck. "We'll leave together tomorrow, and before you ask how I was able to change your flight, I'll remind you I'm still your husband."

"Okay, so if we don't leave until tomorrow, why check out today?"

"That, my dear, is a surprise."

When we wake up, Justice calls Emma to let her know the change in plans, only to find out I already coordinated with her. Em is heading back to California tonight and will touch base once she gets home. We spend the next twenty minutes packing my things before we go back to her room. It's like old times with my wife and her endless commentary on my bad folding skills. Come tomorrow, she'll be back home with me.

By four o'clock, we're heading out of the lobby to the car service. Our next destination isn't too far of a drive. I fall a few steps behind to take her in.

This is perfect.

My life is perfect.

And it's something I will never take for granted.

Chapter 32

Justice

"If you bite your lip any harder, you'll draw blood, sweetheart."

I press my hands into my thighs in a failed attempt to keep calm and not ask Terrence where we're going for the third time in ten minutes. One cannot tempt a lover of Christmas with promises of a magical getaway without said Christmas-lover transforming into Buddy the Elf.

The blindfold over my eyes leaves me in darkness and full of questions. "One hint, *please*."

Soft lips press to my forehead with a tenderness that's meant to soothe but only fuels my curiosity. "Patience is a virtue, princess," he whispers with a smile in his voice. He enjoys the thrill that comes with a good surprise. Me? Not so much.

Minutes pass before our sedan comes to a stop. "This is as far as I can take you, but your destination is only a short walk from here," the driver says.

A short walk? Where are we?

Terrence is out of the car and thanking the driver. The trunk opens and closes. Crisp air shoots a chill to my toes when the door opens and strong arms pull me to my feet by my waist. I have to strain but hear holiday music in the distance and jump at a large vehicle passing by. Terrence kisses my neck and chuckles. "Now you can look." He removes the blindfold.

My eyes adjust to the sunlight. This can't be real. I take a step back. Somehow, our town car left Vail, Colorado, and ended up in a European village nestled between mountains. The buildings look like replicas from *A Christmas Prince* and make me wonder if we'll run into His Royal Highness of Aldovia on our way to wherever our destination is.

I'm speechless.

Terrence takes me into his arms and grins with satisfaction in his eyes. "I know, baby." His kiss is soft but has an intensity that could heat the entire town. Whatever he planned is special, and it's just for me.

"I haven't taken you on a proper date in seven months. Need to change that." He grabs our bags and gestures for us to walk.

"Terrence. This place is unreal. It looks like—"

"One of the many Hallmark movies you've yet to watch taking up space on the DVR?" He raises an eyebrow. "That was the plan. The day is yours to fulfill your holiday movie fantasies. A stroll through the streets to look at shops while sipping hot cocoa. Ice-skating under the lights. We won't see carolers this far into January, but I have a Christmas playlist in case of an emergency. Ready to be Stephanie Tanner for the day?"

I laugh at that. The fact that he calls Jodie Sweetin by her *Full House* character's name is a testament to the many holiday movies he's endured. "Don't act like *Merry & Bright* isn't one of your favorites." I catch a hint of a smile out of the corner of my eye. "Your secret is safe with me."

"It wasn't terrible," he says in a mumble.

Though I took a vow of silence—and promised on my pass to Heaven like that's a thing—to never utter a word about his Hallmark-watching ways, Terrence enjoys it. Our journey into the land of holiday movies began years ago around Christmastime. It's now a tradition to dedicate two weekends in December to matching flannel pajamas and cramming in all the Christmas movies we can. Save the family farm. Meet the love of your life stranded on the side of the road. Retreat to your hometown after heartbreak in the big city. It's all fair game. The plots are cheesy, but they're our thing.

The view takes my breath away when we turn the corner. We're in a fairy tale come to life. If an inn somewhere in the Swiss Alps had a real estate baby with a luxury resort, the offspring *might* look as dreamy as this place. I don't know where this building starts and ends.

I turn to Terrence and stare, unable to hold back tears. "You know how to make a girl feel special."

"If this gives you a glimpse of how much you mean to me, I will die a happy man. Come on, let's go drop off our bags."

We spend five hours as tourists in this unbelievable village, and it only took two minutes to fall in love. Holiday movies have nothing on the real thing. Not that I've been in one. There's something about the touch of Christmas magic and tasting its goodness. We might be in January, but it's here, full of hope and wonder.

I didn't want the day to end, and not because Terrence spoiled me with hot cocoa and marshmallows. This man awakens my soul. There's no shield I need to put up because who I am is good enough. DVR full of Christmas movies and all.

I take one last glance at myself in the mirror and press my hair to make sure it stays in place. We have six o'clock reservations "somewhere special."

Gosh, why are my hands so sweaty?

I open the bathroom door, and Terrence freezes when he takes in my red dress. Unlike the one I wore when we went dancing, this one is a touch more modest with sleeves to my elbow. It still has a slit that lands right above my thigh. I blush under his gaze.

His swallow is audible. "You're gorgeous."

I smile and dip my head. The way he looks at me, with the same fondness he had in his eyes on our wedding day, is too much. The world might see a man who looks like a professional athlete or a model, but I see his heart.

"Turtlenecks look good on you." Terrence makes belly button lint look sexy, but that's beside the point. His sweater stretches across his wide frame and flexes against his forearms when he readjusts his watch. His gray slacks mold to his meaty thighs. If I weren't intoxicated by the aftershave wafting into the bathroom, my knees would've given out by now.

He takes my hand, and we set off for the elevator. Restlessness gets the best of me. I don't mind dressing up from time to time—though

I'm more of a flats and leggings girl—but all of this is overwhelming. My husband doesn't need to spend thousands to win me back. He has me.

"We could've stayed in. You didn't have to do all of this to prove you love me." I shake my head. "It's nice, but it's too much."

Terrence pulls me in for a kiss to my forehead, something he does to calm me when my thoughts go down the rabbit hole like they are now. "You're right. I don't have to do anything. I *want* to spoil my wife and will do so until I leave this earth."

The elevator reaches the bottom floor. I take Terrence's hand as he walks us toward a door that leads outside. He must see the constipated look on my face, because he kisses my hand and gives me a wink. "Relax, princess. I promise we won't get cold."

I brace for the night air, but it doesn't come. We're in an insulated hallway with hanging lights and heaters to keep us warm. After several steps, we arrive in a tented room surrounded by floor lanterns. Moonlight and stars illuminate the makeshift room through a plastic window in the ceiling. A waiter stands next to a white table and chairs. Perfect for two.

"This is." I don't know what to say.

"You deserve the best."

Terrence guides me by the small of my back to my seat before he takes his. A five-course meal is on tonight's menu, and I have to pinch myself under the table to make sure this isn't a dream. "I-I don't know how to thank you for today. I'm at a loss for words." This is a lot to take in.

"You here with me is the only thing I need."

We spend the next two hours eating a fantastic meal and catching up on what happened over the last seven months. This is the fresh start we need.

After dinner, we head back to our room, hand in hand. Full of love and filled with lobster. I'm still in awe over the last few days and how the broken pieces of our lives reconnected to create the perfect picture.

Terrence slides in the key card and holds the door for me. I take off my heels, walk to the balcony, which overlooks an ice rink, and exhale. Flames come to life in the glass door's reflection.

I turn and lock eyes with Terrence. Several seconds pass before we meet each other in the middle of the room. Unlike the last forty-eight hours, we take our time with every kiss.

"I love you, Terrence." My hands wrap around the back of his neck.

"Love you more." He picks me up, and we head to the bedroom to make love for the first time that night.

This is the part of our story where we should ride off into the sunset. The part where we live out our happily ever after until our final breath. We weathered storms that nearly broke us.

But nothing prepares me for what lies ahead.

Chapter 33

Justice

"One tall macchiato and a scone for Reyes."

I grab my order from the counter and head back to my table next to the window. This is my favorite café in Austin, and it's become a second home on Saturday mornings. The smell of fresh-roasted coffee brings me back to the days of sitting inside a shop in Old Town while my mother graded assignments. She had stacks of papers and a caffe latte. I had hot cocoa and a library book for a weekly adventure.

The café is busy for this time of day but is still quiet enough for me to dig into this novel. Teens are lining up to take selfies in front of a backdrop of hanging flowers in the corner. Spring is here, which means endless pastel decorations.

Terrence is still in the middle of a walk-through of the space that will become his new training complex. That leaves me with forty-five minutes or so before he wraps up.

Life has been incredible since we came back from the singles' retreat three months ago. I'm home, thanks to the movers he lined up to pack my studio the same day we landed.

We spent time talking about our future and the things we want to change in our marriage. We also spent a lot of time not talking—between the sheets, in the shower, on the counter, on the floor, in the garage—to catch up on seven months' worth of lovemaking.

Bold espresso coats my lips. I take a generous sip and smooth down my sundress. It's a gorgeous April day. Not a cloud in sight, and the temperature will reach the upper eighties. Everything is perfect.

Then I see him.

Preston Donnelley in full view. We lock eyes and mirror the same bewildered expression. I stare at him for a long minute to make sure my eyes aren't playing games. He's here in the flesh and looks as dapper as usual in a tailored suit.

"Wow. Hey! I didn't expect to see you in Austin." *Or ever again.* I rise to my feet to greet him with a hug.

He gives my back a warm pat and sits down at the empty table across from me with two drinks. "Justice, it's wonderful to see you," he says with a smile that exposes his dimples. "What a surprise."

Why the heck is he in Austin? Is he here on business?

"So, what brings you to my neck of the woods?"

He opens his mouth to answer, but his eyes land on something behind me and light up. "She does." He stands and greets Madison with a kiss.

Wait. Time-out. Preston and Madison are *a thing*? Since when? My eyes flicker between the last two people I expected to see together. He takes her hand to guide her to the table.

"Hello, Justice," she says, to which I smile and nod. Preston has yet to take his eyes off of her, and the heat in his gaze is enough to fan myself.

"So." I point between the two of them. "You and Madison?" He kisses her hands and smiles.

Madison fixes her gaze on Preston, and it's clear something happened. They look...familiar with each other. Like they didn't just meet for the first time months ago. Madison doesn't live in Austin, but, given her job, it's not uncommon for her to pop up.

He turns his attention back to me but never drops her hands. "Remember our dinner, when I told you about a young lady I fell in love with but never found? That was Madison, or Heather Franklin, if I remember correctly."

I scrunch my face at the name. "Heather Franklin? Wasn't she a cheerleader whose parents had a ton of money?"

Madison nods, and—dare I say—her cheeks turn a little pink. "Heather and I were good friends in college. She signed up to study abroad in France but had a last-minute emergency. Since it was nonrefundable, and I was penniless at the time, I took her place."

Her eyes land on Preston, and there are tears in them. *Actual* tears. "I met Preston during a trip to the museum. He asked me out, and that's when our love affair began." She pauses and looks down at their joined hands as if reliving an unpleasant memory. Her voice becomes a whisper. "We were from two separate worlds and had every odd stacked against us. I never told Preston my name because I thought we wouldn't see each other again." She takes a breath. "His family found out and put an end to it. When my time in France was up, I knew I had to leave that piece of me behind."

Madison and I share a look, and in that moment, understanding passes between us. We both lost time with the men we love—only in her case, it was well over a decade ago. In the years I've known her, I've never seen her so emotional.

Did he choose family and status over love?

"So, wait a sec. How did you two reconnect?"

Preston smiles. "At the singles' retreat. The night we had dinner, I saw Heather—sorry, *Madison*—walk in and couldn't believe it." His gaze drifts back to her. "I thought I dreamt it until I had security pull footage to get her hotel room. Heather Franklin didn't have a reservation, but Madison Monroe did. I went to see her the next day, unsure if it *was* her after fifteen years. But when Madison opened the door, I knew without a doubt she was the one who got away."

"I should've told you who I was." She leans over the table for a kiss.

Who freaking knew that a singles' retreat would reunite not only me and Terrence but also Preston and Madison? You couldn't script this. Well, maybe you could, but it's still *wild*.

I hate to break up such a touching story, but there's something I need to know. "If Preston is your person, why did you spend the last fifteen years fixated on Terrence?" She winces at the question. It stings, but I need answers.

Madison brushes nonexistent wrinkles out of her emerald dress and sighs. "Justice, I know my behavior was...inexcusable. And I'm sorry. When I left France, I didn't expect to find love again. I was hurt, and the only person who accepted me for me was Terrence." She squeezes Preston's hand. "I thought I'd lost the love of my life. I knew he'd never find me since I used Heather's name, and I tried to block the pain of never seeing him again. Terrence showed me once that I was worthy of love. I didn't want to lose that. What I did, what I've done, isn't right. I can't apologize enough, Justice. I am truly sorry."

I sit back in my chair and look between them. I've got nothing. Deep down, I'm happy that she found her person. I won't pretend to know what makes her tick, but I don't want to go on with my life hating someone for what they did in the past.

It's time to move on.

I give them a smile. "This is—" I shake my head and replay everything they said. I turn to Madison. "Thank you for your apology. It means a lot. I wouldn't have gone about things the way you did, but I'm glad you two found your way back to each other. I don't know Preston well, but I can tell he's someone special. Plus, he's super loaded, so you'll never have to worry about buying all your designer labels again." We laugh but know it's true.

Twenty minutes pass before we part ways. I give Madison a hug—something I *never* expected to do—and embrace Preston before they walk out hand in hand. He has a business tour in Europe soon, and Madison will be by his side every step of the way.

The ride home is short but consumed with thoughts about Madison and Preston. I can't believe those two dated fifteen years ago and have a second chance at love. Terrence will flip when he finds out.

His black Camaro comes into view when I turn into our driveway. We recently added vines over the garage that drape down the side of the house closest to our front door. There was a home on *House Hunters* that had it, and I fell in love, so my man made it happen. Terrence's handiness with a tool belt is undeniable. Did I mention he looks like a *Magic Mike* extra wearing it and nothing but a pair of jeans and Timberlands?

Our neighbor across the street always keeps her blinds open whenever he's outside with his shirt off. Ms. Agnes might be seventy-three, but the woman has no shame. Can't say I blame her.

I have to squeeze out of my Jeep to keep my door from scratching his. No amount of reminders will get this man to stop parking his car like he sleeps in bed: in the center, with no care or consideration for the person next to him. The garage door is another lost cause. Terrence leaves it open whenever he's in a rush. Ten bucks says I find him in his office.

I close the garage and head to the front door. The sight of our house makes me fall in love with it all over again. The perennials look majestic on the short walk. Light blues and pink florals pop against the beige bricks and hickory-colored shutters of our corner home. We spend most of our evenings on the front-porch swing watching the sun set.

Terrence and Miles spent weeks on renovations to extend the back of the house for an outdoor kitchen. They added floor tiles, a grilling space, a wine refrigerator, a sink, a fireplace, *and* a flat-screen television so they can watch college football. These two pushed each other on platform carts at the home-improvement store and skipped through aisles with linked arms like kids. Miles hops from city to city because of his job, and Terrence was more than happy to play host while they worked on their "special project."

They see each other throughout the year and text more than Emma and I do, and that says a lot. I want Miles to plant roots in Austin, even if I want to throw him from a building on occasion.

I close the front door, drop my keys in the drawer of our foyer table, grab the mail on top, and put my shoes in the closet. Plush carpeting masks my approach to our home office. I don't want to interrupt Terrence if he's in a meeting.

His voice comes through the crack in the door. The tone is soft, like he's trying to tell a secret he doesn't want anyone to hear. When we're both on the phone, one of us usually has to leave the room because his voice rivals a WWE event. I peek my head in to say hi but stop myself when I see him.

He sits with spread legs in front of his computer, and there's a woman on the screen. They're deep in conversation and can't see me from the angle of the door. It's not unusual for him to talk to women, a client or someone involved in his company. But this doesn't sound like a business meeting.

I turn to leave but stay when curiosity gets the better of me.

"I've been waiting to talk to you all day," he says in a faint murmur. "I know things are different now, but maybe there's a way to keep going, Reina?"

Reina?

She's hesitant to respond. It's hard to make out her features from here, except for her flowy chestnut hair.

Who is Reina?

"There isn't an *us*. You know why there can't be." She sighs. "You have to tell her. I know you haven't."

Tell me what?

He rubs the back of his neck and exhales. "I know. Give me time, okay? I need to figure some stuff out first. But I don't want this to stop. This"—he motions between them—"is special."

Your life is about to end, but do continue.

It takes everything in me to step away from the door without a sound. What the hell did I overhear? Is he seeing another woman? No, that can't be. Right?

I enter our bedroom in a rush and make a beeline for the bathroom. Maybe I hit my head and misunderstood the conversation between Terrence and *Reina*. Yes, that's it. I have a concussion or something that requires a trip to the ER, not a divorce attorney. Why would he fight so hard for me only to step out? After everything.

Maybe he met someone before the singles' retreat and had a tough time letting her go?

God, I'm going to be sick. I turn on the faucet to splash water on my face and calm my nerves. *Spoiler: It doesn't work.* I need to keep a level head about this. Otherwise, one of two things will happen: I'll charge into the home office and tear his balls through his throat, or I'll pack my bags and leave him for good.

Or maybe you shouldn't jump to conclusions before you get to the whole "death do us part."

My grip on the sink turns my knuckles white. I've misjudged situations before. He hasn't given me any reason to suspect he's cheating. This could all be a misunderstanding. I didn't hear the entire conversation. When we got back together, we decided to start fresh, and with that comes trust.

The sound of Terrence's laughter fills the halls on his way to our bedroom. "She's still out, but I will tell her you called. I love you too, Mama."

See. How could he have another woman when I'm the one he talks about to his mother?

You just described a side piece.

I stumble over the rug in our room.

"Hey, babe, you're home." He tosses the phone on the bed and pulls me into a hug. I get a grin before he takes my mouth. All my insecurities melt away. I know this man. He won't hurt me like that.

I smile back. "I am. How's your mom?"

"Great. She's back from a visit with Connie and her rug rats." Constance is Terrence's oldest sister, named after a character in *The Three Musketeers*. She lives in Miami with her husband, Emilio, and their two sons, Oscar and Sebastian. Terrence is closer to Audre, his youngest sister he helped raise. Connie moved out when she turned eighteen, attended community college, and found a job in Florida as a medical assistant. She was twelve when their father walked out, and she left New Jersey the second she was old enough. We make the trip to see her family twice a year, though I know Terrence wishes they were closer.

"Sounds like fun. We should go see your mom soon."

He shakes his head. "No need. She wants to come this way now that we're back together."

That makes me smile. Horror stories about monster-in-laws—mothers who keep death grips on their sons—are scary enough. But that's not Robin. Our connection was instant when Terrence and I started dating. She treats me like one of her daughters because to her, I am.

"Let's plan something for our parents to come at once. Mine are itching to visit but wanted to give us our space."

"Sounds like a plan." Terrence puts his arm around my shoulder and kisses my forehead. He won't go five minutes without some physical display of affection. "What do you want to do for dinner? Cook or eat out?"

His conversation with Reina returns in a chill. *I don't think I'm comfortable now that you're back with Justice. You have to tell her.*

"Terrence?"

"Yeah, baby?"

"Who were you talking to in the home office?" I trust him, but that doesn't mean I can't ask questions.

"Another work call," he says in a hurry. "Had to clear up some things." His thumb rubs circles on my shoulder.

It's a lie. The question is, why does he feel the need to do it? It better not be a side piece situation. For his sake.

I swallow to keep my composure and hold back the version of me who's ready to burn all his clothes in his car and walk away smoking a cigarette. "I hope everything is alright...with the business and all."

Terrence searches my face. He looks like he wants to say something but decides against it and gives me a kiss. "Just some decisions I have to make, but nothing too intense, princess." He cups my face for another kiss. "I know I've been busy these last few months with the training center, but I don't want you to worry. You come first. Always will."

Sincerity shines in his eyes. Maybe I have this whole thing wrong. But that doesn't mean my eyes aren't open.

Chapter 34

Terrence

"Do you really have to go? Can't you send someone else?"

If I didn't look up and see my wife, I would think an adult-size child was on top of my suitcase with folded arms and a pout. It's adorable. I'll miss her, even if it's only for a couple of weeks. This is the first time I'll have to leave her since we came back from the singles' retreat, and I hate it.

I kneel in front of Justice, unable to contain a chuckle at her over-the-top performance. "Baby, we talked about this. I have to go on this trip to close out a contract with a client." I kiss her on the forehead. "I know two weeks is a long time, but we'll be together when you come out to visit."

She doesn't budge.

Justice shakes her head and stares at the wall. I lower my mine to keep from cracking up, but it's hard. It's not funny to see her upset that I have to go. Hell, I don't like the thought of so much time away from my wife. Since we came back from Colorado, I've made good on my word to only travel for business when necessary. We've been home for months, and this is the only deal I can't do over the phone.

Construction for the fitness complex is currently underway, thanks to the start-up capital I secured. My relationships with professional athletes and entertainers came through in a major way. I have people lined up to do their strength and conditioning at the new facility, and local schools have expressed interest in using it for off-campus practices and clinics. Even some celebrities I know want to train there for fight sequences.

It's all coming together, better than I'd imagined. I just need Justice to scoot off my suitcase so we can get this last trip out of the way. It's not like she won't be with me in thirteen days.

Los Angeles will be home for a month. Yes, that's a long time, which is why Justice will fly out in a couple of weeks and telecommute once she wraps up things in the office. A former client is on location in Europe and will let us stay in his Malibu home. If I were traveling by myself, I would find a hotel in Los Angeles and not deal with the commute. But I want Justice to be closer to Em so they can see each other more.

"Baby, I'll miss my flight." She shrugs, her eyes still fixed on the wall. "Okay." I stand. "You leave me no choice."

Justice looks up and rolls her eyes. "If you think now is the time for sex, forget it."

My head snaps back with laughter. Only this woman. "You need some rest after the last two nights, princess. But you better believe when you arrive, your ass is mine." I look at my watch. Time for my in-case-of-an-emergency stash.

"I ordered you dinner that should arrive in the next forty-five minutes."

That gets her attention.

"I also have a stash of peanut M&M's, Heath bars, *and* bottles of your favorite white wine in the refrigerator." I waggle my brows. "The big ones."

"Oh, Terrence!" She jumps from my suitcase and wraps me in her arms. When in doubt, stock up on chocolate and wine. Does the trick every time.

I soothe her back and bend down to grab the luggage before she decides to sit on it again. "I'll miss you," I say against her hair. "We'll call each other every night, okay?" She nods on my shoulder. I nudge her to lift her head and kiss her but notice a few tears on her cheeks. "Hey, hey. None of that." It breaks me when she cries. "We'll see each other soon. Plus, you'll be closer to Emma's house."

Justice nods. "I know. I don't know why I'm so emotional." She laughs. "Tell me whose house we're staying in?"

"Nope." I move around her for the front door.

"Oh, come on!" She runs to catch up. "I won't say anything."

I shake my head. "People like their privacy. The last thing I need is my wife geeking out on social media. No."

She runs in front of me and walks backward. My determined firecracker. "Is it a celebrity I know?"

"Not telling."

Her stare is sharp trying to conjure up the answer. "It's in Malibu, so the person has money." *True.* "I know most of the celebrities you train come through the studio because of action movie roles." *Also true.* "So I'll guess the home belongs to one of those superheroes."

I steel my features so as not to give anything away. "I plead the Fifth, princess."

"Thor."

"Chris and his brothers sold their Malibu house."

Silence holds her in deep thought. She bites her lip and scrunches her face. "Robert Downey Jr."

I don't answer but catch her grin out of the corner of my eye. He's the only superhero she'll refer to by his government name.

"Terrence, is it him?"

I stop at the bottom of the staircase to face the version of Sherlock Homegirl known as my wife. "Baby, I will neither confirm nor deny whose house it is. Your nosiness is why there are things like NDAs."

The phone buzzes in my hand. My car is out front to take me to the airport. I sigh. "Time for me to go, princess." I lift her chin up and take her mouth. My dick awakens at Justice's moan. He wants a goodbye kiss too. *Easy, buddy. Have to wait.*

"I love you, Terrence."

"I love you more. I'll call you as soon as I land."

Chapter 35

Justice

Taste tells me I have thirty seconds to make it to the bathroom before my lunch makes a cameo in front of my colleagues. I gag at the unsettling mix of water and butter chicken swaying in my stomach. It's rare for me to be this sick, but at least the writing is on the wall before it's too late.

My eyes lock on the door to the bathroom. I unfasten the button on my blazer and nod at coworkers through this never-ending trek to privacy so I can puke my brains out.

I'll make it. A couple more steps to freedom.

I quicken my pace when my lunch does a backflip up my throat. *Maybe I won't.* The last few steps turn into a sprint. I stagger into the bathroom and head to the farthest stall. I'm alone, which could be deliberate instead of a small miracle. This is the third time today I've hightailed it from my office to offer a sacrifice to the porcelain master of my life. I don't blame anyone who thinks I'm suffering from a bad case of the squirts.

A can of ginger ale and some crackers are next to my computer when I get back to my office.

"I wanted to help." Olivia walks in and shuts the door. "Are you okay?"

I nod at my assistant and wave off her concern. "I'm fine, thanks. I think it's the Indian food I ate. Thank you for this." I lift up the pouch of crackers. "It's very considerate."

"Don't mention it. You've saved my ass countless times. It's the least I can do."

Three years ago, it wasn't uncommon for Olivia to stumble into the office with a hangover. She was an intern fresh out of college and had a very colorful time transitioning into adult life. Still, she had potential, which is why I'll promote her to marketing specialist. She's come into her own, and she's someone I trust and respect.

"Earth to Justice."

"Huh? I'm sorry." I need a nap.

A grin stretches across her face. "You're out of it today. Thinking about your man?"

Don't remind me.

Terrence left for LA a week ago. We call and text each other every day, but it's not enough. I miss him so much, and I don't know why the thought of him away makes me so emotional. Work is no longer enough of a distraction. I need more. I need him.

I sink into the chair behind my desk and rest my forehead in my hands. Death would be an upgrade from whatever this is. "The only thing I'm thinking about is not throwing up again today."

"You might want to see a doctor, Jay. A bad bug is going around the office. Vicki came back to work today after two weeks out. And Alan? He pretty much shit himself for five days straight."

I groan into my hands. "Of course there is." I've been counting down the days on my calendar until the ocean breeze hits my face. "I can't get sick now."

Whatever I have comes and goes in waves. One minute, I'm fine. The next, I want to long jump over desks to reach the bathroom. Sickness and I are distant enemies that don't write, but whatever demon is trying to wring my body of all fluids wants to be pen pals. I need to get to a doctor soon. But it takes weeks to get an appointment, which is why I'm so grateful my mom's sorority sister relocated to Austin and is now my physician.

An idea comes to mind when I finish the text to Dr. Patal asking to see her today. I crack open the ginger ale and let the flavors calm my stomach. "You're right, Liv. Let's close up for the day."

"Sounds good." Her ponytail bounces from side to side as she makes her way to the door. Crimson is such a good color on her. I looked like a frumpy fashion accident when I first landed here after college. Professional clothes for me back then were kitten heels and *Little House on the Prairie* skirts I found at the thrift store. At twenty-five, Olivia is one of the youngest on staff, and she struts through the office like she just came from Milan. Her wit is as fierce as the jumpsuit and gold heels she's wearing today. She turns to call over her shoulder, "See you in a couple days?"

"No." I stand and smile at the lost look on her face. "You know what? I think I'll surprise Terrence in California early and work remotely for the rest of the week. You shouldn't come in, either. To protect yourself from this bug going around."

Her eyes twinkle with mischief. "Yes, of course. We need to be careful." A brow raises. "I'll see you after your trip?"

"It looks that way. You have a vacation next week too, right?"

She nods.

Our company offers generous vacation time, but with the recent accounts we snagged, it's an all-hands-on-deck situation. Management isn't a fan of time away right now, but this two-woman team deserves a break. We handled our business, and then some. Come hell, high water, or a face full of meds, I'll get to California.

"Well then. See you in three weeks."

"I'm sorry, could you please repeat that?"

"You're pregnant, Justice. About five weeks."

My throat works to swallow. The expression on Dr. Patal's face is full of warmth, but I don't think I heard her correctly because she said I'm pregnant.

Me.

"H-how did it happen?" I came in because of the flu.

She laughs. "Well, I don't think I have to explain to you *how* pregnancies happen, dear." Her hands clasp together. "When you said it was urgent, the symptoms you described worried me. The flu that's going around is pretty nasty, so I rushed some tests. Your HCG levels are high and consistent with someone who's pregnant."

She said the p-word again.

Huh.

"You okay, sweetie?"

"Yup. Great." My words come out in a shriek. "I'm sorry, I didn't expect this. Are you *sure* that *I'm* pregnant?"

She reaches across her desk to take my hand. Dr. Patal's office reminds me of my mother. Photos of her and my mom line bookshelves, along with family pictures with her partner Prisha.

"I'm sure, honey. The tests are pretty accurate. You should make an appointment with your ob-gyn soon. Okay?"

"Yes, of course. Thank you so much," I say and wince. "Please don't tell my mom yet." I cringe at the thought of the two of them on the phone. TMZ has nothing on these gossips.

"I promise. Doctor-patient confidentiality prohibits me. It's your business to share whenever you are ready. Congratulations, sweetheart."

I sit in my car after we say our goodbyes, my hands in a death grip on the steering wheel. I called my ob-gyn and made an appointment after I return from California, but I can't will myself to leave this parking lot.

I'm pregnant.

My first instinct is to rush out and buy five pregnancy tests. But what's the point? If my doctor says there's a bun in my oven, there's a bun in my oven.

Motherhood should excite me, but the pain of the last two pregnancy losses has me gasping for air. I choke back a sob and drop my head to the wheel. Terrence and I yearn to be parents. But the thought that lots of sex leads to a baby didn't cross our minds.

Our baby.

I let out a long breath and wipe my eyes. "Hey, little one. Time to surprise Daddy." I call Emma and let her know I'm coming early.

Chapter 36

Justice

"Get in, bitch."

Emma's white Mercedes pulls up to the curb. She loves crowded places, but for me they're up there with an annual Pap smear during that time of the month. She still threatened to cut me when I offered to catch a Lyft.

I put my bags in her trunk and get a big hug after I hop into the passenger seat. She readjusts her rearview mirror before we speed off.

"How was your flight?"

Morning sickness is awful, but you can't know I'm pregnant yet. "It wasn't bad. Sorry you waited longer than expected. Baggage claim is an eternal pain."

California sun bursts through the clouds with a vengeance. I say a silent prayer of thanks that the only threat I have to deal with is solar retinopathy and not upchucking my airplane snack. The last thing I need is to spray my best friend's fancy car with vomit. The top is down. You get the rest.

"How long do I have before you leave me for Terrence?" I catch a glimpse of her smile.

"Aww. Don't tell me you're jealous, Em." I reach to grab her cheek for a squeeze she loves to hate. "He has a business dinner tonight and will get in late, so you have me for the whole day. I went through all of my emails and calls before I boarded the plane. I'm all yours."

The side of her lip curls. She signals to take the 405. "Well, if you want to surprise your man, you'll need more than the Target panties you packed. Let's look through some new pieces at the studio before lunch."

It takes twenty minutes for us to reach her company's office in the Pacific Palisades. Her hips sway in a tight red dress to the rhythm of her gold pumps gliding across the marble floor. She signals for me to follow her through a series of double doors that lead down a hall with a photo shoot in progress.

"This way."

The room is dark except for a white light illuminating the silhouette of a seminude model with her legs in the air. She's on a fancy chaise lounge wearing sky-high heels dipped in crystals that sparkle like a disco ball. A future *Vogue* cover in the making.

Emma walks to the photographer and kisses him on each cheek. They exchange quick pleasantries before he turns back to the model in the sheer bodysuit. Em motions to a rack of lingerie at the side of the room. The hangers are satin, so I know the bras and panties cost more than my mortgage. "These came in from Italy. Find your size, and take what you want."

I stare at her like she asked me to steal the Hope Diamond and stuff it in my bra. "I don't know, Em. This is *really* expensive. I don't want to get you in trouble."

She pauses for a beat and levels me with a glare. "Sweetie, I don't know what they do at your company, but when you're the boss, you act like one. I scored a ten-million-dollar deal last week. I wish someone would flip out over some panties. Now, enjoy."

The next forty-five minutes are a blur. My search for the perfect outfit somehow morphed into me in front of the camera in a black lace teddy. It's backless, does little to cover my breasts, and has a huge slit from the cleavage down to the thigh. Emma stepped in and out to take calls and broke the sound barrier when her eyes scanned me from head to toe. One twirl led to a sultry shoot at her request. Tommaso, the photographer, snaps away with Italian commentary I don't understand. I know *bella* means beautiful, a word he says a lot, but that's all I got.

A sexy boudoir shoot at five weeks pregnant? When in Rome, or Los Angeles in this case.

"We'll print these in black and white," Emma says. "I'll frame them in gold and ship them to your house." Her eyes go back to the monitor. "These are exquisite, Jay."

The hair and makeup team touched me up. My look is still natural, except for the heavy liner around my eyes. Damn, I do look good. This Justice needs to come out more often.

"I aim to please," I say with a wink.

"As you should. Come on." She takes my arm in hers. "Let's get lunch."

Chapter 37

Terrence

The levels of boredom one reaches in a meeting that could've been an email are endless. Here I am, on meeting number five of the day, in a fight to stay awake while someone reads out a slideshow presentation like we're in elementary school. When we set this up, I thought it was to discuss any potential issues and next steps since I received said presentation weeks ago. Is this why I came to California and left my wife at home?

I sit up straight and rest my head in my hand, keeping it upright so I don't fall out of my seat. It's not that I'm ungrateful for the opportunity to have meetings about the training facility. They're just way too long.

Another ninety minutes pass before the presenter starts to wrap up. He's in the middle of recommending the next steps when a text from Justice comes in.

Sweet, merciful Jesus.

"I'm sorry, Mr. Reyes. Do you have a question?"

Every set of eyes in the conference room lands on me. Shit, did I say that out loud? "Nothing. Happy to see this move forward." I cough and wave a hand at the presentation. The hoarse tone in my voice gets me a look from Kenny. He's my attorney, and a damn good one. The guy knows bullshit when he sees it.

I sink back in my chair with my eyes locked on my phone and the Eiffel Tower of erections. My wife stares back at me in a slinky black number that stops above her ass, which is arching off one of those fancy chairs you see in a department store sitting room. Her legs spread in an invitation to a private buffet, and damn it if I don't want to ditch this meeting to rub one out in the bathroom.

Me: *You're killing me, princess.*

Her response is instant and includes lots of laughing emojis.

Justice: *Wanted surprise you. I have another when I see you.*

I. Am. Game.

If she forces me to wear a leash and silk boxers and walk around the block, I'll bark. I don't care. I miss her. Two weeks is too long to go without her in my arms.

Justice isn't the type to wear sexy outfits. She dresses up in lingerie on occasion but usually opts for a knee-length silk nightgown to wear to bed. Her beauty shines from the inside out. Put her in a paper bag and see how fast I create dick holes to touch her.

A pat on my shoulder signals the end of the meeting. Suits cluster in conversation. I say a silent prayer that no one will see the bulge pressed against my pants when I make my exit. A miracle appears in the form of a stack of folders left on the conference room table. I hope they're not important.

After four rounds of handshakes, we're free. I need to nut and grab dinner before I commit murder.

"That went well. It's a good sign Harvey and his team took the initiative with this meeting. He'll come on board." Kenny hasn't lost his optimism since college. The trait is commendable, and it's one of the reasons I'm proud to call him a friend.

"From your mouth to God's ears, man." I pat him on the shoulder.

Chris, my business associate, nods. "If they can meet our number, we should have a deal." Glad to see my frat brother agrees.

I wrap my arms around them and bite my lip to suppress the grin that wants to break free. These two helped me get my dream off the ground. They say it takes a village, but I have gladiators ready to throw down in the arena.

Chris graduated top of his business class at Bodie University before he went for his MBA. How he maintained a 4.0 average and partied the way he did is a miracle in itself. He's a trust-fund kid but is down-to-earth, and he forged his own path that detoured from his father's Silicon Valley footsteps. Chris will be the "numbers guy" who will oversee the financial side of the business and manage stakeholder expectations. He'll stay in LA to keep an ear to the ground but will pop into Austin to stay in the four-million-dollar penthouse he just bought downtown.

Kenny is another brainiac who got his Juris Doctor degree from Bodie. We spent lots of time together on the field and in the library to cram for tests during our undergrad days. Every law firm in a fifty-mile radius did backflips to hire him after we graduated. What did he do? Blew them all off to stay in school for an international business and economic law degree. He packed his bags and took the corporate route that led him to the Big Apple but quit after five years to start his own company. I can't afford Kenny on my best day, but he handles all of my legal needs at a discounted rate, one he makes up for with his high-profile clientele.

Miles is the only one who isn't here. He planned to meet us but had to back out last minute because of work. I'll hit my silent partner up later. A smile builds big enough to expand my chest. I'm so fucking happy. I look between Chris and Kenny. "Have I told you two today that I love you?"

"Come on, man." Kenny extracts himself from my embrace and stifles a laugh. "Not needed."

Chris shakes his head and smirks. "We're here for you, bro."

"Glad to see someone still cares for me," I say with a hip bump to Kenny. He makes it so easy to get under his skin.

His eyes tighten at the corners. "If you try to kiss me, I'll deck you right here."

"You know you love me."

"Rub up on me again and see what happens in this hallway."

Chris and I are both in tears. Kenny acts like gangrene will develop if someone shows him affection that's not tied to fucking. Want to see a six foot five, two-hundred-sixty-pound man in a tailored suit act like a baby? Hug him in public.

Laughter echoes through the empty hall. I put my hands up to collect my composure. "Does my Kenny need dinner and drinks before—" I dodge a fist and jog to put some distance between us, laughing my ass off along the way. "Okay, okay. Let's eat."

"Might I make a suggestion?"

Our heads swivel to see Harvey Miller, a seasoned investor with decades in the game. We clear our throats and stand straighter on his approach. The guy is hard to read. If he sees us in our frat-boy glory, our deal will be dead on arrival.

"Mr. Miller. A pleasure to see you again." We shake hands. Harvey is a heavy hitter across multiple industries. At sixty-four, the man still works hard and plays harder.

He gives the three of us a look. "You guys remind me of me and my friends in our younger years. You can't buy this kind of loyalty. Well, most of the time." We laugh. "You impressed me with your vision for the new training facility. If your schedules are clear, I want to invite you out to one of my restaurants in West Hollywood."

Chris shoots me a glance. This is a good sign Harvey will come on board. I clear my throat. "Sounds great, Mr. Miller."

He smiles and lifts a hand. "Please, call me Harvey."

We follow Harvey out of the lobby. Two town cars arrive within five minutes of his phone call. He motions for us to get into the second one. "The driver knows the address. I'll meet you there." He gives us a nod and disappears into his vehicle.

"Now that's power." You'd never know Kenny has millions if his net worth weren't plastered all over the pages of investment magazines. He's a big kid half the time who acts like he couldn't purchase his own fleet of luxury sedans.

I give him the side-eye and check his shoulder. "Bet you'll let him say he loves you."

"Nah. He'd get decked too. Don't tell him I said it."

We're still at the restaurant three hours later. Harvey closed off the rooftop bar of the swanky fusion joint, and it's an experience. The glass enclosure gives us full access to the nightlife awakening below. We're so high up, people look like ants as they scatter across streets to begin their evening. I'm an East Coast boy but will be the first to admit California has an attractive allure. I can't imagine what it costs to keep the doors to a place like this open. Every liquor bottle on the mirrored shelves is a luxury brand. Wagyu is the cheapest steak served here, and we had Japanese Kobe for dinner *on the house*.

We discussed how Chris, Kenny, and I became friends and got into business, and that earned Harvey's respect. Like us, the people closest to him are the ones he's known for a long time.

Harvey takes a final sip of his scotch and claps his hands. "The night is still young. Let's say we close this deal the old-fashioned way. There's a gentleman's club not too far from here with a private room to go over the contract."

Kenny is the first to his feet. "You don't have to ask me twice. This one here"—he thumbs my way—"needs to get his permission slip signed first."

Bastard.

Strip clubs aren't my scene. The urge to drop bills on women and overpriced drinks never resonated with me. Some men get off on the experience, but that's two steps from a circle jerk in my book. Pass.

I look at my watch and realize it's past nine. I'm an hour late for my check-in with Justice. "I need to make a phone call."

"See, what did I tell you? Permission slip." Kenny's taunt includes a smug grin. I open my mouth to respond, but Chris beats me to it.

"Cut the shit. If you ever grow up and find a woman who will tolerate you enough to become your wife, you'll understand. It's not about a permission slip. It's about respect."

Mic drop.

I give him a nod and head near the elevators to call Justice. Deals in gentleman's clubs aren't uncommon, but that doesn't mean I'll go. It takes three rings for her to pick up, and it doesn't sound like she's home.

A mix of music and loud conversation booms in the background. Does she have the surround sound on? "Hey, baby. Where are you?"

"I'm out with a friend." Justice is out on a weeknight?

Interesting. "Oh, okay. Cool. I'm sorry I forgot to check in earlier. How was your day?"

Three minutes pass in our attempt to catch up, which includes "What did you say?" and "Can't hear you" every other sentence. Justice is vague with her answers, and I'm talking too much about myself. What is going on? "Listen. Harvey Miller, the big fish we want to land, took us out to dinner. He wants to close the deal tonight, but he wants to do it at a club. It's a gentleman's club, and I don't think—"

"Okay, sweetie."

Something is off. This woman has *no* questions? I run through the twenty different anniversaries she makes us celebrate. Did I forget one? The first time I asked her out isn't for another month. Background chatter turns into screams at the start of Ginuwine's "Pony" through the phone.

"Hey, honey, I have to go. I'll check in tomorrow morning. Best of luck with the deal. I love you!"

"I love you."

The call drops.

What the hell was that?

I stare at the number I dialed. Since when is she comfortable with a strip club? And where the hell is she that's playing the *Magic Mike* soundtrack on a school night?

Harvey interrupts my thoughts of calling her back. He puts a hand on my shoulder. "Ready?"

God, I hope I don't regret this.

I slide my phone into my pocket. "I think I'll call it a night, but I want to thank you for today." I run my fingers through my hair. "To be honest, strip clubs aren't my scene."

He looks me over. "Is it because of this permission slip business?"

I chuckle and shake my head. "No. It's not a wife thing, sir. It's a *me* thing. I hope this doesn't hurt our chances to do business together, Mr. Miller."

"Harvey."

"Harvey," I say.

He considers my words, and I brace for rejection. "You know, it's not every day I see a man turn down the opportunity to have beautiful women entertain him."

"What I have at home makes anything else unnecessary. I'm good."

Thank God Kenny isn't within earshot of this conversation. I'd never live it down. But I mean what I said. Nothing against people who enjoy the clubs.

"Well then. That settles it." Here it comes. "I'll have my assistant send over the paperwork in the morning."

I'm sorry, what?

Harvey takes in my expression with a laugh. My eyes couldn't pop further out of my head if I used the Force to fart. Did he say what I think he said?

"Relax, Terrence. No need for a heart attack." His pat on my shoulder brings me back to reality. "These days, integrity is a rare trait to come by in business. It's honorable. Hold on to it. We'll speak soon." He makes his exit, leaving me to soak in the deal.

Holy shit, we did it.

"We need to celebrate. Hell yeah!" Kenny is two seconds from a Tom Cruise moment on the sidewalk. The only thing the man needs is Oprah's couch.

Palm trees blow in the wind, taillights illuminate the mild spring night. We're on Sunset Boulevard, amped up after landing our biggest deal to date, with no destination in sight.

"So, where to now that Mr. Killjoy ruined our night?"

"You're more than welcome to blow a few hundred on some dancers and stroke your dick next to strangers," I say. "Today was long. I want to turn in."

"Amateur hour was fun, but this is where I leave you." Chris puts his phone in his pocket when a town car pulls up to the curb. There are smooth people, and then there's Chris. "Congrats, gentlemen.

I'll see you in the morning." He'll reach his bachelor pad in the Hollywood Hills in a matter of minutes.

I sigh. "And then there were two." Don't get me wrong, I love Kenny, but his frat-boy tendencies didn't fade after he earned his fancy degrees. He looks polished, but on the inside, this thirty-seven-year-old acts like a teenage boy who beats his meat at all hours of the day. I have no desire to keep up with whatever he wants to get into. Miles isn't this bad.

"You sure you want to turn in for the night?" He shakes his head at my nod. "At least let me crash at your superhero pad so I can say I saw the fucking place."

That I can do. "Fine, but only for one night, and you have to wear a blindfold."

"What kind of kinky shit are you into?"

I raise my hand. "I don't want you to bring back some woman to make your dick hard tonight. My spot is not for you to get laid."

He scoffs. "As if I need help. I'm a *lawyer*. I own a successful practice, I'm *very* wealthy, and"—he grabs his junk—"I don't lack downstairs."

I roll my eyes. "If you're such an Adonis, how come every woman you date leaves after a month?" I chuckle at his silence. "Yeah, that's what I thought."

As I open the Lyft app, I hear a woman yell my name. My jaw is too heavy to pick up off the sidewalk. No way she's here. "Reina?" There's no time to register her presence before she leaps into my arms. I spin her around in a bear hug.

"Surprised to see me?" Her grin reaches her coffee-colored tendrils. Reina looks as beautiful as the last time we got together. A year is a lifetime away, but at least we spoke online not too long ago.

"Y-yeah. Yes, I am. What are you doing here?"

"I'm here to see you, silly." She taps a manicured nail on my nose. "My hotel isn't far from here. What do you say to a nightcap to catch up?"

I turn to Kenny. He stares at Reina like a starved man at a buffet. She's in a navy blazer and shorts that rest against her thighs, white pumps, and a white tank. The brunette from *The Vampire Diaries* looks like her twin, if she were Puerto Rican.

At his nod, I turn back to Reina, who bites her lip in anticipation. How can I say no to her? To that face?

I flash a smile of my own. "After you."

Chapter 38

Justice

"*Ciara!*"

My Missy Elliott impersonation flows with precision at the sound of "1, 2 Step" through the speakers. My friend Sierra jumps up from her seat to pop and lock, a performance that earns her well-deserved applause. She's not an R&B princess but is one of my best friends from college.

This track was our go-to jam to hype us up before a big game. As the only two freshman cheerleaders on the Bodie University squad, SiSi and I developed a bond. We don't see each other much, but we pick up where we left off when we do. LA is her home, but overseas has her heart. So does her work as an interpreter. My friend speaks five languages, and her passport boasts of destinations that make desktop backgrounds look like kindergarten art.

"Thank you, thank you very much." She takes a bow and winks at me. "Gosh, Jay. I can't believe you're in my neck of the woods."

"I'll say. It's a miracle we're in the same time zone. Where did just you get back from?"

"Ethiopia. I was with a group that provided translation services for a social-protection-system project." She sips her drink like her life isn't impressive. Sierra is one of the humblest people I know.

We've spent the last four hours together. We toured her new condo, grabbed dinner, and landed at a bar for drinks. Well, she has a drink with liquor in it. I have cranberry juice that I know makes her curious why my lips aren't on a manhattan. But she's not one to pry, thank God.

After lunch with Emma, I went to pick up my rental car and headed back to Malibu. Terrence was in meetings all day, which gave me the perfect amount of time to peek inside our home away from home, which looks more like a compound than someone's private residence. We're in the main house so we don't disrupt the staff who take care of all the animals. I don't think I've seen so many alpacas and chickens in my life and had to fight Emma to let me stay. Her excuse was, and I quote, "No person in his right mind has a zoo *and* a space-age Flintstones house in Malibu." It took an hour of debating before she left, but she did eventually. This was after she told me I can stay with her if I cough up a lung from all of the animal hair.

"When can we see each other again?"

"I have to check in with Terrence, but let's try for dinner with Em on Thursday? You leave on Friday, right?"

She nods. "That works. I know you want to surprise your man. I'll touch base tomorrow about Thursday."

Crap.

I rushed Terrence off the phone so I didn't spoil the surprise I'm in California. Lord knows when he'll be back to the house. I've got time to make my way to Malibu since he'll be out late.

Did he say something about a strip club?

"I better go before I ruin my plan." I stand and wrap my dear friend in a hug.

We say our goodbyes. Ciara's commute is super short, given her condo is only two blocks away. I cross the street to my rental, thankful I found a spot so close. The May night is pleasant yet busy for a weekday. California is an enchanted place, and it gets me excited to see Terrence.

Who's on the other side of the street.

I have to will my body not to dodge cars to get to him. He's in a navy-blue suit and a bronze tie that coordinates with his oxford shoes. His blazer rests against his sculpted forearms, which are on full display with his sleeves rolled up. It should be illegal how his thighs press against his pants. I'm not above sinking my teeth into his ass on this street corner. To yell over the cars whizzing by is pointless, so I open my phone to text him, when he does the unexpected.

Terrence gives the guy next to him a playful shove and puts his arm around a woman's shoulder. She looks up with adoration in her eyes and the biggest smile before he—*my* husband—kisses the top of her forehead.

Her. Fucking. Forehead.

From the view I have of her between parked cars, I can tell she's gorgeous. Her thick, brown hair flows down her shoulders and blows in the wind. She looks put together, matches him in navy, and has petite curves. She reminds me of a Latina version of Elena from *The Vampire Diaries.*

Where have I seen her face?

Two thoughts enter my mind. The first is that this doesn't look like a business meeting. He's too cozy with this woman, who now has her arm wrapped around his waist. The second is more of a math equation to determine how big of a casket I'll need to bury him alive.

I want to vomit, cry, and choke him and Fake Elena at the same time. Well, maybe not Fake Elena. Maybe she doesn't know he has a wife at home, because he sure as hell isn't acting like he does. That question goes out of the window when his wedding ring glints off the headlights of a passing car. They can both go in the same ditch.

This betrayal is a new form of torture. My heart pounds against my chest, and breaths become too difficult to maintain.

After everything we endured, *this* is how it ends?

No wonder he wanted to come out to California for a month. He knows I can't stay the whole time, and that gives him the perfect opportunity to play bachelor.

A car pulls up next to them. I duck when the three of them pile into the back and pass my car. They stop at a red light, which gives me time to follow.

The valet takes my keys. At sixty dollars a night for parking, you better believe whoever's room he'll visit will pay for it.

Oh God, what if Terrence got a room?

I swallow the urge to puke and walk through the main lobby. I'm a woman on a mission without the slightest idea what to do or where to go. Common sense and logic left six streets ago. Unless I bang on every door to ask if my no-good cheating husband is in the room, I'm clueless where to start.

"Can I help you, miss?" I will myself to mirror the front desk attendant's smile and not the look of someone who's about to catch a life sentence. Could I pay her to review the surveillance tapes to see which way Terrence went? Or does that only happen in the movies?

"Miss?"

Showtime. "Sorry, yes. I flew in to surprise a friend, and think I got the hotels mixed up. Is it possible to tell me if a Terrence Reyes is here?" *For his sake, please say no.*

"I'm sorry, but I'm not at liberty to disclose guest information."

My smile drops with my shoulders. Great. Should I fess up that I'm looking for my husband, who might have his pants around his ankles by the time I reach him? It works for scorned wives ready to push their wayward spouses off the balcony in Lifetime movies. *You told her he's your friend. Now he's your husband?*

Just when I think I'll have to pay sixty dollars and wait for my bastard husband to materialize, a small miracle happens. The guy with Terrence stumbles out of one of the bathrooms and heads toward the elevator.

"Never mind. There he is." I grin at the attendant and follow in pursuit. My heels clack against the marble in the empty foyer. I deserve an Olympic medal in speed walking with this hurried pace. A gold one, with chocolate in the middle.

Note to self: I need a snack soon.

I pop on my sunglasses and keep my head down when the elevator door opens. This is Los Angeles, home of celebrities, plastic surgery, and affairs. My look fits. I press my back to the wall, out of his peripheral vision. His face doesn't register as someone I know, but you can never be too safe. He smells fancy and wears a tailored suit. My guess is he's a business partner or a prospect. If he's a partner, why the heck is he going up to a hotel room with my husband and a woman? *Are they going to have a threesome?*

I get his attention when I heave at the thought. *Oops.*

He glances back at me but turns to his phone when it rings. *Saved by the bell.* "Yeah, I'll be there in two." It's hard to hear the person on the line. "Had to take a piss." He pauses. "Room 1004. Got it."

Yes, good to know.

When the doors open, I head in the opposite direction and wait around the corner. Now that I know where Terrence is, *how* will I get to him? What will I say? This is why details are important in a plan. A plan I don't have yet.

The urge to run back to Emma or hop on a flight home rises with my heartbeat. But my feet have a different plan. Guess we're going to room 1004. I startle at two people laughing down the hall. It's Terrence.

Shoot.

A nearby ice room becomes my hideout. I push myself flat against a wall of vending machines. If anyone wants a soda, I'm screwed. Laughter reaches the room before they enter. "Hey, look. They have strawberry Pop-Tarts." The woman's voice rises an octave.

"You still like those things?"

"Of course. Don't tell me you're above them now, Mr. Hotshot. You kept a box for me when I came over for breakfast."

Breakfast? So he's cheating on me *and* feeding her Pop-Tarts? Was this in our house? I close my eyes to level my breath and the wish to maul them both.

"I did," Terrence says. "Those were simpler times."

Someone scoops up ice, and then the room goes silent. I peek my head out and send him a text.

Me: *Hey. What are you up to?*

I put my phone on silent in case he responds.

"It's Justice," I hear him say down the hall.

Yeah, that's right, you bastard. Your wife.

"Will you tell her?" the woman asks.

"I have to, right? I've wanted to tell her for months but didn't know how. This shouldn't be this hard." There's pain in his voice.

What is he talking about?

When I peek again, my heart drops. Terrence's chin rests on Fake Elena's head. The two are in a silent embrace before she speaks. "She deserves to know."

"She does." His voice comes out in a whisper.

"Come on, we'll figure it out together." She looks up at him. "I'm glad you're here."

"Me too."

I wait a half hour for a response. Nothing. The lonely ride back to Malibu takes forty-five minutes. I decide not to call Emma. Her desire to chop off his balls will tempt me to find an axe. I have to think beyond instant gratification. I also like his nuts.

There's a baby on the way. *Our* baby.

The stages of grief hit me in waves throughout the night.

Shock.

Denial.

Pain.

Anger.

Depression.

Why did he do this?

Tomorrow, I'll go to Emma and book a flight back home to Virginia to decide what to do with my mess of a life. I'll move to California or somewhere new. The mountains in Montana are beautiful this time of year, or so I hear. Either way, this is over. Terrence will be part of his baby's life, but we're done—for good this time.

An answered prayer in the form of sleep comes at two o'clock in the morning. I nestle into the pillow to give my body the rest it needs. This house is empty, just like my marriage.

Chapter 39

Justice

Terrence didn't come back to the house. It should turn my anger into fury, but how is that possible when I'm too numb to hurt more than I do?

I look at my phone for the fourth time in ten minutes.

No missed calls or texts.

My throat burns at the thought of last night. The Terrence from yesterday is not the man I married. Or maybe it is, and I missed the warning signs. He does travel a lot. Was I dumb to expect him to be faithful?

I huff into my pillow. Monogamy is a choice. Marriage is hard, but it doesn't take an act of God for someone to commit to one person. Hell, the superhero who lives in this house is faithful to his wife. He has millions in the bank, his own action figures, and ladies lined up for their chance at the man with iron.

The woman with Terrence looked familiar. Is she the same one from the video call weeks ago? Did he meet her when we separated and never broke it off?

My stomach lurches, a countdown to my morning appointment with the toilet. The exit from the king-size bed into the en suite bathroom is made with the grace of a baby giraffe on a tightrope.

The motion sensor light illuminates white walls and gray slate tiles. Alpacas roam a fenced enclosure from the steel-framed window over the freestanding tub.

This place is mag—

Hold that thought.

Last night's dinner and cranberry mocktails erupt from my stomach in a repulsive mix. Beads of sweat tickle my brow, which is inches from the bottom of the toilet that I wish would flush me away. Nausea wasn't my companion—at least not like this—during my last two pregnancies. It takes what little strength I have left to rinse out my mouth and brush my teeth with steady feet. Pain surges through my chest.

I'm alone.

How do I begin to deal with the nightmare that's become my new life? Running away is the easiest option. It's one I'm acquainted with, but it will get me nowhere. Let's say I take off a few weeks. Then what? I still have to face the fact that the man I thought loved me is a cheater.

They say you shouldn't do life alone, so I trade my pajamas for a vintage shirt and leggings and call the one person who's been my anchor through the darkest storms.

Emma picks up the video call on the fourth ring. She's still in bed but she's camera-ready with a glow like she had morning sex. "Was video necessary?" Her voice is rough.

"Terrence is cheating on me with Elena from *The Vampire Diaries*. Do you want to go on a coffee run? I can't work the machine here. Tony Stark left no instructions." Not sure if any of that made sense. My sanity is somewhere with my self-esteem. Long gone and not in this room.

"Wait, slow down. What about Terrence and *The Vampire Diaries* girl and coffee with Tony Stark?"

I blow out a deep breath. "I went out with SiSi last night over in West Hollywood."

"Uh-huh." She squints at the screen as if it will help her decipher my meltdown.

"Terrence was out after a business meeting. He was across the street with some guy and a woman when I went to my car."

"*Okay*. Drinks after business meetings are normal."

My nostrils flare on an inhale. "He put his arm around her and twirled her. They took a Lyft to a hotel. I followed him and tracked them down but jumped into an ice room when I heard them coming. They reminisced about Pop-Tarts for breakfast, hugged, and confessed I need to know about the two of them." My voice chokes. Here comes the ugly sob. "Tony Stark's coffee machine requires security clearance, and I can't even have caffeine right now because of my current state."

"And you call me *now*? What the hell, Jay?"

This hurts too much. "Well, you know, I had a breakdown." The tears and snot smeared across my face are souvenirs.

Her voice softens. "Hey, hey. Everything will be okay, Justice."

My laugh morphs into the pitch of a hyena. I scrub my hand across my eyes and nose. "For all I know, they've been dating since we separated. You should've seen him, Em. He looked so happy."

The rumble of a deep growl interrupts my tears. My eyes dart across the room until I realize the sound is coming from her end the phone. Muffled whispers ping-pong before the camera whips from Emma's face to one I didn't expect to see in the same room, let alone her bed.

"I'll fucking kill him myself."

No.

No.

My lips stumble to form his name. "*Miles?*" His eyes are pitch-black and his muscles tensed. The sight is enough to make me want to hide under the bed.

"Are you still at the house?"

At any moment, someone will jump out of the closet and point at the hidden cameras of a reality show. A god-awful show where my husband cheats on me, and my best friend sleeps with his on the low. This train wreck writes itself.

"Justice?!" I jump at the bite in his voice. This level of anger is new territory. "Are. You. Still. There?"

"Y-yes."

He tosses the phone back to Emma. "Stay there." His voice is a bark in the distance. It's pointless to beg him not to come over. The man is as stubborn as I am. He also can't hear my pleas because of his argument with my best friend. The camera shakes in a scuffle that goes from a view of the ceiling to Miles.

Head to toe naked.

The screen is small but still needs an "objects are closer than they appear" warning label.

"His *dick*!" I turn in complete horror. This is now the second time I've seen every inch of him.

"Sorry, sweetie!" Em's face fills the screen. Holy eggplant. I need therapy. Lots of it.

"Listen, I'm happy that you two want to protect me, but he doesn't need to come over here." Not with *that* weapon. "Terrence isn't back yet, and he and I need to talk."

The distant sound of a door slam informs me I'm too late. The Hulk is on his way. Fitting, when you consider Tony Stark's relationship with him. I clutch my phone and head for the hall. Emma's house isn't far, which means Miles will be here in less than ten minutes. The front door opens before my toes hit the landing. "Terrence is here," I say in a whisper.

"Keep me on the phone. I got your back."

Emma stays silent on my descent downstairs. I manage to walk without so much as a creak on the hardwood steps. Maybe I was an assassin in a past life. I turn off the video on my approach to not make Em want to vomit like I have to right now. If ever I needed my best friend free of headaches and nausea, today is the day.

Terrence tosses his keys on the kitchen counter. His back is to me, and his head is down glued to his phone. I'm too far away to get a glimpse of what has his attention. He puts it down and runs his fingers through his hair. His hands brace the exotic marble on a sigh.

I go back on camera and flip the view for Emma to see him. She tilts her head and shrugs with the same confusion as me. We spar in whispers. She tells me to talk to him, and I tell her I'm not ready. Minutes pass before my phone buzzes with a text. I take in her wide eyes that lead me to my husband's gaze. He steps back and covers his mouth with his hand. His eyes dart from his phone to mine like he summoned me from his thoughts. There's a pained expression in his eyes.

He lifts his phone in the air. "I forgot to respond to your text last night. Sorry about that."

Time to put words to my pain. To say how much he hurt me *again*. I *want* to form them, but his stare keeps me frozen in place. If I didn't already know something was wrong, the way his eyes bore into mine is a dead giveaway. He's not the slightest bit curious why I'm here a week early? God only knows how many nights he spent with other women. The idea of him living a double life makes me see red.

"I guess I don't have to ask if you had a long night. Too much fun at the strip club?"

He shakes his head. "Didn't go." His tone registers on the lowest audible setting.

I cross my arms and laugh, careful to keep my phone up so Emma can have a front-row seat to the downfall of my marriage. "Of course. You don't need to watch random women shake their asses in your face when you can stick your dick in your mistress." Emotion takes over. I might burst into tears or punch him in his wayward penis. Both great options.

"Justice, what are you talking about?"

"I saw you on Sunset Boulevard last night. How long?"

He drops his head. The bastard can't look me in the eyes.

My head shakes several times to fight back tears and the pain of his betrayal. "How *long*, Terrence?" The echo of my scream bounces across the kitchen.

"You better answer her, dickhead, before I come over with a shot-gun and two shovels!"

His head snaps up at Emma's voice. "You have Em on the phone? Jesus, Justice. What happened to privacy between a husband and wife?"

"Emma never hurt me the way you have."

He nods. "I deserve that."

My lip trembles at his confession. So this is it?

"I can't believe you. After everything, *this* is how you want to end it?" Tears burn my eyes. "I deserve more respect, but God only knows how many women you have across the world the second you go away on"—I use air quotes—"business."

Quick, shallow breaths contort his face, as if he now realizes the error of his ways. He holds up his hands with wide eyes. "Wait a minute, baby. I don't think you understand."

"Oh, I understand fine. You are both an asshole and the biggest disappointment in my life." He flinches at the stab of my words. I hope they twist straight into his heart. I pull off my engagement and wedding rings and hurl them at his chest. Our eyes fall to watch the once-prized possessions plummet to the floor with a thud. Terrence swallows hard, his eyes locked on the floor. "It's over."

"I'll be okay. I'll be okay." Those three words leave my lips on repeat as my feet take me up the stairs to pack my things. It's a struggle to breathe.

"Yes, you will, sweetie," Emma says from the phone. "Get your stuff and come over."

Terrence grabs my waist to spin me around and steadies me in his grasp. Sweat beads on his forehead, and his chest heaves with the intensity of a man who sprinted a marathon. His eyes, wet with tears, meet mine. "Please let me explain."

"You don't have to sneak around anymore." I make it up one step before he grabs my arm.

"It's not what you think." There's a plea in his voice.

The ghost of a woman fed up with her husband's shit possesses me. My legs deserve a high five and a handclap of praise for the steps I take up the staircase. They're shaky, but I'm on the move.

"She's not my mistress!" Terrence calls out. The only part of me this man will see from here on out is my back. "I would never cheat on you, Jay!"

Like hell.

His voice strains. "She's a fucking therapist!"

I still, unable to discern what he said. My mind tells me to leave him, but my body has other plans. I gasp when I turn and lock eyes with him. Terrence grips the railing like he doesn't have the strength to stand. He looks broken, so broken. I've never seen him this emotional before, not even when I left him over a year ago.

Pissed?

Yeah.

Angry?

For sure.

This is new territory.

There's pain he can no longer mask buried in his words. Vulnerability shines in his eyes and how terrified he is that I'll walk out of his life forever. He opens his mouth to speak but has to catch his breath. "Reina gave me resources on how to cope with our separation."

Reina. The woman who was on the video call. If she's his therapist, why is she here? "So that justifies you going back to her hotel room? Let me guess. It was a house call?"

His reply is instant. "No, baby, you got it all wrong. Chris, my business partner, told Reina where I was. She's at a hotel in West Hollywood with her fiancé. Reina is marrying Chris's little brother, who plays soccer for the Los Angeles Mambas. Kenny and I went back to their hotel to see them. It got late, and Ethan, Reina's fiancé, thought I should spend the night and skip the hour commute since I had plans to train him this morning." He takes a breath. "Remember when I said I'm here to finish out a contract?"

I nod.

"That's Ethan."

Gravity forces my body to sit. For a multimillion-dollar home, these steps aren't comfortable. I look at Emma's wide eyes. She stares with her hand over her mouth. Her view is still on Terrence, and if my eyes don't deceive me, there are tears in her eyes. She *never* cries.

"How should I feel? You kept therapy a secret from me, your life partner. The way your hands were on her, I thought you two were lovers."

"We have history."

I can't help but roll my eyes and laugh. The actual nerve of this man. "Of course you do." I rise to my feet.

He holds out a hand. "Wait! I can explain. I know I'm doing a shit job, but it will all make sen—"

Three things happen. The front door chimes, a flash of black and gray speeds into Terrence with the force of a bullet, and Emma and I scream. Miles pulls him to the foyer, lifts him in the air, and slams him to the floor.

"Please don't kill him!" I scream. Terrence clutches his gut from the blow that has me scared for his life. He's big, but Miles is a tank. Every muscle in that man's shoulders, chest, and back is on full display. He left Emma's house in nothing but sweats and sliders and looks *pissed*.

Miles crouches down to put a finger in Terrence's face. "What the fuck is wrong with you? Is this how you treat your wife? Your fucking *wife*? You know better! If you want to do that shit, don't stay married." He shakes his head. "You were supposed to be better than me, T."

Terrence grimaces. If I went airborne and got rag-dolled, I'd be in pain too.

"Bro, I swear I didn't cheat. I was with Reina. She's been a listening ear from time to time," he winces, "unofficially."

"Why didn't you tell Justice about her the second you two got back together?"

Bingo.

"I wanted to..." He grips his side and pushes against the wall to stand. "You know how it is. Guys where we're from don't talk about feelings. It looks weak." He turns to me. "Life became meaningless when you left. I couldn't eat, barely slept, and drove past your apartment each night to be closer to you. I didn't know how to live without you or get you back. It's not easy to admit my shortcomings, so I got help to become the man who deserves you."

"Justice?" Miles's gaze is on me, but my eyes are on my husband. A man whose stare pleads with me to believe him.

"Don't you think I deserved to know?" It sounds like I ate a bowl of rocks for breakfast.

He runs a hand through his hair. "I planned to tell you on this trip. Reina referred me to another professional who's been helping me, but she sends me general tips from the trade on occasion. I want to go to couples therapy if that's something you still want to do. I wasn't ready when you asked the first time, but I found a Christian counselor to help us."

He continues at my nod.

"I don't always have the words to express myself, so I wrote you letters every week, from the time you walked out until last week." Terrence smiles at my confusion. "There are over sixty upstairs in the nightstand for you. I thought they would make a good anniversary gift since we'll spend it here and last year's wasn't spectacular. I want this one to be special."

More tears streak my cheeks. Every part of me wants to run into his arms and never let go. But I can't. "That still doesn't explain how intimate you and your therapist looked. Is sex with her part of the history you two share?"

His smile falls at the same time Miles grabs his shirt to press him against the wall. "Bro, back off!" Terrence says with force. He pushes past him to get to me. "No, baby. I told you, I've never been unfaithful."

"Really? What about the Pop-Tarts?"

His face scrunches. "What Pop-Tarts? You don't like them, Jay."

"*I* don't. But your therapist *does*. I followed you to the hotel and heard her say you kept a box for her for breakfast."

I throw my phone to Miles. Emma will have to deal with the motion sickness. I'm past the point of anger. I'm nuclear and ready to explode. "Whatever *relationship* you have with your thera-pist—sorry, *former* therapist now—is inappropriate. The hugging, the Pop-Tarts for breakfast? I can't trust you. This is too stressful for me, and I refuse to put this baby's health at risk!"

Chapter 40

Terrence

It's amazing what you hear when everything goes silent. My heart sounds like it will burst through my chest. Miles and Emma gasp. A hush falls. And I think I heard Justice say something about a baby. *Our* baby. She rambles on about Reina, but the only thing my ears register is that she's carrying our child.

"You're pregnant?" My eyes drop to her T-shirt. I don't see a bump, but that doesn't stop me from imagining Justice's swollen belly over the next several months. My hands burn to hold her.

Her eyes peer through me with enough force to send me to the pits of Hell where she thinks I belong. "We'll raise this child together, but I can't stay in this relationship anymore. You and your therapist deserve each other."

We're back to this again? I count to five and respond. "Princess, Reina is Audre's childhood best friend. I helped take care of her when she was little. She stayed at our house on Friday nights when her mom worked at the hospital with mine. That's why there was a box of Pop-Tarts for her."

Audre and Reina were as thick as thieves and a pain in my ass. They still are today. I left for college when they were in middle school but spent a good chunk of my high school years in big-brother mode. Thelma and Louise wanted to follow me everywhere I went, which kept me out of trouble but cramped my style.

I can't believe Justice believed Reina was my mistress, of all things. The thought makes me want to gag. We might not be blood, but she's a third sister.

Justice studies me. The rage from her face dissolves into a questioning gaze. "That's who Reina is?"

I nod. "She finished her doctorate of psychology, and she's opening up her own practice. When Reina graduated last year, I reached out because I want to offer teletherapy to my clients. I hoped she could be my therapist since I'm comfortable around her, but she shot me down because of our history. We have monthly check-ins about how she wants to set up working with future clients." I reach for Justice's hands and say a silent prayer of thanks she doesn't push me down the steps. "Baby, I never meant to hurt you or make you question my faithfulness. *You* have my heart. I fought all of my life to become a man who's nothing like my father, and I harmed the one person I vowed to protect in the process. I'm sorry, Jay. I'm so sorry."

And now, the moment of truth. This woman has every reason to leave me, but I hope we're strong enough to make it through this. I can't lose her again.

Time is such a blur that I don't register her arms around me until she says, "We'll be okay." I'm on my knees, which explains why Justice is taller. My head presses against the womb that carries our child, and my arms wrap around my wife's waist like a lifeline. I'm sobbing, and I don't give a damn who sees. I need this woman as much as I need air.

An eternity passes through our embrace until I stand. My mouth is on her with gentle kisses to her lips, her cheek, and down her neck. I wanted to do this earlier but freaked after I heard her phone behind me. It's hard to think when your nuts leap into your stomach. I press my forehead against hers and take her lips again. "We're having a baby."

Tears spill. She nods. "Yeah, we are." Justice's smile reaches the deepest parts of my soul.

We're having a baby.

Miles clears his throat. "I'm going to be an uncle." If he grins any harder, he'll crack a tooth. He moves to wrap Justice in a hug and presses a kiss to the top of her head. "Congrats, kid."

"Thank you," she says to his burly frame, which covers most of her body.

When he turns to me, we share a look that chokes us up. We clap each other's backs, unable to speak. I get to share this journey with my brother.

He coughs and puts his head down. "Yeah, congrats, bro." His sunglasses come out of his pocket to hide his swollen eyes. That they didn't break when he hemmed me up like a professional wrestler is a small miracle. With one last pat on the shoulder, he heads to the front door. "Now that everything is good, I'll go back to the feast you interrupted. Congrats again." He tosses Justice's phone back to her.

She looks down at Em. "I thought brunch is later?"

Miles responds for her. "She'll need to eat after I finish with her."

Wait.

The corner of his lips curl.

Don't say it.

He shrugs. "I had a taste during the singles' retreat and can't shake the addiction."

My eyes whip back to Justice. "Did you know about this?"

"Nope." She stares at her phone. "I guess this explains all those times something came up. *Miles?* Em, *really?*"

"I'm still here," he says.

I lean against the wall. My wife surprised me, thought I cheated, and told me we're pregnant. Well, not me. Her. *Now* I find out my best friend is with my wife's best friend. I want to celebrate their relationship, but they're both not into long-term commitments. If this hits the fan, I'm guilty by association. That means the doghouse.

Fuck that.

I'm in front of Miles in four steps. My hands wrap around his traps. "Be right back, princess," I say over my shoulder and push him out the front door.

When we get a good distance from the house, I shove the bastard as hard as he came at me. He's older and bigger, but I'll put him on his ass if I need to.

"Are you fucking kidding me?" I bark. "*Emma?* Out of everyone, you go after *her?*" Miles is a loyal friend, but he's a shit lover at best. The guy rotates women like tires and only cares about what they do for him. "I'm not paying for your mistakes when you screw this up. I love you, man, but this one is too close to home. End it now."

"Can't do that, bro."

"When you break Emma's heart, you'll hurt Justice. I won't have it."

I can picture the "men aren't shit" fest that will take place in my living room. Chocolate wrappers and tubs of ice cream everywhere. Lifetime movies like *When Husbands Cheat* and Mary J. Blige albums on repeat. Emma acts like breakups don't hurt her, but the last time it happened, I couldn't use my own movie room for a week and got the stink eye any time I dared to breathe.

And sex?

Forget about it.

Justice was on strike in solidarity.

"This is different. *She's* different."

"You're ready to commit to one woman, one pussy for the rest of your life?" His jaw ticks at that last part. I'm as protective of Em as he is of Justice. If he's serious about this, he needs to prove it. I let out a sigh and fold my arms across my chest. "Is your community dick worthy of her?"

I brace for him to swing at me, but it doesn't happen. He takes a deep breath, and that's when I see it.

"I can't explain it, but I'm drawn to her, man. It's like I've been blind for so many years and can finally see," he says.

My smile turns into a full-on grin. "You're in love with her."

His eyes drop to his shoes, and he nods. I've never seen him like this before. *Ever.* "Do you take care of her? Treat her like she's the only person in the world who matters to you? Are you faithful to *only* her?"

"Yes, yes, and yes, *Dad*. I'm a prick at times, but I'm not that much of an asshole."

I stare at him, deadpan.

"Okay, okay." He raises his hands. "I'm an asshole. I never thought what you and Jay have was in the cards for me. But I want that with Emma."

"Holy shit."

He exhales. "I know. This is new for me, but she's worth it."

I pat him on the back. "Then I wish you two the best."

The alpacas shriek at his unexpected laughter. "You're going to be a father, and I want to *settle down*. If you'd told me a year ago this would happen, I would've said you're full of shit."

Chapter 41

Justice

The sting from Terrence's slap sends a wave of heat through my body. I squirm against his thighs, trapped on his shaft pumping, in and out of me. His neckties gag my mouth and restrain my hands. He laughs and mouths *behave* before he reaches for the mute button on his phone. "I agree with Chris." The scent of his aftershave lulls me into a trance at the flick of his finger on one of my nipples. "Let's have our grand opening in September but offer exclusive access in August for any professional team that needs the space."

His tongue swirls around the peak, and my whimper earns me a warning glare. I shudder with every graze of his teeth on my sensitive skin. A hushed moan escapes the gag in my mouth. Terrence rustles papers on his desk to drown out the sound so his business partners can't hear us having sex like the professionals we are. His tongue moves to my other nipple, his thrusts become more forceful.

It's too much.

Terrence presses the mute button again and sits up in his office chair. "You wanted to play this game, princess." He drags his tongue from my breasts to my neck. "Now be a good girl and keep that pretty mouth quiet before I find a use for it somewhere else."

He raises my hips to slam into me. I see stars when he does it again and again until my eyes roll back. There's no need to see the smirk on his face.

Why did I think it would be a good idea to tempt this man with skimpy outfits during work calls? I have on one of his button-downs that lands high up on my thighs with no panties or common sense. We've been at it like animals since we came home from California a week ago. Maybe the pregnancy hormones are the culprit, but it doesn't take much for me to spread my legs for Terrence.

Yup, that damn grin is still on his face. We lock eyes, and one of his eyebrows raises when I lift myself off of him and drop between his knees. "What are you doing, Justice?" He pulls the tie from my mouth, and a smirk of my own forms. His groan is immediate when I guide him into my mouth. I practiced my deep-throating skills and want to scream when he reaches the back of my throat.

That's right, baby. I own you and this dick.

Terrence leans back and wraps a hand around my hair, the other grips his office chair arm. He jerks, a tell that he's close. When I think I have him, he frees himself to pull me to my feet. My hands find freedom from his tie, and I yelp when Terrence lifts me against his chest and pushes everything except the phone off his desk. The wood's cool surface sends a chill up my spine. "Nice try, baby."

That's all I get before he wraps a hand around my throat and lets me have it. My legs pull him closer like a Venus flytrap and shake when he tilts my hips to reach the spot that drives me crazy. He raises one leg to his shoulder and trails his tongue to my ankle. "Come for me, princess."

My back bows off the desk at the pressure that builds. I have to cover my mouth to keep from screaming when Terrence hits the mute button. "Yes, I think that will work." His breath strains. "I think I know the perfect spot," he says at the same time his thumb circles my clit. He continues to plow into me. I'm thankful for this man's reflexes, like hitting the mute button again before the people on this call hear the howls of a woman chased by another orgasm.

"We should check in with our new marketing expert first. Is Justice there?"

Justice can't come to the phone right now. Please leave a message.

Terrence makes a guttural sound and thrusts deeper before his finger finds the mute button. "Nope. Occupied at the moment, but I can try to schedule something with her later this week."

He slams on the mute button again and comes in a roar. There's no way they don't know what we're doing. I reach up to wrap my arms around him as he ends the call. We share a deep kiss, our bodies sliding against each other from sweat.

This never gets old and never will.

He leans to press his lips against my earlobe. "Do you have time for a meeting with the team later this week, Mrs. Reyes?"

"I think we can arrange that." He moans when I take his bottom lip between my teeth.

We're up and on the move, with Terrence still inside me. He sits me on the vanity in our bathroom, and replaces himself with toilet paper to grab a warm washcloth.

This is my life, and it's good.

In the last six weeks, we spent time in the superhero-who-shall-remain-nameless's house. We made love, celebrated our pregnancy news with Emma and Miles, went on our first double date with them, and made love some more. Then Terrence took me on a mini getaway that was the surprise of my life.

He wanted to have an intimate vow renewal. When I asked Terrence about our sunset beach ceremony, he said he planned it months ago. I bawled my eyes out when Em, Miles, my parents, his mom, and Audre approached our spot on the sand. Even Reina made the trip, which gave us time to connect and for me to meet Ethan. My husband thought of everything, from my wedding gown to his khaki ensemble and the most delicious feast. We decided it's best not to share our baby news until I hit the second trimester. It was hard to dodge the side glances from our mothers, but we survived.

This man continues to amaze me, and I couldn't be more in love with him.

Construction on his 15,000-square-foot facility wrapped earlier than expected, thanks to Harvey and the strings he pulled. The Austin location is perfect to capitalize on the sports teams in the city, as well as San Antonio, Houston, and Dallas. Requests from teams and universities to conduct training camps and host clinics come in on the daily. Terrence puts so much thought and love into his business. He'll get his free summer camp for kids who can't afford it and put a childcare area in the facility for employees.

I wish things were great at my job, but I found myself unemployed when we arrived back home. My company is under investigation for embezzlement and marketing fraud. *Can you believe it?* But the end of a chapter for me was an opportunity for rebirth for Terrence. He worked with me to create a business plan for my marketing consulting company. In two weeks, I had a name, an LLC, a logo, a website, and Emma's, Terrence's, and Kenny's companies as clients. Olivia now works as my digital marketing strategist to keep a finger on the pulse of the online landscape. We don't have an office yet, but we all work from home and meet weekly for our staff meetings. To be a business owner is a reality I never dreamt, but I love the extra authority over the projects I take on.

I'm in the middle of fighting with Terrence to keep my shirt on when my phone rings. "Babe, I should get it."

"You *will* get it," he says, sucking the spot on my neck that curls my toes. His length pulsates against my stomach. This man's reboot time is impressive.

I duck under his arm fast enough to get to my phone on our bed. It's Dr. Gayle. I put it on speaker and turn to Terrence, daring him to act nasty while she can hear. "Hi, Dr. Gayle."

"Justice. You sound out of breath. Is everything okay?"

I bite my lip to suppress a giggle. Terrence wiggles his eyebrows in victory. His arms hang off the doorframe, putting his broad muscles on full display. He took his shirt off and stands in gray sweatpants slung low enough to see his crown over the waistband.

Our eyes stay locked on each other, and my legs part like the Red Sea in a slow tease, ready for his staff to perform another miracle. "I finished a pretty intense workout." My hand circles my clit. "I'm a little tired but want to do another one soon."

Lord, the things this man makes me do.

"That's good. Do you and Terrence have time to swing by my office today? There's something I need to go over with you two."

My gaze falters at her request. We had our first appointment a week ago. Why does she want to see us again so soon? Terrence and I share a look.

We can't lose this baby.

"Justice?"

"Sure—yeah. We'll come by today."

"Good. It's best to go over this in person. I will see you both at three o'clock, if that works?"

I swallow the lump in my throat. "That's fine."

Terrence is by my side before I hang up. Emotion wells in me. I want to cry and scream. One pregnancy loss was horrific enough. Two almost made me lose hope. If it happens again...

"Don't go there, baby," he murmurs. "We don't know what she wants, so let's stay positive." Strong arms hold me. "Stay with me, Justice. Don't get inside of your head."

"I don't know if I'm strong enough." My voice cracks.

He kisses me again. "Then I'll be strong for the both of us."

The smell of disinfectant overwhelms my nostrils. Paper crinkles when I shift my weight on the examination table. Each minute that passes before Dr. Gayle enters traps me in my thoughts.

"Breathe, baby." Terrence kisses my hand interlaced with his. He's in the chair next to me and does his best not to look nervous. He's terrified, but he won't show it.

I jump when the door opens. "Good afternoon, Justice. Hi, Terrence."

"Good afternoon," we say in unison.

"Thank you both for meeting me here today," Dr. Gayle says. "Something caught my attention when I reviewed your chart again. I want to reexamine you today."

At my nod, she lowers the table and the lights in the room. She puts on the glasses that hang around her neck. With kitten heels, Dr. Gayle is five-three at best and reminds me of my Grandma Edith. She was a short little thing but quite the firecracker who served her community and the church. Grandma was a sweet woman who loved baking cookies but would be the first to tell you when she'd had enough or if it was time for you to go home. I was her favorite and only granddaughter, and we enjoyed our time together until she transitioned on when I was fifteen. She led a full life, passed in peace, and headed into the arms of her Maker with the joy of reuniting with my grandpa, who died five years before her.

I miss her so much.

Dr. Gayle sheathes the transvaginal transducer—the alien dildo, as Terrence likes to call it—and applies a gel. "This might feel cold and a little uncomfortable. Same as last time."

She sits on a stool and rolls next to me. I squirm at the pressure from the transducer; I'm still sensitive from what Terrence and I did hours before we got here.

"Is everything okay with the baby?" He frowns at the monitor.

Dr. Gayle doesn't take her eyes off the screen. "One second, please." She moves the wand inside until she lands on the spot in question.

If something's wrong, I need to know now. I squeeze my eyes shut to focus on my breathing. Terrence runs this thumb over my clammy hand, but it's not enough. We're so close to the second trimester. We've never made it this far and had plans to tell our parents and friends about our pregnancy next week. If we... If history repeats itself...

"I knew it," she says to herself. She takes a screenshot and turns to face us. When she opens her mouth to speak, I cut her off.

"We lost the baby, didn't we? Like the last two pregnancies."

She covers my hand closest to hers. My lips quiver. *Please not again, God.*

"I'm very sorry you experienced that, sweetie." Her voice carries the tone of a loving grandmother. "Miscarriages are much more common than people think. But that's not why I called you in today."

Huh?

"Your HCG levels were higher than most at ten weeks. I had a suspicion that proved to be correct."

My brows pull together. "I'm afraid I don't follow."

She smiles and twists a button on the computer. Silence blends with our baby's heartbeat. "It appears our first ultrasound did not catch the little bean, or strawberry, I should say now that you're eleven weeks along."

She smiles at our blank stares.

"Listen closer," she says. "You're expecting twins."

Her words roll into me like a person regaining her memory after years of amnesia. It takes some focus, but I hear two heartbeats.

Twins.

Terrence's grip on my hand is stiff. His eyes stare at the monitor, and I don't think he's blinked. I call his name three times before he swallows and answers. "Y-yes, baby, I'm here. Twins. *Shit.* I mean—sorry, Doctor."

Dr. Gayle laughs and turns off the monitor. She rises to her feet to get the lights. "No apologies needed, Terrence. You'd be surprised how common that reaction is when people find out they're having more than one child." She hands us two sonogram pictures. Our *babies*. "Everything looks healthy so far. Nausea and fatigue will increase, so make sure you get plenty of rest and drink lots of water, Justice. Any questions for me?"

Yes, here's one: how?

She smiles again. "I'm sure you two have lots to discuss. Schedule your next appointment at the front desk before you leave. We'll do a noninvasive prenatal screening in the coming weeks to make sure everything is fine. I'll have the sex of the babies once I get the results, and I'll tell you if you want to know."

Again, silence.

Dr. Gayle pulls open the door and turns to smile at us. "Take all the time you need. Congratulations. I'll see you soon."

Time passes and tears flow. We hold each other and thank God. Terrence can't stop kissing me. "I love you so much, Jay."

"I love you too, baby."

Chapter 42

Terrence

Mariah Carey's "All I Want for Christmas Is You" plays on repeat for the *fourth* time today. I now regret my decision not to soundproof the walls in this house. Mariah doesn't want a lot for Christmas, but I'll take a silent night.

In the last five days, I've tasted enough crinkle cookies and hot buttered rum to last me an eternity. The more ugly sweaters Justice forces me to wear, the more I empathize with the Grinch. He wasn't an asshole. He was a survivor, forced to endure the antics of Whoville.

"Ouch." Pain from the needle sears my skin. I have blisters from hanging up lights on our home for the International Space Station to see. This is what happens when your wife's nesting phase collides with the holidays. "Remind me why we're doing this?"

Lee Garvey keeps his eyes glued on the TV and grabs more popcorn. "Do you want to face the firing squad? This is the only way we can watch the best Christmas movie of all time."

I learned early on never to second-guess my father-in-law. He's a wise man who's taught me over the years the power of "Yes, dear" and to keep my head down to dodge arguments.

It's a Christmas miracle the women haven't kicked down the door to the home office and forced us to make *another* gingerbread house for the small town swallowing up the kitchen island. If that means we have to hide out here and string popcorn garland together until our fingers bleed, so be it.

At least we have beers, snacks, and *Die Hard*.

The last several months came and went in a flash. One minute, I'm planning for the grand opening of my facility. The next, I'm preparing for the arrival of our twins.

Twins.

My heart swells with joy and terror at the thought of two babies' love and screams in this house. I can't thank God enough for the rainbow after the storm, our light at the end of a very dark tunnel. I'm in awe of my wife, which is why I'll wrap this whole damn house in popcorn garland if necessary.

What my baby wants, my baby gets.

Justice had to take it easy but didn't slow down her hustle too much. Her marketing campaign for my training facility helped us gain more business than anticipated. Sales have tripled since we opened our doors in September. Justice had to hire a marketing assistant *and* an intern to help her and Olivia juggle the demand ahead of her maternity leave.

I'm so proud of her.

"So." Lee slaps the back of my shoulder and reaches for his beer. "Only a few weeks left."

I rub a hand over my chin and nod. "Yeah. Justice hit week thirty-seven. The doctor told us she could have them any day now."

Which is why you all are here.

It's no coincidence her parents and my mother decided to visit us for Christmas. They hope two little gifts will make an appearance this week.

"Are you ready?"

"I think so."

Babyproofing. *Check.*

Car seats installed. *Check.*

Hospital bag packed. *Check.*

Nursery complete. *Check.*

I read every pregnancy book, attended childbirth classes with Jay, and bookmarked natural childbirth videos on YouTube in case we're on the side of the road with no doctor or help.

My father-in-law shakes his head and smiles. "I'm sure you have everything crossed off that checklist." He turns to me and studies my face. "I know you'll take care of my daughter. I want to know if *you* are ready."

A few moments pass. Justice was my only focus this entire pregnancy. "I...don't know," I say. "I think I am, and I know I'll do what's needed to keep my family safe, but—"

"You question what type of father you'll be since you didn't have one to look up to when you were younger."

Bingo.

The only memory I have of my father is when he walked out on us when I was seven. I became the man of the house at a young age, not because my mother demanded it, but because she didn't deserve to bear the weight of the world on her shoulders. I did my best to be someone I'm proud of, the husband Justice deserves. But part of me questions if it's enough.

"You're a good man, Terrence, and you'll be a great dad. If you ever need anything, I'm here for you, son. Always am."

We stand to hug and pat each other on the back. "Thanks. That means a lot."

Lee put me through the wringer when Justice and I started dating, but I expected nothing less. She's his pride and joy, and I was a football player on one of the most popular college teams in the country. God knows I'll do the same with our girls.

"Hope I'm not interrupting anything."

Justice stands in the doorway with the biggest grin. Her glow is undeniable, even in that hideous "There are cookies in this oven" Christmas sweater. She takes in my sweater that says, "I put the cookies in that oven."

Damn right I did.

Her eyes darken. She licks her lips and eyes the package she wants to unwrap. It's subtle, but I catch it.

I give my head the slightest shake and shoot her a look that says, *Not in front of your father.* This woman's hormones have her on edge. "Need something, princess?" I ask to snap her out of eye-fucking me next to her dad.

"Yes. You."

I raise an eyebrow.

"I mean," she giggles, "I'm taking a nap. Care to join?" She looks to her dad. "Mom and Robin told me to get you. They want to go out for lunch and get a few last-minute items."

"Sounds great." Lee walks to Justice and plants a kiss on the top of her head. For a guy in his sixties, he looks like her older brother. I know he breaks hearts with that salt-and-pepper situation. "Rest up, sweetheart. Later, Terrence."

"See ya, Lee."

She shuffles over to me to plant a kiss. Her movement mimics a duck, and it's adorable. "Hey," she says in a whisper against my lips.

"Hey, baby." I slide my tongue into her mouth. She moans and deepens our kiss. My arms coast down her body to cradle her belly. I chuckle at the *thump, thump, thump* on her right side.

"Do my other babies need some attention too?" I squat down to press a kiss where my hand is and get another *thump*. "So feisty. Just like your mama."

Justice laughs. It amazes me she doesn't have bruises with all the punches and kicks inside her belly. Our babies are acrobats.

"Come on, Mr. Reyes. Your surprise awaits." She runs her fingers through my hair, her thumbs making soothing circles against my scalp.

I moan. "If you keep that up, we won't leave this spot."

She giggles. "Come on. Your food will get cold."

"Food? Should I go out to eat with our parents? You need to rest, baby."

"I will, but I want to take care of my man first." She grabs my hand and tugs. "Come on."

I smell it before we enter our bedroom. If I close my eyes, I can see Abuela Reyes in the kitchen whipping up a mouthwatering Christmas feast.

"Your mother helped me make you a special lunch."

I raise a brow.

"Okay, she did most of it." She laughs and waves a hand over her belly. "Our mothers didn't let me stay on my feet for that long." She nods to the tray table next to my side of the bed. The small *charamico* stands proud on the nightstand, an assortment of colorful ornaments on painted white branches. "There's a *puerco asado* sandwich, yuca patties, and spiced bread pudding. All made from your grandmother's recipes."

I take her face in my hands and kiss her. God, I love this woman.

She looks up at me with eyes that reflect the same adoration. "Let's slip into our pj's and watch *Die Hard 2*. That counts as a Christmas movie, right?"

"Yes, it does." I kiss her again.

"Good. I want you to rest with me before these babies come. You're so good to me. I want to take care of you too."

"I love you."

"I love you more."

~ ·ee· ~

"Am I hurting you?" I ask with a heavy breath. "I can stop."

"Terrence, you better not."

Sweat trickles down my face and coats my back. Each stroke is on the lowest setting possible to glide in and out of Justice, who's on all fours. I recite the lyrics to Usher's "Nice & Slow" in my head to keep from thrusting too hard or finishing too soon. She's *super* tight.

One major change during this pregnancy is Justice's appetite. The woman eats for three and can't get enough sex. Under normal circumstances, I'm all for it. The doctor gave us the thumbs-up to keep our physical activity. We can't hang from the ceiling, but we make love on the regular.

And you know what doesn't help you blow your load as fast as it takes Sonic the Hedgehog to collect seven rings? Reciting Usher's "Nice & Slow" in your head.

"Come on, baby. Give it to me." Her moan mixes with a whine for me to pick up the pace. "Please. I need you." She arches her back, and damn if I can hold back my release much longer. My performance has been shit. How the hell can my dick compete when Justice clenches around me like that?

I grab her hips and roll into her center. It lacks the force of piston thrusts, but it's enough to hit her spot. Call me a pansy, but I'm nervous I'll hurt her.

"That's it. Yes. Give it to me. *Harder.*"

I hesitate but don't want her to grab my dick like she did last time. This woman has a death grip.

"Justice."

Her head snaps back to meet my eyes with a gaze that makes me jump. "Terrence," she says as calmly as possible. "We went over this, thousands of times. We spoke to the doctor, honey. I'll be okay. The babies will be okay. We'll be okay. Now *fuck* me, *please.*"

That's the end of that. Her forearms fall on her pregnancy pillow when I sink deeper. She'll cuss me out later for not driving her into the headboard. Based on her moans, this pace is just fine. I'm afraid to break my wife and poke my children in the head with my dick, but other than that, pregnancy sex is incredible. Her walls are a warm vise.

"Yes, baby. That's it." Justice rises back onto all fours and moves against me. My balls lift when she clenches again. *Jesus.*

"I'm going to come, Terrence!"

I move faster, my orgasm in a chase after hers. I thicken when she closes around me.

Shit. I'm done.

"Yes, Terrence!"

Thank God our parents aren't home. I expect only my seed when I pull out, but a clear fluid comes with it. Justice is in postcoital bliss and doesn't notice.

"Hey, baby...did you pee on yourself?"

She looks down and frowns at the wet spot on our bed. "No." Her head shakes. "I peed before we started. That must be you."

"Well, if you didn't pee, what the hell is that?" It looks like pee but doesn't smell like it.

We look at each other. Holy shit, her water broke. Our babies.

I jump up and hold the dresser for stability. I'm not ready. "Our babies are coming! We have to call the doctor, our parents, and go to the birthing center."

I sprint around our bedroom in search of the hospital bag I packed weeks ago. "Where the hell is it?" I rush to the nightstand to look for the stopwatch and come up short. "Where is everything?" It's a fight to get control of my breath. I spin in circles. Where are the hospital bag, the stopwatch, and what's left of my sanity?

Justice sits on the bed in tears from laughter.

"What's so funny?" I bark on accident. Here I am a mess, and she thinks it's comedy hour.

"You," she says. "You're adorable." She rises to her feet with a hand on the bed for balance. "You put the hospital bag in my trunk three weeks ago. And the stopwatch? It's on the doorknob."

I knew that.

Liar.

I grab a pair of basketball shorts and a T-shirt. "Laugh all you want, but when I pass out on the delivery room floor, don't scream at me. I might not make it, princess."

It's normal for first-time dads to lose it, right? All the birthing class training is out the window.

Get it together. You aren't about to push out two watermelons. She is. Be strong for your wife.

Right.

I wrap her in a hug and kiss the top of her head. "I'm sorry," I say against her hair. "I'm...nervous."

She grins and kisses me. "You're not the only one. We'll be fine. Now let's go get our babies."

Our gazes linger until her face morphs into a pained expression.

My eyes go wide. "What's wrong, baby?"

Her nails dig into my biceps. She hunches over. "Contractions, I think," she says in a strained breath. "Wow. So that's what it feels like?"

"We're leaving now." I scoop her into my arms, careful not to crush her belly.

"What about our parents? Shouldn't we wait for them?"

"No." I shake my head. We're halfway down the steps, feet from the garage door. "I'll call your dad once we're in the car. You're my top priority."

"Why only my dad?"

"Because he's the only one I trust to keep Lucy and Ethel away from the birthing center until we say it's time to come."

She tries to laugh but scrunches her face.

I stop to see if she's okay.

"This is uncomfortable." She groans.

Chapter 43

Terrence

The days blend into each other. A month has passed since we welcomed our daughters on December 23. Christmas was a little different this year, but it came early in the best way. We settled into our home and couldn't be happier. Much of that joy came in the form of two eager grandmothers who stayed with us for three weeks. They were godsends. Our guardian angels of much-needed sleep.

With two extra sets of hands, Justice and I stocked up on shut-eye while my mom and Angela tag teamed Gracie and Edie without a drop of sweat. They changed, burped, and bottle-fed the twins with pumped breast milk. Justice still nursed them but had more time to recover, which was all that mattered to me.

Lee flew back to Alexandria a couple of weeks ago for work. He had full confidence "the Gigis" could handle it. He has yet to pick out a nickname for himself, so *Grandpa* will have to do for now.

Emma and Miles have come out to see their godchildren. It's still weird to see them together. They swear they aren't into commitments, but the spark between them is bright.

"What have you two been up to?" Justice closes her eyes and moans. She's on the opposite end of the couch, giving me full access to rub her feet.

Miles and Emma share a look as they pace around the living room with our month-old babies. "We got back from a trip," Em says. Her eyes hold Miles's.

I squint at them both. "Did you two elope?"

Her reply is instant. "Of course not." I glance over at Miles, who stares at her with an emotion I can't register. Disappointment, maybe?

Interesting.

He sighs. "We spent last week in Vail."

Colorado?

My eyes dart to Justice. She opens her mouth and pauses. "You two went to the singles' retreat...again?"

"Yes," they say in unison.

"Why?"

"Is everything okay?" I thought things were good between them. Maybe I'm wrong.

Emma waves a hand in the air, careful not to disturb Gracie, who's nestled in her other arm. "It's fine. We thought it would be fun to go back to where it all started."

Silence falls on the room like a heavy weight. Something happened, and whatever it is, it's big.

My brow furrows, and I shoot Miles a look that says, *What the hell did you do?*

He mouths something back to me that takes a second to register: *Won't marry me.*

"*What?*" Crap, I said that out loud.

Justice sits up. "What's wrong, baby?"

Emma stares at me, and I know she knows that I know. She frowns but gathers herself when Justice turns to her.

I look between Em and Miles and roll my eyes. "Nothing," I say through gritted teeth. "Just...tired."

"Oh, okay." Justice goes on to talk about the girls. She's clueless about the shitstorm that is our best friends' relationship, and that's fine by me. My wife is only one month postpartum. I don't want her to stress out.

I'll talk to Miles offline. We haven't spoken much these last few weeks, for obvious reasons, but the topic of marriage came up when we did.

"How did you know Justice was your person?" I remember him asking me. My response was something like your soul finding its counterpart.

Yes, it's from *Wedding Crashers*, a movie in which men up their body count at random weddings, but it doesn't make it any less true. Something in my spirit leapt the moment I laid eyes on Justice sixteen years ago. I never had an instant connection to someone that went beyond physical attraction. It's like we found our way back to each other.

The more time we spent together, the more it confirmed what I knew: Justice is my person. I would marry this woman every two years if she'd let me, and I hope Miles and Em find a love that fills them, whether they end up together or not.

Justice's cheeks flush. Shit, I'm staring.

She gives me a coy smile. "What?"

My eyes reflect nothing but adoration for the woman who holds my heart. I reach to pull her to my chest and drop my head to capture her mouth. "I love you so much," I say before I take it again for another kiss.

A moan vibrates from her body. She wraps her arms around my neck. My soul isn't the only thing that recognizes something in her. The pressure of her against me has my dick hard in my jeans.

Have to wait a couple more weeks for her to heal. Sorry, buddy.

I'm about to give her space when she grinds against my erection. *Jesus.*

"Princess," I say against her lips.

Am I horny? Hell yes. Does my right hand hurt? Of course. But the doctor says we have to wait.

"Baby," I say in a warning. If she keeps this up, I'll blow right here on this couch. "Hon—"

She deepens our kiss that turns frantic. My hand goes to her ass and hers grips my thigh. I wrap a hand around her hair to pull her closer.

I read about lower libidos after childbirth. It looks like Justice is in the other category.

Fuck.

She sits up and covers her breasts over her shirt, her eyes as wide as saucers. "Uh-oh." Her voice is a whisper.

We look down to see two wet circles. My baby is turned on. "Hey, don't," I say when she lowers her head. "Look at me, Justice."

Her eyes rise to meet mine.

"You are beautiful. This"—I rub my thumbs across the wet spots, arousing her—"is beautiful." I shower kisses on her chin and lips. "You've never been more gorgeous to me. I also think you found a loophole to the no sex for six weeks rule."

She chuckles. "You're okay with dry humping?"

I pull her back to stare into her eyes. "Baby, I'm more than okay with anything you give me."

If I have to bust a nut in my boxer briefs until we get the green light and she's comfortable with sex, so be it.

Her eyes drop to my mouth and linger before they rise to mine again. She bites her bottom lip in the adorable way she does when a kinky thought crosses her mind. "I need to pump first, but I'm down."

"We'll leave you to it. Go handle your business." We turn in horror to Miles, who stares at us with a grin.

Emma drops her head to hide her smile and walks toward the kitchen. "Your mama is a freak," she says in a voice that mocks a whisper to our daughter. "I taught her well."

I look to Justice. "Mrs. Reyes?"

Her eyes glow with desire. "My pump is upstairs in our bathroom."

I nod. "That's good."

She drags her gaze down my chest to my dick, and damn it if my nipples aren't hard too. Her lips part for her tongue to sweep from one side to the other, and she says in a sultry voice, "I can think of something else I can...milk."

Check, please.

"Welp." I rise off the couch and bring her up with me. "I think we'll have a nap since you two have the kids."

Miles bursts into laughter. "Glad one of us will see some action."

"Heard that!" Emma yells from the kitchen.

"You were meant to," he calls over his shoulder. He turns to us and winks. "Scram, you two. I need some time with my goddaughters."

You don't have to tell us twice.

~ee~

Justice and I sit in our children's nursery, each rocking in a glider with one of our daughters. When they're both down, we put them in their cribs, turn the baby monitors on, and crack the door.

I still can't believe I'm a dad. I wanted this for a long time, and I'm in awe that it finally happened. To this day, I don't know how we pulled twins out of the hat, but I can't thank God enough.

It's a brisk evening for February in Austin. We sit on the front-porch swing to watch the sun set, with the baby monitors turned to max volume. It's just the two of us here now.

Justice cuddles next to me. "Can you believe this is our life?"

I shake my head. "When my father walked out on my mom, I wasn't sure I would ever be ready to become one. But it's something I wanted." I reach for her hand and weave my fingers through hers. "Thank you for making my dreams a reality."

Before our split, I thought it wasn't right to let her see my emotions, that I had to carry the weight of our burdens to protect her. But now I realize that's far from the truth. Our connection deepened in ways I didn't think were possible. I wanted to be the one to save her from every hurt and fear, but the truth is Justice saved me.

She smiles back. "Thank you for making mine a reality too."

We sit in silence for a half hour before our children wake.

THE END

Epilogue

Justice

*T*wo *years later*

"Do I look okay? The other veil was better. Do you think it will rain? It looks like it."

I exhale and look to the ceiling. *It will be okay.* Another two years, another wedding. The thought brings me back to reality with a smile.

I give Emma a big hug to shut her up. She'll hyperventilate if she keeps up this pace. "Em, look at me." I grab her arms and make her mimic my breaths. "You look perfect. This day will be perfect. There's nothing to worry about, okay? One step at a time. We'll get there."

She nods. "One step at a time."

I stare at my best friend and let the tears slide down my face. Em once used lovers for their hardware. I didn't think she would meet her match, but she did in Miles, and I'm so happy.

The two people in my life who dodged commitment like the plague will dedicate their lives to each other.

"Is she done? We need to line you two up."

"Yes, Madison," I say with an eye roll. "Our girl is ready to go."

She steps through the door. "Perfect, because we're ahead of schedule, and if we—"

Emma's face twists at her pause. "What?" Her eyes search her body for the problem. "It's the veil, right? I knew it." I have to slap her hands so she won't mess up her hair and makeup, which took two hours.

Tears fill Madison's eyes. "No." Her voice cracks. "You're breathtaking, Em." She laughs at herself and fans her face with her hands. "Sorry, hormones. I'll see you both outside."

And with that, the woman I once loathed struts out the door. From the back of her formfitting dress, you'd never know she's seven months pregnant. Madison Donnelley looks like a million bucks—or should I say a billion bucks, since she married Preston—in her backless yellow dress. That she can balance herself and that baby bump in sky-high heels is quite the talent.

Preston and I reconnected after he caught wind of my marketing company's campaigns for Terrence and Emma. That led to emails, meetings, and exclusive rights to oversee the marketing for his hotel brands.

In two years, my little company took home three national marketing awards. We expanded our reach and opened up an office in New York City to handle the East Coast and European business. Olivia relocated to the Big Apple as the chief marketing officer, and I hold down the fort here in Austin to cover the West Coast, the Caribbean, and the remainder of our international operations. Each location employs fifteen people, and I'm so proud of my work family and all we've accomplished in such a short amount of time.

If you would've told me I would lose my job and start a business that would grow into a multimillion-dollar brand, I would've told you to get your head examined. That's on top of Madison and I becoming close friends.

She and Preston are inseparable. Though it took time, we were able to have our come-to-Jesus moment that turned a nightmare situation into the most unexpected surprise. Underneath her layers, Madison is kind, caring, and pretty sweet. Double dates were awkward at first, but we're all happy in our relationships, which allowed us to bury old drama once and for all.

Terrence and Preston are now good friends. He became his personal trainer, and that led to his company creating an exclusive training program for Preston's hotels that's a hit. We don't see the Donnelleys much since they relocated to Paris, but we meet up with them a few times a year—in Austin when they visit, New York City, or Los Angeles. We'll see them in the City of Love next year when we celebrate our sixteenth wedding anniversary.

It took some coaxing for Emma to let her guard down with Madison, but we're now a trio. Our annual girls' trip rivals the yearly "bro retreat" Miles, Terrence, and Preston take.

No matter how busy our lives get, we make time for each other.

I stand behind Emma and gaze at my friend's reflection in the mirror. My chin rests on her shoulder, and I place a hand above her heart. Words can't convey how gorgeous she is. Em looks radiant in her illusion wedding dress that fits her like a bodysuit. Diamonds drip from her ears to accentuate her neck. They look perfect with her summer updo.

We've been by each other's sides for every major life event since we first met in freshman homeroom twenty-two years ago. Terrence is the love of my life, but Emma is my sister.

"If you keep up that look, I will cry," she says. She places her hand above mine.

The five-carat engagement ring on her finger winks at us in the mirror. Two small diamonds flank the central pear-shaped stone Miles cut himself from an ethical mine in Australia. Yes, the man is that sprung. They join part of the ring that his grandfather gave to his grandmother. Both have passed on, so it's a way for him to honor their legacy and build one of his own with Emma.

"Come on, Mrs. Walker. Your husband awaits."

She smiles. "I like the sound of that."

We step out of the white tent to the flutters of violins.

"Ready, Em?"

She nods with a smile. "Let's do this."

I take her hand and guide us to the partition to make our entrance. Miles and Terrence should be in position. Now it's time for my kids to take their places, and I say a quick prayer they don't throw one of their tantrums. They had their nap and snacks. The only thing left to do is bribe them into obedience.

I crouch down to Edie and Gracie. They're almost three and aren't strangers to public meltdowns without a moment's notice. My daughters act possessed when a bout of the terrible twos takes over, but they're calm right now. A miracle in itself.

"You both will walk down the aisle like we practiced. If you toss these flowers"—I point to their baskets—"on the ground, the Gigis will have candy for you. Okay?"

Please let this work.

I know we don't negotiate with terrorists, but I'd like to see the Anti-Terrorism Advisory Council try to talk these two-year-old twins into following directions.

Gracie yells with a thumbs-up, "Okay, Mommy!"

One down, one to go.

Edie looks at her sister, then down at her flowers. I wouldn't put it past her to make a run for it. She could hot-wire a car with all the tech lessons Uncle Miles teaches them.

"Edie." I raise an eyebrow.

She huffs but nods. "Okay, Mommy."

I kiss them both and peek past the partition to give the signal. My mom and Robin sit in the front row across the aisle from each other. They pull out a handful of candy from their bags like they're about to make it rain on trick-or-treaters.

Malcolm X wasn't lying when he said, "By any means necessary."

"Okay, girls. Now."

They walk out to the sound of adoring guests who *ooh* and *ahh* at their every move. Gracie and Edie look pretty darn adorable in their tulle off-the-shoulder flower girl dresses. The lilac color matches the bouquets tied to each of the aisle chairs.

Terrence's eyes light up on our daughters' approach. Petals spill from their tiny hands, and I struggle not to get choked up. Everything goes as planned until Edie gets closer to the end of the aisle.

"Papa, you're pretty!" She runs at him full speed and bypasses her grandmothers' bounty of sweets.

He squats down to wrap her in a hug. His arm stretches out for Gracie once she catches up. The girls giggle at something he says and each take a seat next to a grandmother.

I turn back to Emma to see her count the steps in her head and snap.

"Sorry, Jay. I'm nervous."

I take her into my arms and smile. "There's nothing to worry about, love. This is your day. Enjoy it, because it goes so fast." She lets out a laugh and nods. "Don't make me cry again." I step back to take another look at her. "You're such a beautiful bride. I'll see you down there."

My turn.

The day is perfect. We're in a Malibu vineyard that puts any Hallmark movie to shame. Rolling hills surround us as far as the eye can see and provide the perfect backdrop for two of my favorite people in the world to say I do.

My breath catches when my eyes lock on Terrence. He stares at me with a hunger in his eyes that hasn't waned after all these years. I drink in the black tux draped over his hard muscles and lick the edge of my mouth to keep from drooling. My man could start a wildfire with his penguin suit.

He grabs my hand to pull me in for a kiss before I make it to my spot. "You look amazing, Mrs. Reyes," he says in a whisper. His eyes never leave mine.

My cream chiffon matron of honor gown is a simple A-line silhouette with spaghetti straps and a deep V-neck that shows off my other girls. The dress splits up my leg, which has Terrence's full attention. His eyes travel from my lace-up heels to my exposed thigh.

Our children and parents are a few feet away, but that doesn't extinguish the heat in his eyes or between my legs.

I lick my bottom lip and keep my voice to a whisper. "Thank you, Mr. Reyes."

The music changes, and the partition opens again for Emma and her father to walk through. Guests stand, and I have to recite the alphabet backward in my head to stop the tears.

I turn to look at Miles, who wipes an eye. This is one of the first times I've seen him so emotional, and it makes me happy to know he'll care for Emma.

Or I'll make him wipe the other eye after I pop it.

The ceremony lasts twenty minutes. Emma and Miles tongue each other down in front of God and fifty guests. They jump the broom after the pastor announces Mr. and Mrs. Walker and walk down the aisle to an eruption of cheers.

They did it!

Terrence takes my arm in his for our departure. "I'm fucking you in nothing but those shoes tonight," he says in my ear.

My nipples perk. *Yes, please do.*

I brush my shoulder against his and smile at the guests still seated. "Language, baby."

He turns to his mom on my side of the aisle and gives a nod. "Sorry." He plants a kiss on my shoulder. "I want you to ride my face and come on my tongue. Better for you, princess?"

"Can't I have both?"

"Greedy girl." The lick to my ear sends a chill up my spine.

I shake my head and take in the happy faces. Reina is here with her husband, Ethan. They had an intimate wedding on Catalina Island two years ago during his off-season and are expecting their first child. Reina and I still keep in touch, though she spends most of her time in California with Terrence's younger sister now that Audre relocated to Los Angeles. She's here too, and she looks rather cozy next to Chris. They both live in the city, and with Reina and Ethan's move to the Pacific Palisades to start a family, I'm certain they're living together.

Terrence hasn't caught on, but his business partner dating his baby sister will send him into a fit of rage. He'll flip about the age difference, but five years isn't that big of a deal.

Kenny is on the other side of Chris, drenched in sweat. He looks at his phone like he's got an appointment to face the firing squad. My guess is he wants to get back in Olivia's good graces. This playboy follows her around New York City ever since she turned him down. They really like each other, but Liv needs more assurance he can commit before she "wastes her good years" on someone twelve years her senior.

Good for her.

I catch a glimpse of Miles and Em with the photographer out of the corner of my eye when firm hands wrap around my waist.

Terrence lifts me over his shoulder and makes a sharp detour to the tent.

"Baby, we have wedding pictures to take."

"Calm down, woman. We have ten minutes."

Huh?

"Ten minutes for what?"

He walks in silence.

"Ten minutes for what, Terrence?"

We go through the partition we used for hair and makeup. He steadies me on my stilettos, closes the curtains, and locks the fabric in place. His eyes are black when he turns to face me.

"Terrence." I put up a hand and take a few steps back to put some distance between us. "This is Miles and Emma's special day. We'll survive if wait a few hours until we're alone."

He takes slow, measured steps. "Sorry, princess. Can't do that." He undoes his tie and wraps it around his hand.

"Terrence." I eye the tie and take another two steps back.

"Justice." He takes two steps forward.

I'm out of options when my butt hits the vanity. There's no negotiating with my husband when he's this turned on.

He stops between my legs and places his hands on the counter to corner me. His tie finds a home around my mouth before I have a chance to plead with him.

"Now, before you try to talk me out of what I'm about to do, this is for you." He knots the silk fabric at the back of my neck. "I love when you scream my name, but I think it's in poor taste given the occasion."

I whimper at the touch of his hands on my straps. Down, down they go. He unleashes a series of kisses from my neck to my breasts. I arch when he devours one nipple and takes the other.

"I don't know how you expected me to behave." He bunches up the fabric of my dress to expose both thighs and hisses.

I chuckle into my gag. I forgot to put on panties. *Oops.*

His eyes jump to meet mine; his voice strains with lust. "Jesus, princess."

I lean back to lift my heels onto the counter and spread wide. The old Justice would head for the hills in embarrassment, but the new me knows better. I'm safe with Terrence and happen to like living on the wild side from time to time. I embrace my sexual appetite in my marriage and no longer shy away from it.

He lifts my legs to his shoulders and sinks down to sit on the ottoman. With the height difference, he has an uninterrupted view of his destination.

"I know better than to mess with your hair and makeup," Terrence says on my inner thigh. His tongue drags up my leg and latches on to my clit. "I want my dessert now."

And with that, he grips the back of my legs to pull me closer and feasts.

Bonus Epilogue

Terrence

Emma and Miles's wedding reception lasts for six hours. Our kids will sleep like rocks tonight for our moms.

I arranged for Justice and I to have a special date night tonight. We don't get many moments with the two of us like this, and I plan to take full advantage. My wife doesn't know that I booked a room by the ocean for us. The girls are in "the Gigi suite" far, far away.

We walk to our rental car for the night. Justice wanted to know if we should change out of our wedding attire, but I said no. She looks too beautiful, and I need another taste of her in that dress.

I hold the door open and help her into the car for a drive down the Pacific Coast Highway.

"Terrence, where are we going?"

"Relax, you'll see." I take her hand and press my lips to her knuckles.

When I found out the wedding wasn't too far from Emma's old house, there was one place I knew Justice needed to see in person. We didn't have time to do it when we were here two years ago, so this will be our last chance for a while.

Emma sold her home before the wedding. She and Miles are moving to Austin to be closer to their godchildren.

I find the perfect parking spot and walk around the car to open her door. She's so clueless. It's freaking adorable.

"This is beautiful," she says.

"Just wait."

I take her hand and guide her past the café to the pier. It dawns on me she's still in her heels. "Want me to carry you?"

She laughs and pats my shoulder. "You're too good to me. I'm fine, I promise."

We walk toward the end of the pier. Justice looks around. Maybe she'll notice where we are. I'm not sure.

"This place looks familiar, but I don't think I've been here before."

Not in person.

When we reach the end, I turn to her and tuck one of her curls behind her ear. "It looks a little different since they filmed the movie, but I thought you would want to see Paradise Cove."

Her eyes widen when it clicks. She looks to the left and the right like a celebrity will appear. "This is where they filmed it?"

I nod.

The smile she gives is contagious. I grin from ear to ear. "Yup. They filmed *Indecent Proposal* here."

"Oh, I can't believe it! I wonder how many times Emma drove by here." Her hand caresses my cheek and seals my heart with her gaze. "Thank you for this." She pulls me in for a kiss.

People might think it's silly that she likes a movie about a married couple who agrees to let the wife sleep with a stranger for money.

That shit would *never* happen in a million years if it were Justice. But the movie wasn't horrible.

David and Diana's love went through the fire. They started said fire, but they were able to find their way back to each other. Like us. Hell, there was even a billionaire involved.

"The movie came on while we were in Vail and made me think of us. I always wanted to get back together but was so afraid to take the first step." She lowers her head.

I lift her chin, meet her eyes, and kiss her. "I wanted the same thing. There's no need to feel bad about the past. It's where it should be, in the past."

Her smile ignites a fire in my soul. I kiss her again and wrap her in my arms and turn us to face the water for the sunset. The wind brushes against our faces. She nestles into me for comfort, and I reach down to place a hand on her growing bump.

Justice is four months pregnant. Our son is on the way, who we'll name Matthan, which means "gift of the Lord." The twins are on the fence about their baby brother because of the whole sharing thing, but they'll come around.

I hope.

We stand in silence and let the saltwater air consume us. My family is healthy and happy. Justice is a force in the marketing world and continues to take it by storm. This woman never ceases to amaze me.

My training facility is more successful than I expected. We still book far in advance and have free summer camps for young athletes on the rise. It's something I wanted to do that makes me think about my days in Newark.

Justice lets out a sigh. "I never imagined we'd reconnect at a singles' retreat, of all places?" She laughs. "What are the odds?"

"Pretty high."

She turns to me and searches my eyes. I look down and smile. "I knew you were going to be there."

Her brows furrow. "H-how?"

"When I was in Japan on a business trip, I got an alert about our emergency credit card. There was a charge, and I figured you mixed up the cards again by accident." She has a bad habit of doing it, so I made the alerts come to me.

For once, she's speechless.

"I saw the trip to Vail and figured it was another girls' trip with Emma. But there was a separate charge for some singles' retreat package, and I had to follow you. We spent too much time apart, and I refused to lose you for good."

She leans into me. "You mean to tell me you *planned* to find me there? Did Emma or Miles know?"

"No. Miles wanted me to go out more. I made a bet with him that I knew I would lose so we'd end up at the singles' retreat."

She nods. "He wanted you to get over me."

"I flew from Japan to Colorado with every intention to get you back."

Justice takes another second to process everything. When she looks up, her eyes are wet. "I...I don't know what to say."

I wipe her tears. We kiss, and I rest my forehead on hers. "Did I tell you I love you today?"

She lets out a giggle and looks up. "No."

"It's true."

"Even now?"

"Forever."

Want more of Justice and Terrence? Subscribe to my newsletter to receive an email with the links to my deleted scenes!

https://tanvierwrites.substack.com/

Emma and Miles's story is next in the Chance at Love Series. Stay tuned for *Miles Apart*!

KEEP READING for the first chapter of *Ella Gets the D*, my divorce rom-com!

Chapter 1

Ella

I remember when he bought this house. *Our house*. That day, the glare from the sun seared the back of my neck, which struggled to crane up the ivory brick facade. Sweat dripped from my brow onto my one-year-old squirming in my arms while I chased after my three-year-old, who was determined to break an Olympic record for sprinting down the sidewalk. I was tired but couldn't get the stupid grin pasted on my face to fade.

Six bedrooms.

Six bathrooms.

A corner lot executive home, perfect for an executive and his family.

For three years, I scrubbed every floor, washed every sheet, and prepared every meal in appreciation of a house that was mine in every sense except in name. It became routine, like the birthday parties, swim lessons, and PTA fundraisers that eat through the weekend before you turn around and restart the clock on Monday.

That's the funny thing about routines. It's not hard to spot something out of place.

Take these black pumps at the foot of the staircase. They're fierce but look three sizes smaller than the size ten I wear.

And those moans ping-ponging off the walls? Not mine, either.

The likelihood that a robber—with expensive taste in shoes—waited for the perfect opportunity this Saturday morning to break in and pleasure themselves for the hell of it is slim to none.

I don't need routine to tell me my husband is upstairs exploring someone's insides with his unfaithful dick.

Today is April Fool's Day, and it looks like the joke is on me.

"God, Charles! *Yes.*" The knock of our upholstered headboard against the wall quickens.

What the hell am I supposed to do? Run upstairs with a kitchen knife? Sneak out and pretend I don't hear him rearranging someone else's guts?

I just changed those sheets.

I've seen this scenario play out in hundreds of Lifetime movies. Wealthy husband cheats on wife. This happened to three women at my son's elementary school this year alone.

And it looks like I'm joining the club.

"Oh! Ohh!"

He's close. A few more pumps and—

"*Arghhh!*"

Jack Sparrow got his booty.

Fight or flight, Ella.

I should feel something. Anger. Hurt. Betrayal. *Something.* My mind registers the indiscretion—I hear it, for crying out loud—but I'm numb. My fingers wrap around the refrigerator door handle. I pull out the uncorked wine and drink straight from the bottle.

Shock.

That's what this is. Sadness will come any minute now. Except it never does.

Huh.

Jade-green eyes I once fell in love with widen when Charles turns the corner. His steps falter. "Ella. You're home."

I tip the bottle at him. "Quite the perceptive one you are."

He scans around for our kids. *They're not here to see you for the bastard you are, dear husband.* It's bad enough Jackson heard "Daddy hurting Mommy." How do you explain the birds and the bees to a curious six-year-old, or that his father got caught pollinating another flower?

He adjusts the teal tie the kids and I bought him last Father's Day. His tailored gray suit is back in place. Not a wrinkle or an ounce of shame in sight. "Thought you had a party today."

And I deserved more respect than hearing you go to Pound Town with another woman in our home.

"I left Duke's gift," I say with a nod toward the front door. His eyes follow mine to a blue and green Minecraft bag I forgot to pack in my rush to get Jackson and Haile to their swim lessons on time. "Who's in our bedroom?"

He holds me in a stare, one meant to shrink me down a size for challenging the powerful Charles Hudson II. "No one important."

"Let me guess, you took a detour from the conference you're supposed to be at to give a personal tour of our house. She tripped and fell on your penis," I deadpan. "Hope she enjoyed the new headboard. Sounded sturdy."

Oh, look, I pissed off Charles the Cheater. He hates when anyone questions his authority.

Too bad.

I stand from the kitchen counter I spent countless hours cleaning and head to the staircase. Charles moves in front of me. His voice is low when he speaks. "You don't want to do this, El."

My eyes travel up his frame to reach his gaze. "Don't I?" I step around him and grab a heel to bang on the railing. "Oh, mistress!" I singsong. "Come out, come out, wherever you are!"

"*Ella*," Charles says through gritted teeth.

Hit a nerve, did I?

Footsteps pad down the carpeted runner. Charles and I watch the woman he propelled into our memory foam mattress descend the oak staircase.

She's shorter than me—five-five to my five-eleven, if I had to guess—and looks young. High school young. God, I hope she's at least twenty-one.

Champagne hair fans over her eyes, which refuse to meet mine. I look down at her red-painted toes to search for whatever has her attention. Her hands twist in front of her sheath dress like she's working on an imaginary Rubik's Cube.

She's nervous.

She should be.

"Look at me." Her head lifts at a snail's pace to reveal a flushed face and hazel eyes. She's pretty, the type who bites the sides of their mouth to contour the cheekbones they see in high fashion magazines. She has a narrow nose and plump lips that look like she sucked dick for two hours. If she wasn't screwing my husband, I'd ask where she gets her eyebrows done. They're thick like mine but look airbrushed. "How old are you?"

"Tw-twenty-nine."

I glare at Charles, who looks back unamused. Their twenty-one-year age gap is on brand with this cliché. Of course he picks a woman nearly half his age. I hope she can separate her whites from her lights and darks.

The twenty-niner opens her mouth to speak, but I cut her off. "Nothing you say will change the fact that you had sex with a married man. And don't insult my intelligence, because he's wearing his ring." I sigh. "You're young. You can still make better choices." Hope blooms in her eyes. I smother it. "Don't look at me like that. You're still a bitch. Go do better; I know I will."

"Enough!" A large vein strains against Charles's neck. "Go wait in the car," he says to his mistress, his eyes fixed on me.

Our gazes remain in a tug-of-war. Silence thickens the air until we hear the scurry of feet and the mud room door close.

"I'm going to the airport."

"If you think you—"

His hand raises. "I'll drop her off and come straight home. I won't go to the conference."

I scowl. "And you think *that* makes *this* better?" Reality sets in. "You were going to keep her in your hotel room." The audacity of this man. "Do you two work together?"

"It doesn't matter."

"You're right. We're done."

That felt good. Let me say it again.

"Done." I close the distance between us, my confidence building with each step. "Go to the conference, Charles. You're free to fuck whoever, whenever, as a single man."

I've questioned Charles's faithfulness over the years. Long hours. Endless business travel. I was too afraid of the answer, and now I know the truth. The tilt of his head and tick of his jaw tell me he's not just a bastard, but a liar and a cheater too.

I laugh. It's a ridiculous laugh—with snorting to top it off—that won't stop. I laugh at the white walls and beige decor that are a full-time job to keep clean with a four- and six-year-old. I laugh at the three pieces of furniture in every room because "less is more." And I laugh at the man in front of me. A man I wasted sixteen years with, who grunts like a pirate when he comes.

I walk back to the kitchen, grab my purse, and head to the front door for Duke's gift. Strong hands grab my waist to pin me back to his chest.

He's hard.

His breath is a whisper on my neck. "You drive me crazy, you know that?" I gasp when he tightens his grip. First he cheats. Now he wants to suffocate me? My life really is a Lifetime movie. "I'm not done with you," he says in a low voice.

I bite my lip to hold back a laugh and a little vomit. Money pays for lots of things, but not common sense. "You think we'll work this out?"

His hands lower to trace the curves of my hips. "Of course. We're perfect together."

I turn and grin. "And the women?"

Like the one you sent to the car like a dog. Does she fetch on command too?

He reaches around to cup my ass. "They don't matter. Only you."

It's not lost on me he said *they* and not *she.* How many are on his roster? I need to Lysol this house.

But first.

"Charles?" His breath hitches at my hands on his shirt. The bastard just had sex and is ready for round two. He really believes we'll turn a new leaf. My nails dig into his chest.

He's panting. "Yes, El?"

"Go. Fuck. Yourself."

I drive my knee into his balls. He squeals and drops to the floor. His eyes bulge at my sneaker on his wayward dick. If only I'd worn heels today. "Don't you *ever* touch me again."

He cries at the pressure.

"Let me make myself clear. I want a divorce. The kids will stay at my mother's house for spring break. I'll be back for my things after the party. You better not be here."

With that, I turn the knob and step into the sunlight at the end of a very dark tunnel. He can close the door whenever he gets up. I'm that petty.

"El!" he whines. "Come back here! You can't leave!"

Like hell I can't.

"We'll do couples therapy. I'll change." He staggers to the front door and holds it for support. I catch his pleading eyes through the passenger window. It takes a second for him to morph into the monster he is. "You'll regret this!"

I open the door and stand on the inside of my SUV. "You're making a scene, Charles. You don't want the neighbors to know how much of a bastard you are!"

His eyes roam across rolling lawns. I know people are looking at us, and the thought of shattering this picture-perfect facade widens my grin. "Don't forget about your mistress in the car! She needs to get home before the streetlights come on!"

His eyes are practically out of their sockets.

Good.

I jump into the car, blow a kiss, and peel out of the driveway. The rush gives me the assurance I need that everything will be okay.

I tell myself I'm fine, but it's a lie.

Acknowledgments

Where to start? Thank you (yes, you) for taking a chance on an unknown indie author with a long French name that's hard to pronounce. (Spoiler alert: It's Tawn-vee-aye.) You don't know me from a stranger in a Target aisle. Or maybe you do. Either way, I'm grateful.

This book was my first attempt at pouring into a community that's become a self-care destination. My therapist suggested I find an outlet outside of my day job, public policy. Stress surrounded me from all sides, and I needed a happily ever after. One romance book turned into 20, and before I knew it, I drafted a very rough version of *The Seven Month Itch*. It collected dust for some time, and now, it's finally here.

Justice has a special place in my heart. She's a part of me, a woman who second-guesses herself, is awkward at times, and is still discovering untapped kinks. Once you hit a certain age, there's this expectation you're supposed to have it all together. But that's simply not true. Everyone evolves and heals at their own pace. There's beauty in our imperfections that don't make us any less worthy of love. Justice is that reminder to me. I refuse to go on record about whether the "art" in those scenes imitated life (look away, Mom and Dad), but Terrence's goodness does come from my husband.

The road to publishing my first romance novel was bumpy, caused a few bruises, and had many detours. I'm thankful to the mini team that formed because putting out a book is hard—especially if you take the indie route.

To Caroline Knecht, my editor, thank you for the notes in the margin, written-out GIFs, and your excitement while combing through my book. Where would I, or the punctuation in this story, be without you?

Thank you to my community, which has morphed into a second family. Your confidence sustained me when I questioned myself and whether I could work on policy by day and write about pleasure at night. To my first family, thank you for supporting my random dream. Nobody batted an eye when I told them I was writing a romance book. They nodded, said, "Okay," and asked how they could help. Whether you were a soundboard for a scene that popped into my head, prayed for me, encouraged me, or asked for updates, I'm grateful for the love.

Finally, to my dear husband, the person who holds the ground so I can fly. When I said I wanted to write a romance book in 2020—during winter break before the last semester of grad school, no less—you never questioned the randomness or my ability. You've been a constant beacon of support, a wrangler of our sons when I needed quiet time to write, and my biggest cheerleader. You read every rough draft and were the unofficial technical advisor to the spicy scenes. #AnEngineerIsGonnaEngineer. Thank you for being you, believing in me, and entertaining my rambling. Terrence's best qualities reflect your heart, and I'm blessed to have you in my life as my own cinnamon roll.

So, that's it for now. Thank you all for the grace to stumble and the kind words that keep me going. Writing is an ever-changing process, and I'm excited to go on this journey now that I've stepped out of my comfort zone.

Onward.

Tanvier Peart is a future bestselling romance author with a healthy obsession for snacks and happily ever afters. She is a good girl with kinks who spends her days working on policy and enjoys the wild life of being a wife and soccer mom. By night, she writes and reads romance books with steamy scenes. When she's not lost in the land of smut, Tanvier enjoys long walks down snack aisles and the chorus of grunts at the gym.

Want to stay up to date on all of Tanvier's bookish news? Sign up for her newsletter:

https://tanvierwrites.substack.com/

Connect with Tanvier online:

@tanvierwrites

(Instagram, TikTok, Threads, Facebook)

www.ingramcontent.com/pod-product-compliance
Lightning Source LLC
Chambersburg PA
CBHW011846300726
48970CB00009B/2678